VIRA
MODERN
416

Violet Trefusis

Remembered by Enid Bagnold as 'luxurious, gay, elliptical, witty', Violet Trefusis was born in 1894, the daughter of George and Alice Keppel. Mrs Keppel was a prominent and much-loved figure in Edwardian society and the mistress of Edward VII. In 1918 Violet embarked on a passionate affair with her childhood friend, Vita Sackville-West, but in 1919 agreed to marriage with Denys Trefusis in order to suppress the scandal. The affair with Vita ended traumatically, and Violet and her husband moved to Paris. In 1927 Denys Trefusis died, soon after her first novel was published in French. She wrote six further novels, in French and in English, as well as two volumes of memoirs. She lived in England during World War II but afterwards divided her time between her Paris apartment, her villa near Florence and a tower near Paris which she had restored from 1927 on. Renowned as hostess and wit, she moved in glittering international circles, and was awarded the Legion d'Honneur and the Italian Order of Merit. She died in Florence in 1972.

PIRATES AT PLAY

Violet Trefusis

New Introduction by Lisa St Aubin de Terán

To Princess Marthe Bibesco
In long-promised token of my friendahip and admiration. V.T.

A *Virago* Book

This edition published by Virago Press 1996

First published in Great Britain by Michael Joseph Limited 1950

Copyright © Estate of Violet Trefusis 1950

Introduction copyright © Lisa St Aubin de Terán 1996

A CIP catalogue record for this book is available from the British Library

ISBN 186049 234 7

Typeset by
Keystroke, Jacaranda Lodge, Wolverhampton

Printed and bound in Great Britain by
Clays Ltd, St Ives plc

Virago
A Division of Little, Brown and Company (UK)
Brettenham House
Lancaster Place
London WC2E 7EN

Contents

Introduction

Pirates at Play is an apt title for a novel by a social pirate who played with people and places on the page with the relentless flirtatiousness that she applied to her own life. Violet Trefusis was a profoundly passionate woman, whose passions overlapped like rock strata. When she writes about falling in love, about flirting, about manipulating the world around her, she is writing about what she knows. Since she writes here about England and Italy, passion and betrayal, and about the social stratospheres of Florence and of a great English country house she can provide an insider's details. She pokes fun at snobbery while underlining a character's lack of taste. She praises her Italian middle-class characters, endows them with beauty, only to tear them apart for their social pretensions. This constant sand-papering away of hopes and aspirations within the novel, the building up of characters only to knock them down like coconuts at a fair, is in itself an act of piracy. As the author schemes and the characters scheme, each to deceive, disturb or betray, the effect is of a world in microcosm, ruled by prejudice and by misconception which produces various states of alienation – which in turn produces the author herself, irredeemably alienated emotionally from so much and so many.

Within the story there are two families, two bands of pirates, two factions at play. One is the Italian Papagalli (parrots). The quiet father is the Pope's dentist and has been made a Papal count. The mother, a plump, pretentious Neapolitan, is 'curiously drawn, not to Naples, but to Florence, which seemed to her the acme of the *signorile*, exclusive yet cosmopolitan, romantic yet disciplined, ancient, yet up to date as regards plumbing . . . ' So the family of five sons and Vica, their lovely sister, are 'torn away from their beloved Calabria, forced into gloves and boots, and compelled to behave outwardly, at any rate, like the people they so much despised'. This is the first pirate ship, launched on foreign waters with a crew seething with inward and outward mutiny. Four of the brothers are handsome clones of each other, the fifth, Amerigo, has 'just escaped being a dwarf, if not a hunchback'. The flawlessly beautiful and ambitiously scheming Vica is captain of this ship at war with the world.

The second family and rival clan are the very English Caracoles (pronounced 'Crackles'), who decide to send their own angelically beautiful daughter, Elizabeth, to learn Italian in Florence. She is to be the paying guest of the Papagallis. Even before she leaves, her trunks are being packed with prejudice and misconceptions: her father, Lord Canterdown, tells her that some of 'these dagoes' are 'pretty personable chaps, I admit – but we don't want an ice-creamer for a son-in-law'. Ensconced in the English countryside and shielded by their wealth and titles, the Caracoles look down on the Papagalli, who in turn look down on the English (they imagine that Elizabeth is bound to have protruding teeth and flat feet) while longing to be accepted by English society as well as by the Florentine nobility.

The two backgrounds and the two rival societies are drawn with an informed eye. Few writers could be better equipped for such expert exploratory surgery. Violet Trefusis was born Violet Keppel in 1894, the daughter of Alice Keppel, the Edwardian society hostess who was mistress of Edward VII. Violet Keppel's luxurious childhood was spent in England, Scotland, France and Italy. Her London life was spiced by unofficial visits from the king. As a child, the pretty, precocious Violet was both spoilt and left to indulge her fantasies. Even then indecision was an integral part of her self: she was trilingual, switching continually between English, French and Italian. She does this in her writing too, peppering her sentences with foreign phrases. As an adult she was never quite able to separate her real life from the life she imagined. She longed to shock conventional society (and often succeeded in doing so) yet ultimately was too enmeshed in it to ever truly break away. It was not so much a case of her not having the courage of her convictions as of not knowing what her convictions were.

Violet is better known for the scandal caused by her love affair with Vita Sackville–West than for any of her writings. Earlier, in 1913, Violet had been engaged to Lord Gerald Wellesley. In 1918, during her public flirtation with him, Osbert Sitwell declared himself to be 'very unhappy about the way Violet Trefusis treats me'. In 1918 Violet and Vita, friends since childhood, became lovers and ran away together (and were to elope, frequently if briefly, several times during the next two years), creating a scandal that rocked English high society. That same year, pressured by her mother, who hoped to silence the gossip, Violet got engaged to Denys Trefusis, whom she married the following year, though still desperately in love with Vita. By then Violet Keppel was twenty-two and a year into her lesbian passion, yet upon discovering the facts of life she wrote to Vita, 'Thank goodness, I have been spared this horrible knowledge for much longer than most people . . . We will eliminate the words Lust and Passion from our vocabulary, they are dirty and hideous . . . No wonder I have always lived in a world of my own – or as much as possible . . . no wonder I have preferred fairy-tales to facts'. Yet this is the same young woman who, a year earlier, had shocked the none too saintly mother of Vita Sackville-West by chatting about her louche private life in such a way as to elicit the comment that 'she {Violet] certainly has very immoral ideas of a supreme desire to amuse herself'.

Pirates at Play might seem to be only a flirtatious comedy
of errors wrapped around two love stories if it were not for
the unbroken thread of the author's own psychological
dilemma. She despises society while longing for its accep-
tance. She licks her own wounds while inflicting wounds on
others. She laughs at rules, then sneers at servants who try
to circumvent them and at middle-class social climbers.
Her treatment of the servants in her novel is as ruthless
as her real-life treatment. During a visit to Saint-Loup,
Violet Trefusis' last home in France, Vita Sackville-West
was appalled at Violet's behaviour towards her ancient
maid: 'It's really more than a little mad . . . It is a sort of lust
for power, I think she must have someone to bully'. In
her novel, Violet bullies the servants so skilfully that
she provides great insights into their characters. 'In those
days, in the heart of every large untidy upper-class British
family, like a large untidy cabbage rose, lurked a small
black useful parasite: the name of the species was
Madamzell'. Likewise, at the heart of the Papagalli family,
there is poor Mademoiselle Crispin, in reality a seamstress
but elevated by her socially ambitious employer to the
status of governess. The past loves and future aspirations of
these humble creatures are probed unlovingly. Perhaps the
writer's palpable dislike of penury is tinged with fear, since
it was the prospect of losing the lavish allowance bestowed
by her mother that finally made Violet relinquish the
almost mesmeric hold she had over Vita Sackville-West.

By 1921 her two year marriage to Denys Trefusis was on
the brink of divorce with Violet caught up in a scandal of
her own making. Her husband agreed not to divorce her
on condition that they lived abroad and were subsidised
by Mrs Keppel. Violet capitulated and, in the charge of an
old French governess, was sent to Clingendaal, a Keppel
property in Holland. It was there that she started to write
her first novel. She was lonely, bored and humiliated, but
still rich and still (just) socially acceptable, if only at a

distance. Later, she joined her husband in Paris. He died of TB in 1929, on the brink once again of ending the unhappy marriage. It can thus be conjectured that, in love as in social *mores*, this novel is an essay in wish fulfilment. Published in 1951, though set in the 1920s, this is a book in which outrageous behaviour is praised and accepted, and true love wins the day without any penalties.

Many novelists portray themselves, thinly disguised, as one of the characters in their stories. Here, however, Violet Trefusis has not only conferred many elements of herself on both the two heroines but has also painted a suggestive self portrait in the character of the scapegoat and buffoon. The two beauties, Vica and Elizabeth, are transparently modelled on the author's ideas of herself; they are fascinating to all who behold them while standing above their friends, families and foes, and are set apart, too, by their superior intelligence and wit. It is less obvious by far, yet more telling, that Violet Trefusis, the wealthy society beauty, is transformed into the charming, intelligent but grotesque outcast and object of ridicule, Amerigo Papagallo. Amerigo is as wide as he is tall and dresses absurdly. Both outwardly and inwardly Rigo is a freak, a rebel and, precisely because he doesn't fit in, he is accepted, feted and chosen to be part of the patrician world his four handsome brothers are desperate to enter. And it is only Rigo who understands the potentially incestuous nature of the love Vica and her brother Guido have for each other, a love that is echoed less strongly in all four of the Papagalli blades. As Vica explains to the newly arrived Elizabeth, 'my brothers have always preferred me to anyone'. Only Rigo will dare to speak openly of it, earning himself nothing but boxed ears and a stream of abuse from the indignant Guido. He may get called a 'filthy dwarf' and a 'disgusting abortion', but he sees and speaks the truth. Another brother, Mario, explains his homosexual involvement to his sister by telling her, 'Vica, I can never love any woman but you.'

This is a novel with many male characters but, apart from Rigo, Signor Papagalli and an elderly Florentine astronomer-prince, they are not gifted with intelligence. The two older men have no interest in the machinations of society and are out of the battle for most of the novel. Rigo, however, is central to the plot, as is Gian Galeazzo, the Italian nobleman who plays the field of love with an arrogance that is softened by his experience of the two families. Privately, Violet Trefusis wrote, 'I hate men. They fill me with revulsion. Even quite small boys.' But she didn't hate Gian Galeazzo when she created him, which makes him all the more believable. He is not a mere caricature like Charles, his bumbling English counterpart, but is portrayed in all his unlikeable vanity and pride, then hurt, and finally pulled through the fire as someone worthwhile.

Behind the teasing and the bravura portrayals of social manners this is a novel about wish fulfilment, both in text and sub-text: the unacceptable is accepted, the unlikeable are liked. We are shown the mask, the face and the forensic report of two apparently conflicting but often overlapping cultures. Some of the writing is flippant and some is profound, as for instance the silence of Lord Canterdown's house observed by an outsider:

> The silence of the banqueting hall, used only on great occasions, was quite different from the silence of, say, the Yellow Parlour. In the banqueting hall, there reigned a silence that had been, as it were, enforced with difficulty, it was an effort, and a resentful one, as though it were holding its breath until you got out of the room. The silence of the Yellow Parlour . . . had an attentive vigilant quality . . . whereas the Red Drawing Room's silence was sulky, satiated.

The following description of the author, given to someone who was about to meet her for the first time, in 1941, could easily be a description of *Pirates at Play*:

She will amuse you, but you must beware her. She is a siren (not the air raid sort). Her appearance will startle you, as she has lost her eye for make-up. She has the loveliest voice in the world; interlards her conversation with French slang so up-to-date that one doesn't understand half of it; is a mythomane as well as being profoundly untruthful; is witty; is an extravagant and fantastic personality; is a bore in the sense that she loves living in a world of intrigues and is determined to involve one in them; is in fact one of the most dangerous people I know. You have been warned.

This novel takes just such characters and allows them to bask in the glow of society's approval. And it toasts them, raising now a glass of cordial, which might be whisked away and replaced by wine, champagne, tinctures and a poisonous cocktail.

Within this novel there are so many loves that each chapter is sated with them: there is love of place, of houses, family love, love of position, of the stars, of teeth; there is self-love, romantic love, sensual love, unrequited and requited love, heterosexual, homosexual, incestuous, religious and platonic love. The reader is manipulated, sometimes to the point of confusion. Violet Trefusis, the arch-manipulator, not only enjoyed it, she made her victims enjoy being manipulated, which is no easy task. The pirates here pose and parade and push, while probing society's values and the politics of love, and the reader is manipulated into endless intrigues. This guide doesn't stop for stragglers. She knows her way blindfold: it is the world she lived in until her death in 1972, the microcosm she both loved and loathed.

Lisa St Aubin de Terán, Morra 1995

CHAPTER ONE
La Famiglia

'I THINK it is time,' drawled Vica from her horizontal position on the floor, in that voice, that even in those days constituted an attempt on people's self-possession, 'I think it is time we had a coat of arms. When I *say* coat of arms, I *mean* coat of arms; something full of style and bravado,' here she lifted her pencil with a flourish – ('What next?' muttered Mademoiselle Crispin, biting a woolly thread off her 'petit point' with some savagery.) 'Why not,' the sauntering voice resumed, 'why not a cock, *gallo*, surmounted by the papal tiara which, after all, *always* looks well? – Or a tooth, say, a molar, enclosed in the papal tiara? We *may* be descended from a pope, for all we know.' . . . 'From a *pope*,' roared one of her brothers. 'I say,' he interpolated the youths scattered about the room in varying attitudes of abandon, 'did you hear that?' . . . 'From a *popess*, more likely! What price Pope Joan, she would look well in the family tree, emerging from a tiara!' . . . 'Say what you like, I cling to my tiara, it is a tactful reminder that we are papal counts. People, I assure you, like to be reminded of the favours they have bestowed. As to the molar, I agree that it is sometimes preferable not to define the reason of the favour. We would be known as *papal*, rather than *dental*, Counts. . . . A cock, something like this, emerging from a tiara, papa-gallo,' Vica continued serenely. 'Whereas our

previous efforts tend to resemble a parrot in a cage. A parrot
in a cage is all very well over the door of an inn, but it looks
frivolous on writing paper.'

'Do you propose,' another voice intruded, not unlike
Vica's, but less deep, 'do you propose, may I ask, to put the
papal tiara on *our* writing paper? . . . You will be arrested, my
poor girl, before you know where you are!' Simultaneously,
her two favourite brothers hurled themselves on the floor,
one on either side of the designer in heraldry. 'My dear, it is
not a papal tiara it is a balloon, a mongolfier,' verified Guido,
the youngest. 'It is in deplorable taste, though arresting, like
Vica,' murmured Mario from the other side. 'Repeat that,'
rapped his sister. 'You heard,' she struggled to her feet with
the awkwardness of a young colt. Now, as Mademoiselle
Crispin watched them cuffing and snarling like cubs on the
floor, she sighed, for even then it was better not to come on
Ludovica unawares. One is not as beautiful as that; *Si avverte*,
one warns people, as old Conte del Sugo complained to her
mother, the first time he saw her romping with her brothers
in the *podere*. He was right, it wasn't fair. It was hitting below
the belt. Your first reaction was incredulity, scepticism: we
are not taken in, there is a snag somewhere, there *must* be.
This perfect co-ordination of impeccable parts, this timely
encounter, this unanimous effort in the common cause? She
made other people's faces look like reach-me-downs, bought
in a jumble sale; she was so clear, they were so confused.
Unique, flawless, she was the perfect specimen with which
one would endow a bankrupt zoological garden. At the time
of which we write, the try-outs and displacements of her
'teens had been satisfactorily settled; her features, by devious
routes, had reached the same conclusion: surprisingly, they
all plumped for perfection. Mademoiselle sighed again.
What could be the future of one so favoured, physically and
intellectually, as Ludovica, what the temptations, what the
surrenders? Who would put spokes in her wheel? Not her doting mother, to be sure, still less her awed, if absentminded,

father. Her brothers? Mademoiselle herself? Ludovica made short work of her flimsy defences. Mademoiselle would be swept off her feet, and danced round the room, or, worse still, Ludovica would lay her head in Mademoiselle's lap and gaze up at her with those jewelled eyes which made her feel quite dizzy. No. The only hope was her brothers. Potential suitors had already nick-named those tutelary giants, the 'duennas.' There was nearly always at least one duenna in attendance; there were five in all, including Amerigo, who had just escaped being a dwarf, if not a hunchback.

Someone said that a medal ought to be struck of Vica and her brothers (Amerigo excepted), her profile preceding theirs, surpassing theirs, the perfected specimen escorted by the rough copies.

She was just beginning to discover her power. It was fun, just as a new pocket-knife is fun; fun to carve one's initials on people's hearts. Once she had done so, she gave them no further thought and danced off to join her brothers. They had their jokes and their language; though they were admired and feared, it cannot be said they were very popular. As well invite a horde of locusts to a meal; and food, in Calabria, has never been very plentiful.

How, it may be asked, was it possible that a person as civilized as Mademoiselle Crispin should deliberately expose herself to the privations, discomforts, climatic excesses, such as living in Calabria entailed? Her title of 'governess' to the Papagalli family was, it must be confessed, a purely honorary one, and had, for that matter, better be gone into at once. Mademoiselle Crispin, was, 'de son métier,' a dressmaker. She had originally settled in Naples, which, she was aware, for a self-respecting Tourangelle, was a most eccentric thing to do, because she had inherited a small sum from an aunt which enabled her to indulge in the commendable *period* desire to 'see Naples and die.'

It had been love at first sight.

She saw Naples and lived.

Naples, ce cher Vésuve, his plume a little crooked like a
dissipated musketeer's, the town rising sparkling tier upon
sparkling tier of houses, white as a wedding cake! Naples,
full of fatuity and congratulations, pommarded curls, white
kid gloves, confetti and compliments, the stage of perpetual
'Nozze,' as old-fashioned as valentines and dance cards. The
ridiculous delightful men, with coral hunchbacks on their
watchchains, who muttered 'belle gambe' as you passed, and
sighed as if their hearts would break; the officers who nearly
swept the glasses off the tables in their attempt to fling their
capes over their shoulders with a sufficiently superb gesture.
No wonder Mademoiselle Crispin fell for Naples!

Given her nationality, it was not difficult to get a job as
assistant dressmaker in a shop on the Via Carracciolo.
Mademoiselle Crispin prospered until the evil day when la
Signora Artemisia's nephew, Angiolino, appeared on the
scene. Angiolino was her undoing, and must have been the
undoing of many prosperous middle-aged spinsters since.
In appearance he resembled the improbable fiancés you see
on glossy French postcards, holding a branch of lilac over
their betrothed's head and accompanied by syrupy captions
such as: 'Écoute ma belle, c'est l'oiseau fidèle qui chante
toujours le retour des beaux jours.' In his way Angiolino
was perfect: he had poise, charm, brio, and not the shadow
of a scruple.

For several months Mademoiselle Crispin was very happy.
Angiolino's slightest whim was law: poor pet, he had had
such a wretched childhood; his father, a profane parucchiere,
had inflicted incredible humiliations on the sensitive lad.
Nothing was sacred to the fellow, not even Angiolino's
beautiful satin curls which his father forbade him to cut as
he used them to try out feminine coiffures. 'Think of the
indignity! At the age of 16, io maschio, with a woman's bun
on my head!' And the tears would rise to his beautiful eyes,
and Mademoiselle Crispin would suggest an evening at the
opera, followed by a little 'souper galant' to inter these

unpalatable memories. Everything went swimmingly until Mademoiselle Crispin's savings began to give out; as they dwindled, so, alas! did Angiolino's affection. He would remind her that she was not as young as she was; that the Neapolitan ladies were prepared to go to any lengths (financial or otherwise) to obtain his favours; that there seemed, on the other hand, to be singularly little competition for those of Mademoiselle Crispin. . . .

Then, one terrible day, she returned home to find that Angiolino had removed his belongings from her lodging, also, incidentally, some trinkets of hers, leaving, however, a charming compensatory note saying that he was taking them as souvenirs of her; every time he looked at them he would be reminded of her embraces. . . .

Poor Crispin found herself penniless; moreover, the unfeeling Zia Artemisia chose this moment to say she no longer required the services of one who had behaved with such brutality, such lack of imagination, to this angel in human form, her nephew. Things, indeed, could not have been worse, when blinded by tears, she ran into la Signora (not yet Countess) Papagalli, whose dresses she had designed for many months past and whose fugues to Naples were becoming more frequent. 'Ma, cara Crispin, what *can* be the matter?' exclaimed the warmhearted Signora. 'You cannot be seen weeping thus in the Via Carracciolo, come, we will go into the nearest café.'

Seated in front of a cup of steaming coffee, Mademoiselle Crispin told her sad little story, not omitting the farewell note. Signora Papagalli was indignant, rather than surprised.

'Really, cara, at your age! You ought to have known better than to leave your knick-knacks lying about. If you had been an old English 'Mees' you could not have been more gullible. But, stia tranquilla! No good will come to this young man.' She lowered her voice: 'I will cast a spell, ah! you smile! only Wait. I am very good at spells. Intanto,' she said in a brisker tone, 'you shall come and live with us and make all the children's clothes. No, no, thank me not! In this way, I shall be remunerated.'

And so it happened that Mademoiselle Crispin came to be living in Calabria; only, as the Papagalli family mounted in the social scale, it had been decided to confer on her the status of governess.

'The children are so devoted to their old French governess. Of course, I know, modern parents sent their children to school, but in my family we are so conservative; personally, I always think school tends to turn girls into hoydens, do you not agree, Baronessa?'

In those days they lived fifty miles from Reggio Calabria. They might be living there still had their gregarious mother not wished for company. She loathed Calabria, and all its ways. Her husband, as befitted His Holiness's personal dentist, had a *pied à terre* in Rome, where she occasionally visited him, but where she was not encouraged to bring the children. Artemisia, in spite of her entry to lesser Vatican circles, felt swallowed up in Rome; although she acknowledged it to be every inch a capital, she found it impersonal, prejudiced, standoffish. You had either to be a prince or a peasant, and Artemisia was neither. The daughter of a Neapolitan *avvocato* who had emigrated to Florence, she was curiously drawn, not to Naples, but to Florence, which seemed to her the acme of the *signorile*, exclusive yet cosmopolitan, romantic yet disciplined, ancient, yet up to date as regards plumbing and hygienic amenities. Then there were the dressmakers, the bridge parties, all the delightful futilities unknown in Calabria. . . .

At last her opportunity came. La Nonna (her husband's mother), had died, leaving them a large apartment in one of those cliff-like houses on the Lung'arno. To the immense chagrin of Vica and her brothers, they were torn away from their beloved Calabria, forced into gloves and boots, and compelled to behave outwardly, at any rate, like the people they so much despised.

The apartment on the Lung'arno was gloomy, roomy, uniformly hideous. It had very high ceilings, mostly sprinkled with swallows, bearing sprigs of mimosa in their beaks, narrow windows with narrower stone window seats. The walls were hung with threatening landscapes, and pictures of very old saints. The furniture, spuriously quattrocento, was agony, no more, no less. It was almost impossible to sit down without hurting oneself. The dining-room table for instance, was a jumble of legs which hit out at you in all directions. Chair backs were perpendicular and inquisitorial, just the height guaranteed to produce a crippling backache. Maria Teresa was inclined to be sympathetic about the chairs though she considered the furniture as beautiful as it was distinguished, for what was austerity, but distinction? Apologizing for her own, less ascetic tastes, she would usher you into her boudoir, where she had really let herself go, and which she had furnished with all her Neapolitan exuberance. Everything looked richly edible. . . . There were consoles, apparently made of brawn, nougat cabinets with tiny perspectives in barley sugar, a peppermint mantelpiece, little round tables curiously aspiring to be taken for 'flans' – and covered with a perfect plethora of diminutive objects in arch pastry. As to the ceiling, it was clotted with cherubs, Mamma had always been partial to 'cherubbish.' . . . A variety of operatic photographs menaced, ogled, swaggered from the piano: Van Rooy as Wotan, Jean de Rescke as Don Josè, Tetrazzini as an elephantine Butterfly, for Signora Papagalli had sung minor parts in Grand Opera in her youth. She had a small sweet soprano, and enough beauty to make any talent seem superfluous. 'Can't you be content with your looks without pestering me to take singing lessons?' her mother, a handsome irascible Irishwoman from County Cork, was for ever complaining. She had come to Italy as companion to an ailing British dowager. Neapolitan Avvocato Ticchio administered her Florentine estate. One look at Shelagh was sufficient to convince him that he was not worthy to call himself a man if in less than three months she

had not succumbed to his honourable – per forza! Irish girls
had the reputation of being as chaste as English girls were
accessible – intentions. The marriage was a success. Avvocato
Ticchio, who was also a house agent in his spare time, turned
out to be an astute man of business. A great many foreigners
were settling in Florence at that period. At once plausible and
ruthless, he adapted history to suit each individual taste. The
number of Medici 'follies' he sold to rich Americans, the
quantity of Beatrice's 'bowers' he disposed of to the more
sentimental British are not to be lightly dismissed. He died a
wealthy man, in the overwhelmingly respectable apartment
on the Lung'arno. It is possible that Vica inherited her extraordinary gift of embroidering on the most homely themes
from her grandfather. She was never at a loss. Her hypnotic
Scheherazade voice turned gasometers into minarets with
the greatest possible ease. Potemkin, we are told, dazzled
Catherine the Great with the prosperous-looking papier
mâché villages which he had hastily erected on the banks of
the Volga in honour of her tour. Vica, likewise an illusionist,
excelled at conjuring up just such village mirages.

It is rare enough, God knows, to be two against the world,
but when it comes to being ten against the world, why,
thrones have rocked for less! Drastic, decorative, devoted,
they started as a family, but might well end as a movement.
They were Papagallis and Papagallists. In the fifteenth century
they would have probably coined their own currency.

For the time being, they were self-contained, self-sufficient,
self-satisfied. Their horizon was bounded by the Appennines;
they were content to exercise their budding tentacles in
the cascine; they did not suspect there were worlds to be
conquered, victims predestined to become the prey of the
Papagalli. . . .

They did not know they were an act of God.

Occasionally, a few foreigners were invited to Mamma's tea
parties. She was anxious to keep in touch with her musical

past. A French mezzo soprano, two Czech pianists, a Portuguese singer of 'fados,' came and went. There was a perennial mutter of music in Casa Papagalli. . . .

Mamma would readily accompany her friends, a much resented pincenez balanced on the tip of her nose. Sometimes, she would be pressed to sing. Her ghostly little soprano did not match her (by then) contralto physique. She adored being pressed to sing. It made her very happy. . . .

There they would be, Mamma singing, preferably something fragrant with 'memories,' for at least one man present (she had been a flirt in her youth). Concepcion Valdez, a Swiss violinist with the Spanish type, from which she had wrung the last drop of complicity, beating time with the black-sequined fan which she was never without; and a few habitués: il dottore Felice Buongiorno, a Neapolitan punchinello, dapper and deafening, old Conte del Sugo who was supposed to have had a duel with d'Annunzio in his youth, Baron Hummer, like a huge bland pink coral pig off some giant's watchchain, and, last but not least, an Englishman dressed entirely in symbols like an Englishman in a charade, with tweed knickerbockers, a pipe and a drooping moustache one suspected of being false. He was known as 'Mephisto' Macpherson, because he was always humming snatches from *Faust*.

Then, into this charming, chubby salon, as coy as an old dance programme, would begin the Infiltration; a brother would slink in, lean gracefully against one of the brawn pillars, to be presently joined by another brother, who would make straight for the piano, where he would tower over the accompanist like the statue of Doom, turning the pages either too slowly or too quickly – he would then politely offer to take the flustered accompanist's place. This accomplished, he would play one finger the first bar of Malbrouck s'en va-t'en guerre. This was the signal for the door to open admitting Vica flanked by two even more spectacular brothers. The three seemed like beings from another world, serene, disdainfully benevolent. They toil not, neither do they spin. . . .

The spell of poor Mamma's salon was broken. Concepcion would agitate her fan in articulate protestation: Mephisto Macpherson would mutter twirling his du Maurier moustache: 'I say, what have we here?' Hummer, turning his crimsoning nuque away from the newcomers was the only one who made some show of resistance, inasmuch as he would try to ignore the whole procedure by starting a stentorian conversation with Concepcion, too unnerved to make adequate reply.

Del Sugo, on the other hand, would bend over Vica's hand as though she were a duchess. She adored him; as a little girl in Naples, he had asked her what she would like for a birthday present. 'Your monocle,' was the unexpected reply. For months she wore it round her neck on a pink ribbon. This theatrical gesture accomplished, he would draw her down beside him: 'You should not do this, Vica . . . ' 'Why not?' 'It isn't fair.' 'Fair to whom?' 'Fair to your mother. Why must you disturb her innocent pleasures? She doesn't intrude on yours.' 'But it's such fun, we might be a band of pirates, you all look so scared.' 'That is exactly what you are, a band of pirates and *you* are the ringleader.'

Vica looked pensive, her cleft chin cupped in her narrow hands. 'I can never get married,' she announced sombrely. 'And why not, pray?' 'Because I can never leave my brothers. We would wilt and pine away if we were separated.' 'What nonsense. You are but a child,' the old man said tenderly. Vica gave one of her sudden chuckles: 'I should be sorry for the man who married me, he wouldn't realize he was marrying my brothers as well!'

This scene was enacted, with variations, every time poor Mamma 'received.'

CHAPTER TWO
The Other Family

'WELL, they *sound* all right,' said Lady Canterdown, peering over her letter, over her spectacles.

'What's that, my dear?' inquired her husband, turning his 'good' ear towards her.

'I said, they *sound* all right,' she repeated raising her voice and her spectacles, 'these Italians, I mean the Italian family,' she shouted, 'we are sending Elizabeth to stay with to learn Italian.'

'Most unnecessary, I should have thought,' he grunted.

'You were saying only the other day, Christopher, what a pity it was we were such bad linguists.'

'We seem to have got on pretty well, in spite of being bad linguists. I don't hold with Englishmen who are good linguists except when they happen to be diplomats.'

'Oh, Christopher, why do you pretend to be so insular, like an Englishman in a French play, sir Rosbif, I believe you do it on purpose.'

'That's not the point, if you send Liza to Italy, there is no knowing what may happen to her. Be raped in the train, I shouldn't be surprised.'

'Darling Christopher, it's the girls who do the raping nowadays, believe me.'

'Well, look what happens to Liza in Taunton, let alone

Florence! The other day I left her sitting in the car when I went into the Bank. What did I find when I came out? Two strange young men under the car, which had nothing whatever the matter with it, and a third lighting her cigarette. She's a public nuisance, is our Liz.' He chuckled proudly as he stuffed his pipe.

'Well, all the more reason for sending her to stay with a family of Italian dentists. Nobody could go wrong with a dentist – even an Italian one.'

'I thought they never went near a dentist because they had such good teeth.'

'Don't be puerile, Christopher, *of course* they have dentists! Besides, this is a very exceptional dentist, he was ennobled by the Pope.'

'What for, in the name of all that's holy?'

'For stopping the Pope's teeth, of course. Even Popes have teeth.'

'Well, I'll be blowed! Should never have thought popes had anything so carnal. Liza won't stay there twenty-four hours,' he remarked after a pause, pulling at the pipe he had just lit.

'Why not, pray?'

'Can you see Liza spending her life in a dentist's waiting-room fingering back numbers of *Punch* or whatever the Italian equivalent is?'

'She won't have to wait if she lives there. Besides, there's nothing the matter with her teeth. We are sending her there to learn Italian.'

'Nobody wants to know what "Step this way, please" is in Italian!'

'*Must* you be so silly, Christopher,' pleaded his wife. 'She won't have anything to do with the dentist part, besides I have already explained, he only attends the Pope.'

'Disgusting snobbishness, I call it.'

'These people, Papagalli their name is,' said Lady Canter-down adjusting her spectacles and reverting to the letter, 'live in a "lordly" apartment. They must mean "signorile," over-looking the Lung'arno. I used to sketch the Ponte Vecchio from there when I was a girl – two saloons on the "noble floor" – it all sounds very aristocratic, "the young lady will have the companionship of the Countess's daughter and also of her five brothers,"' read Lady Canterdown *diminuendo*, unable to keep the dismay from her voice.

'Speak a little louder, I didn't catch the last part.'

'It only says this, there is a girl of the same age as Liz,' faltered his wife, 'and, "and plenty of young people in the neighbourhood."'

'No young men in the family?'

'Yes, no, the girl has two baby brothers, twins,' bawled Lady Canterdown bravely, thinking she might as well be hung for a sheep as for a lamb, and somehow liking the idea of twins.

'Just as well,' grumbled her spouse, 'otherwise I might have been tempted to put my foot down. Have you told Liza it's all fixed up?'

'No, I have not seen her since this morning.'

'Of course the Italian family will all speak perfect English in less than no time, and Liza's Italian will, with luck! remain in the same class as yours,' twinkled Lord Canterdown, relighting his recalcitrant pipe.

'Anyhow, I don't refer to "Benozzer Gozzly" like *some* people,' retorted his wife.

'Have I ever pretended to be an æsthete? How long do you propose to leave Liza with the macaronies?'

'As long as necessary.'

'What for?'

'Oh dear! you *are* maddening, anyhow, here she is; nobody bangs so many doors in rapid succession as Liza.'

'I like it meself,' muttered Lord Canterdown, 'makes me feel my hearing's perfect. That last one sounded very near.' Only a few seconds elapsed before the door burst open. Both parents raised their heads with the same anticipated pleasure.

Was it possible that Liza was all their own work? All the light in the room rushed to meet her, became absorbed, transmuted. It was as though they saw her for the first time. Liza once remarked: 'I must put in an appearance at such and such a place.' An admirer rebuked her gently: 'You mean you must put in an apparition.' She possessed the element of surprise of the apparition: its mercilessness, luminosity, Tobias and the Angel.

Everything about Liza shone; her hair, eyes, teeth, skin. She was made of gold, the pale gold you see in seventeenth-century stained-glass windows, the greenish gold of Gesso mirrors. Lady Canterdown's heart failed her. And she was sending this celestial being, this untried angel to Italy, a country notorious for its appetite for women, its lust for blondeur? 'O Mummy, must you sit there looking like the Soul's Awakening?' There was nothing celestial about Liza's voice; on the contrary, it had a rousing, astringent quality that revived the victim and brought him to his senses. It acted as an antidote. Maybe she wasn't as dazzling as that, after all?

'No, no I suppose not,' sighed Lady Canterdown, recovering slightly.

'Even Father looks pretty queer, now I come to think of it,' stated Liza running a practised eye over that parent. 'Are you about to tell me that the time has come for me to wed the ill-favoured but well-intentioned princeling to whom you betrothed me in my cradle?'

Lord Canterdown sat up suddenly. 'No, no, God forbid! Another year in the schoolroom at least for you, my girl.'

'Oh well, that's nothing new,' Liza slung her long legs over the arm of her father's chair. 'I can't think why you continue to look so momentous?'

'Well, dear, it's like this.' Lady Canterdown smoothed the crumpled pages. . . .

Canterdown was very different in those days from what it is now. A large staff of class-conscious servants ministered to its many wants. Raw-boned country lads with huge clumsy hands (like Michelangelo's David) encased in hereditary white cotton gloves that were handed down from footman to footman, were ruthlessly drilled by Mr. Crawle, the butler, who resembled one of those fullblooded portraits by Raeburn with his mottled cheeks and incipient side-whiskers. Scared and starched housemaids were hunted from grate to grate by tiny red-haired Margaret, the 'Head,' who, being Scottish, had a vocabulary as extensive as it was caustic. . . .

Upstairs, in self-imposed reclusion, reigned the sybilline figure of Nana, whose most trivial utterance was quoted with respect by the family. The nursery still retained its symbolic smell of scalded milk and Elliman's Embrocation; a high fender conjured up visions of drying flannels; there was always a kettle on the hob. Photographs of Liza as a baby, playing with her toes, of Charles, Liza's brother, sitting on his mother's knee in an attitude of deplorable affectation, of Charles at his Prep. school with his first cricket bat, of Liza in plaits and a 'plate' during her notoriously brief *age ingrat*, cluttered the mantelpiece. Supernumerary snapshots of Liza diving, beagling, ski-ing, skating, seemed to hint at possible favouritism on the part of Nana. You were not left long in doubt, Nana never tired of boasting of the exploits of her darling; Charles' commendable achievements in cricket and hunting-field were barely glossed over. No wonder he was such a nice boy! Nana had briefly aspired to the post of housekeeper (as a weary Empire builder might covet a peerage after a lifetime given up to the service of his country), but Lady Canterdown held other views. Nana as oracle, confidant, 'Eminence grise,' in the nursery was one thing; Nana as bully, informer, dictator, in the housekeeper's room, was another. Mr. Crawle would never have stood for it, let alone Miss Rapp, her Ladyship's maid.

Hence Nana's Buddha-like, if deceptive, aloofness: it was a far, far better thing to be the confessor of the entire Caracole family, including aunts and cousins, than the *maître*

du protocole of the housekeeper's room; besides, it entailed
the additional privilege of being waited on hand and foot by
a miserable and anonymous creature known as the Girl,
who was to be met with staggering up the backstairs with a
groaning tray at least three or four times a day.

In those days, in the heart of every large untidy upper
class British family, like a large untidy cabbage rose, lurked
a small black useful parasite: the name of the species was
Madamzell. It was the parasite that kept the rose together,
that prevented it from shedding its petals all over the place.

The process of mutual assimilation went on for years. The
Madamzell learned to endure chaff, draughts, rock cakes,
nicknames. Her pupils, on the other hand, learned that
Volume was not necessarily an adjunct of Power, that you
could, for instance be tiny and tremendous. They also learnt
the departments, rather than the deportment of France, and
a curious castrated lingo, that could, however, be relied
upon to procure them the necessities of life on the other side
of the Channel.

After five or six years exile, the Madamzell herself was apt
to disregard that pizzicato element in the French language
which makes it sound as though it were pronounced on tiptoe, each vowel acute, steely sharp; her accent would tend
to become blurred and furry. Why bother? Only a French ear
could detect the difference. To English ears it all sounded the
same. When she went on her yearly holiday to France, her
nephews and nieces would tease her about her 'English'
accent, her low heels, her loose woolly jumpers. She would
begin to feel less at home in France than in England. As time
went on, the catalogue she had been sent twice a year from
the Bon Marché became an irrelevant and tactless reminder.
French clothes made one conspicuous, a thing she had
learned one must never be. Ten years' exile had taught her
to prefer comfort to fashion, friendship to passion, flowers to
salads, dogs to human beings.

The boys had taught her cricket, the girls had taught her

nothing. France had become very remote, a place where you shake hands all day long and talk about nothing but food. Nothing short of a war, or threat of war, could impinge on this acquired phlegm. *Then* a huge map of France would appear out of the blue, occupying the whole of the school-room wall. The most trifling mistake in French would be stringently corrected. All Madamzell's relations, dead or living, would be triumphantly reinstated, *le cousin militaire* occupying the place of honour on the mantelpiece. The Fachoda Incident would be taken out and dusted. The last days of Napoleon at Saint Helena would be significantly read and dwelt on; the children were reminded that for 180 years England was governed by a French dynasty. . . .

Even Madamzell's appearance would seem to undergo a change; long discarded ear-rings (that ornament inseparable from the Frenchwoman) would reappear; it would be remarked what square blunt peasant hands she had; only France could have produced those hands, that staccato mincing walk. . . .

France had reclaimed her child.

The Canterdown rose did not differ from other roses; it had a particularly efficient parasite.

Second only in importance to Nana, was Mademoiselle Cujac. One might have assumed that their spheres would not overlap; morally and politically, they did, however. It was suf-ficient for Madamzell to advocate woollen socks for Elizabeth, for the child to be sent down barelegged, in sandals, by Nana; if she was prescribed cod liver oil in the nursery, Madamzell made a point of discounting the dose in the schoolroom. This guerilla warfare had lasted for fourteen years and showed no sign of abating. Nana had come to the family when Liza was three; this, she considered, gave her precedence over Madamzell, who had arrived on the scenes four years later. Madamzell was accordingly treated as an upstart who should be kept in her place. Poor Liza's childhood had been made hideous by this rivalry. She was in the habit of referring to

Nana and Madamzell as her 'Sicilian lovers.' Brother Charles, on the other hand, lazy and unperplexed, could afford to ignore these underground conspiracies, besides, Madamzell really preferred him; when he was home for the holidays, Liza took a back seat in her affections, but Liza was a Principle ('it is against my Principles to allow Elizabeth to stay up later than nine'), whereas Charles was a mere Sentiment, transitory, unofficial.

To-day, however, an event without precedent was about to take place in the nursery: in view of the imminent removal of their pet, Nana had sent a message by the Girl to Madamzell asking her to come to the nursery at five.

Lady Canterdown had announced her irrevocable decision to both parties that very morning, a decision which Madamzell had greeted with irony; 'Ees it not a peety, Lady Canterdown, to precipitate what ees bound to 'appen, anyway?' and Nana with open and lachrymose censure: 'I shouldn't have thought you 'ad it in you, M'Lady, to send the pore little thing to a barbarous country like that with never a soul to turn to.'

The outcome was, that Madamzell and Nana had decided to join forces for a major offensive against this unnatural mother's project. True, Liza had been abroad before, to Switzerland, to the Riviera, but escorted by Madamzell. True, she would be accompanied on her journey to Florence by her cousin, Frances Mildew; on her way to Rome, once there, who was to protect her from the lascivious Florentines? Besides, Madamzell or no Madamzell, her English would remain intact; serene; inviolate. She spoke it with equal firmness in Lucerne and in Cannes, in fact, she was an excellent teacher. Her pupils were legion. Hence the proposed divorce from Madamzell: hence Florence; hence the Papagalli.

Madamzell, as was customary, had lived so long in England, that she could speak neither English nor French. Rapid and reckless, she never paused for a word; her literal translations from the French were little masterpieces; in her zeal to show how different English was from her own tongue, she was apt to give English words whose pronunciation scarcely differed from the French a knowing tweak, with curious results. She had been heard to say, for instance: '*Imagyne the peasants,*' '*Liza, you are eunuch,*'* etc. . . .

Now, her diminutive person clad in superimposed woollies, humouring Nana as it were, in her dress, and fully conscious of the importance of the occasion, she set out for the nursery: François I meeting Henry VIII on the field of the Cloth of Gold. . . .

Not to be outdone in chivalry, Nana half rose on her rheumaticky old feet as she entered the room. 'I wouldn't 'ave asked you to come up, Madamzell,' she wheezed, 'if it wasn't for them stairs. I just felt I couldn't face 'em, me legs 'as been that troublesome of late!'

'I know, I know,' interposed Madamzell quickly in the 'tirez les premiers, Messieurs les Anglais' spirit, 'I would 'ave come to see you in any cases, when I knew what was going to arrive to Liza.'

'Far be it from me to pick 'oles in 'Er Ladyship,' proceeded Nana heavily, 'but it do seem crool to let that pore young thing fend for herself in Hitaly, of all outlandish places!'

'But for Liza, more dangerous,' insinuated Madamzell with perfidy, ''ow many jeunes filles 'ave turn bad there?' (Serenades, oranges, tarentellas, d'Annunzio: on pouvait s'attendre à tout.) 'It is sufficient she show 'er face once in the train. I know. I 'ave seen it 'appen, all the women they 'ad to carry their own baggages.'

Nana nodded, gracious but uncomprehending. She merely wanted Madamzell's support, her mark, so to speak, on the petition; she was not interested in all this verbiage.

'If 'Is Lordship should ask my hopinion as, sooner or later 'e will, I shall tell 'Im, you think as I do, Madamzell,' she puffed, wishing to seal the situation, thereby landing heavily

* 'Unique'

in the first gaffe of the interview, forgetting both the laws of
etiquette and Gallic susceptibilities.

Madamzell whipped round as though she had been stung.
'*Eef* Lord Canterdown consult anyone, Mrs. Spankey, it will
be me! I will tell eem you are au courant of this project,
'owever, you 'ave been so long in the family, I conceive you
'ave voice in the chapter,' she completed with a flourish
worthy of François I.

The manner, rather than the words, implied that she was
making a gesture.

Gestures, Nana knew, called for only one thing, 'tea.' She
knew she could not go wrong if she produced a cup for her
guest. She rose painfully to her swollen feet. It became
immediately apparent why Charles and Liza had nicknamed
her Smet Smet, after Rupert Brooke's hippopotamus goddess.
She trundled to the cupboard; with difficulty reached for
a small brown teapot. Madamzell watched her with some
trepidation but realized it would be tactless to interfere with
the ritual. Nana placed the teapot, milk jug, and two cups on
the battle-scarred nursery table with its green baize cloth.
'There!' she panted, 'I always think there's nothing like a
cuppertea to 'elp to talk things over.'

At last she allowed herself to relax. It was the happiest
hour of the day, the time when her legs ached least. A
kind of Morland mellowness invested Nana, the teapot, the
shining kettle on the hob. Her eyes like small bright birds
came and went, as though caged in that immobile face.
She became symbolical of a certain aspect of English life, the
most endearing, perhaps the most enduring. She stood for
the England that curtsied, but did not cringe, that made rude
songs about 'Boney,' and which later would refer to 'that
there 'Itler.'

Lord Canterdown's 'study' bore testimony to the fact that he
had been a gay dog in his youth. 'It's not so much a study,'
his irreverent daughter was wont to remark, 'as a "study" in

the nude!' Ladies of every nationality and dimension, ladies in every position, painted, photographed, sculpted, leered, yearned, *reminded* Lord Canterdown from every shelf, table, console, pedestal, that he had been the devil of a fellow until – quite recently.

It confirmed his wife's theory that it is not necessary to be handsome, let alone intellectual, to be successful with her sex. Lord Canterdown's uncompromising grey bowler (worn on the back of his head), bubbly blue eye, slightly bow legs and inveterate pink carnation had been the joy of every caricaturist in Europe, from Spy to Sem. His arrival at Monte Carlo, Deauville or Carlsbad was the signal for the season to begin. Pretty aspirants to the favours of the rich 'milord' hurried to the places where he was to be met with, the bars, the 'rooms,' the springs. . . . Lady Canterdown rarely accompanied him on his continental trips; a certain blameless itinerary was nevertheless reserved for her: Florence, the Italian lakes, Pau, was Sylvia's beat. Here, no candidate, however attractive, had the slightest chance of success.

Now (alas!) things were very different. 'Cracker's'* day was over – as a seducer at any rate. He felt he must make it up to Sylvia for years, not of neglect, but of dissipation. He was easily able to persuade himself that *au fond* he had always preferred his wife to any of the flower-maidens whose portraits adorned his walls; no doubt he had, in a way.

Sylvia's gradual detachment, gentle mockery, had served her well. How many predicaments had she not teased him out of? Besides, there was Liza. . . . They knelt on either side of her in the hushed attitude of donors.

If there was a room more revelatory than Lord Canterdown's 'study,' it was his bathroom. Here piety and pruriency were forced into startling juxtaposition. Reproductions of

* 'Caracole,' the family name, is pronounced 'Crackle.' Christopher Caracole was inevitably known at his private school as 'Christmas Crackers'; the name stuck.

Luini, Fra Angelico, Ghirlandajo, Simone Martini, gaped with astonishment at Kirchner girls, swinging long silk legs from cocktail stools, at *fausses ingénues* by Domergue in the best 'Vie Parisienne' tradition. Some of the religious paintings had been a source of embarrassment to Lady Canterdown when travelling. 'I say,' her spouse would remark in ringing tones in front of a guide and twenty tourists, 'don't you think that little madonna has a tremendous look of "Chiffon" Cropperfield? About the mouth, I mean? Or is it in the way she does her hair? I'd like to buy a photograph of that one.' This scene had been reproduced (with variations) all over Europe.

The morning Liza was leaving for London, and incidentally, Florence, she sat, dressed for travelling, on the edge of Lord Canterdown's bath, a rich affair the shape of an éclair, in lead, encased in mahogany.

'How you have the face to admit anyone into this scandalous apartment, let alone an innocent girl,' she remarked, raising her eyes to her father who was engaged in scraping his chin with a razor resembling a miniature scythe, he did not hold with 'these new-fangled Gillettes!'

'Can you be referring to yourself, Elizabeth?' he inquired, turning on her a pushed-up eyebrow, as ferocious as that of any Samurai, 'I hardly . . . ' scrape, scrape, 'think you come under *that* heading. In fact,' he added, relinquishing the scythe at last, 'you may even teach the Florentines one thing or two.'

'Well, it's a pity you did not give me the run of your bathroom library,' his daughter replied airily, indicating a small bookshelf containing nothing but works of then popular sauciness, such as 'Le Roi Pausole,' 'La Garçonne,' etc., 'before sending me to a country where little boys of twelve already shave on the sly. You may live to regret your head-strong decision.'

Lord Canterdown suddenly realized that this badinage had gone on enough and that the parting paternal injunctions must be crammed into a few minutes. 'Now, listen, Liza, this is all very well. A joke's a joke, and all that, but don't you go messing yourself up with one of these dagoes. Some of 'em are pretty personable chaps, I'll admit – but we don't want an ice-creamer for a son-in-law. You may turn their heads as much as you like, so long as you keep your own.'

'If I look into the future, Father, what do I see?' She pretended to peer into a crystal globe. 'Wait! Wait! It's becoming clearer. Yes! A dark stranger, tall, with matchless teeth. He bends over me. I recoil. He snarls: "Open wide! Wider!" What does he hold in his right hand? Horror! A drill!'

This was the kind of joke Lord Canterdown could appreciate. Roaring with laughter, he gave his daughter one of his resounding Elizabethan smacks on the buttocks. 'It's time you started, my girl. Now mind you remember to give Francie my message.' . . . Francie was Lord Canterdown's favourite niece. She was accompanying Liza to Florence.

Poor Francie! . . . She was one of those popular elderly girls whose happiness was purely vicarious, inasmuch as she looked on at other people being happy. It had taken her the best part of ten years to realize that popularity could become a substitute for love; that, in fact, the loved were seldom popular; that, in order to acquire popularity you had to be not necessarily, but preferably, plain, obliging, self-effacing, a good listener, always available for a last minute invitation to luncheon or dinner. When young, no plainer than other girls, Francie had aspired to matrimony. Her parents had done their duty by her, had presented her at Court; given a ball. It was up to her to find a husband. The year of her début, she endeavoured to dance with eldest sons; the second year with younger sons; the third year with men who attracted her, and who came under the more nebulous heading of 'business.' ('He is in some kind of business, I believe.') She had had one or two 'nibbles,' but alas! they never came to anything. Her lack of technique was deplorable. She never kept the nibblers waiting, aired no caprices, never cut their dances and assured them of her wholehearted devotion.

Of course she never got married. It was about then that her popularity started, opening, so to speak, out of a long and painstaking career as bridesmaid. She was the ideal brides-maid, not pretty enough to detract from the bride, nor plain enough to mar the wedding group, sufficiently well-born to be an asset to humbler brides, not sufficiently exalted to make the bridesmaids' presents appear inadequate. (Her small crocodile jewel-case was filled with these.) Her wardrobe consisted mainly of bridesmaid's dresses shorn of their more frivolous trappings and converted into plausible evening dresses. As she was the soul of loyalty, she never repeated any gossip, however amusing; she took other people's children to the pantomime and other people's husbands (the boring ones) for country walks. She took advice but never umbrage.

Much in demand for week-ends (Francie is such a good mixer) the only tribute she exacted was a caricature or a ribald verse in her visitor's book, which was her most valued possession. It was a stout tome bound in green morocco; the addresses of nearly all the stately homes in England figured in it; neatly cut out of the writing paper and placed above a view of the house, there would follow the signatures of her fellow guests, some laboured doggerel on the hunt ball, or a frieze of the local 'meet' done in coloured chalks borrowed from the nursery. There were also a few meticulous water-colour sketches of salmon flies, and half a dozen dance programmes with tiny white pencils attached. . . .

Poor Francie, platonic when she should have been prolific, protégée when she should have been patroness. . . . No one would ever know the struggles she had had with a tempera-ment which would not have been misplaced in a Mexican film star, but which now, thanks to her new vocation, was becoming mercifully atrophied. For her cousin, Francie experienced an affectionate awe, an uneasy admiration.

The five hundred a year she had inherited from her parents enabled her to rent a four-room flat in Knightsbridge. Putting up Liza was like having a peacock to stay in a rabbit run. She knew only too well the effect she would have on her surroundings: what was the good of buying daffodils to put on Liza's dressing-table? Her hair was a brighter gold. Why bother to drape those Paisley shawls on the sofa? Liza's faultless form had no need of protective colouring. Still, she trailed about the flat in a dispirited way, patting a cushion here, removing an imaginary speck of dust there.

This time to-morrow she would be in the train. Though she mistrusted foreigners, she liked the thought of staying with her uncle, the Ambassador; it was pleasant to see the play from the Royal box, so to speak. She questioned the wisdom of sending Liza to Florence without Madamzell, though one was forced to admit Liza was able to take care of herself. No clinging ivy, was Liza. I wonder if she has had any proposals, I suppose so, though she is only seventeen. She seems older, in a way. Experienced. She need never worry about it's being her last one, her last proposal, I mean. There'll always be another. I wonder if she has ever been in love like I was with Angus McPhaill? No, of course not, she doesn't know the meaning of the word, yet she is not exactly a flirt. Too direct, too outspoken. How wonderful to be able to say one is tired, that cricket bores one stiff, that one doesn't really care about fishing. She can afford to be truthful. She has a truthful face, as truthful as – as a drawn sword. What an extraordinary simile! I must be getting fanciful in my old age.

Well, we've got grapefruit, and cutlets, and rhubarb-fool for dinner. Mrs. Gannet came in on purpose to do the cutlets, jolly decent of her, I call it. If I were alone I should cook myself a poached egg, I don't suppose Liza has ever dined off a poached egg in her life, pampered little thing! I wonder how she will like that messed-up Italian food, very fattening I should think. Not that it will affect Liza, if anything she is a shade too thin. I can't help feeling glad, in a way, that she's

not coming to the Embassy, I shouldn't have had a look in.
O dear! How spiteful I'm becoming. Why, there's the bell,
the train must have been in time for once.

Francie went to open the door. Liza stood on the threshold.
She was not alone. A very large young man, shaggy – his hair
was like burnt-up turf – stood by her side.

'Francie, this is Peter Speight, he came to meet me at the
station. Wasn't it sweet of him? Peter, this is Francie, my
guardian angel, you don't mind if Peter stays to dinner, do
you, darling?

Francie *did* mind, very much. A cosy little meal for two,
everything calculated to a nicety, was one thing, a no doubt
ravenous, uninvited giant, was another. Really, Liza was too
inconsiderate! It was easy to see she was used to a house
with twenty servants.

Peter Speight ate two out of the four cutlets and nearly all
the potatoes. As for the rhubarb-fool, poor Francie had to
pretend she didn't like it. Now, with one of Francie's
precious Worcester cups precariously perched on a patched
and tweedy knee, belatedly conscious that he had eaten
nearly all the dinner, he was endeavouring to ingratiate
himself with his hostess, a conquest it was politic to make,
as he intended to marry her cousin.

'I *do* think it was nice of you to let me stay to dinner,' he
beamed.

'You ought to have said that hours ago,' interrupted Liza;
'it's too late, now you've bolted all her dinner. The least you
can do is to send her orchids, or asparagus to-morrow . . .
Oh! but I was forgetting: we shan't be here to-morrow, shall
we, Francie? But you could bring the orchids to the station.'
How could Liz be so brazen? The difference in generation
and upbringing asserted itself more strongly.

'I should be very much embarrassed if you did any such
thing,' Francie hastened to atone.

'He couldn't really, even if he wanted to, he hasn't a penny
in the world,' proclaimed Liz, enjoying his penury.

'Did you catch that gloating note?' Peter said. 'She's proud of my destitution, I'm her only poor friend; the only one who lives in lodgings, smokes what her mother calls "footmen's cigarettes," and buys ready-made clothes. I can see you're wondering how on earth we got to know each other. I was up at Cambridge with her brother – got there on a scholarship – '

'Charles,' said Elizabeth, 'was more than flattered at Peter taking any notice of him: you see, Charles, bless his heart, is scarcely an intellectual, is he, Peter?'

'He doesn't have to be. It's probably part of his charm that he isn't. Got a cigarette for me, Liza?'

'I'm not supposed to smoke, but Francie does, and has. Chuck us a fag, Francie.' Francie glanced rather dubiously at the two recumbent figures sprawling on the not so very broad divan, and did as she was bidden.

'You see,' resumed Elizabeth, bending over Peter's match, 'he is going to become a politician. Left Wing, of course' – (she was conscious of a mounting snobbishness) – 'in the meantime he writes articles for the papers.' Her cigarette described the flourish of a pen.

'Oh come now, Liz, you talk as though editors were simply falling over one another in their haste to carry off my steaming pages. When I think that only yesterday two of my most brilliant efforts were returned. . . . '

'Good Heavens!' exclaimed Elizabeth in her most lordly manner, 'what can you expect at your age? What genius has ever succeeded right away? If you did, I should take it as a sign of mediocrity.'

Francie began to feel *de trop*. They seemed to have forgotten her existence. She could not help liking the young man, though he obviously wasn't of their class; he had a disarming grin and square beautiful teeth.

'Look here, Liz,' he now said in a voice both peremptory and proprietory, '*no* nonsense about not having time to write once you are in Italy. It won't wash, see!'

Francie felt an involuntary thrill. She had always longed to be spoken to like that.

'Well,' came Elizabeth's self-possessed voice through the smoke, 'you know what I am: either I write *reams*, or not at all, but I expect it will be reams, if the family turns out anything like what I anticipate.'

'I can't help wishing you were going to be there too.' The young man nodded graciously in the direction of his hostess. 'Not, I fear, that it would make much difference: she'll have them all in the hollow of her hand before twenty-four hours have elapsed. So bad for her, it doesn't do to encourage her latent narcissism.'

Francie resented the implication that Italy would naturally assume that she was Elizabeth's chaperone. It was sentences like this, uttered in public, that had cheated her of a husband. Of course, any young men that were on the premises would fall in love with Elizabeth. Did she feel more than her usual gruff affection for this one? It was doubtful, but you never can tell. Meanwhile the two had resumed their dialogue, based on mutual appreciation and candour.

Francie was free to return to the packing that was her pride and only talent.

The Simplon Express lurched and rattled through the night. Elizabeth, in her upper berth, reviewed the exciting day: the train journey from Victoria to Dover, in a train that seemed of toy-like dimensions, compared to its high steep French colleague. The crossing in a boat that was a floating *résumé* of everything the British tourist would pine for, when abroad: tea, continuous and unstinted; chintzes (in the cabins); good manners; an optimistic outlook. ('Is the sea going to be rough, steward?' The invariable reply, in view of a mounting gale: 'Maybe a bit choppy, Miss, but nothin' to speak of.')

Even the burly boisterous sea, of a rocking-horse grey, with a tendency to practical jokes, was all-British, likewise the scampering unincommoded children, so different from the silent greenish foreigners. It was evident from the word 'go,' that we belonged to a superior race. At Calais, however, the foreigners came into their own. Galvanized, competent, they stood up to the horde of blue-chinned, blue-bloused porters, with accelerated voices, faces, who grabbed your luggage before you had time to give any explanations and bore it off to the customs, where British families, looking taller and more hygienic than ever, towered over the douaniers like Gulliver over the Lilliputians.

Once in the Paris train, with your luggage safely stacked, you could relax at last. Francie, an excellent sailor, knowing it was the last 'decent' meal they were likely to get for weeks, had taken the precaution of lunching on board, but the more squeamish were now confronted with the perversities of the French menu (written in purple tears) with its suspect sauces, and lonely vegetables, served by themselves.

Francie nostalgically evoked the sensible cutlets and honest rhubarb of the previous night, while Elizabeth, who had a more eclectic appetite, tucked into her hors d'œuvre, and the pale spacious landscape flowed past . . . here were no hedges, no clustered villages, no cosiness. One felt exposed, vulnerable. 'I've never cared much for France, it seems so empty, except, of course, the Riviera, which is fun,' confessed Francie.

Elizabeth's angelic countenance assumed that air of sagacity that sat so oddly on one of her years. 'I think,' she said slowly, 'I *could* like France very much, it doesn't *gush* at one, you would have to take a lot of trouble to make friends, real friends, I mean, not just bowing acquaintances.'

They reached Paris late that evening; the steep blackened houses, round the Gare du Nord, anonymous, unanimous, appeared much more sinister to Francie than London's tiny individual hovels, with the sooty flowerpots, and their square yard of 'lawn.'

They had driven across Paris to the Gare de Lyon, in a taxi

with a demon driver who had given them a thrilling series
of hair-breadth escapes. Poor Francie's syncopated: 'Pas . . .
si . . . vite!' had merely raised a sadistic grin.

They bounced, they grazed, they feinted, they lunged, they
bluffed, they escaped – by the skin of their teeth. Elizabeth
enjoyed it. Francie, pale and decomposed, kept on muttering:
'Never again, not if I know it, never again!'

And now it was night, and Francie was snoring with
moderation in the berth below. Elizabeth didn't feel like
sleep: she cautiously reached down for the bag of *pralines*
they had bought at the Gare de Lyon and which was in the
net suspended over Francie's berth. No, she decided, munching gingerly, she didn't want the train ever to stop. She would
like it to absorb country after country, with picturesque
pauses now and then, at stations with outlandish names
ending in CZS, full of peasants in high boots and fur caps, or
else, vehement embroidered women singing in chorus like in
'Cavalleria Rusticana' . . . She had forgotten all about Peter
Speight for the time being.

CHAPTER THREE
Male Chorus

'I WOULD remind you, bambini,' said Countess Papagalli sententiously, 'that the English are inclined to be fussy about baths. Yes, I am well aware that your father sticks all his dental negatives on the walls of one bathroom, and that Gina sleeps in the other.'

'I don't see why il Babbo's negatives should prevent one from enjoying one's ablutions,' objected Vica. 'After all, once she knows whose teeth they are.'

'Hush, my child, we do not speak of such things in public – '

'But we are not in public, Mamma, siamo tra di noi – '

'Zitto, Vica! I detest this flippancy. *In ogni modo*, Gina must remove her clothes, they can be kept in the *ufficio*.'

'How often will she want a bath?'

'At least once a day.'

'She must be very dirty.'

'My dear child, the English are eccentric, it is a well-known fact, but remember, there was no haggling about the price of her room. It is more than any of our friends get for their Signorina inglese.'

'There was no need for us to emulate our friends. Nothing compelled us to have a signorina inglese.'

'I bet she has protruding teeth and flat feet' – from Ugo.

'I think not. La Contessa Canterdò' has laid much stress on

the fact that she must not be left alone for long with young men.'

'*Meno male*! In that case I will go and change my tie.'

'It is quite unnecessary to go to the station, but remember, *ormai*, we all change for dinner.'

'But I have only got one evening dress!' wailed Vica.

'Never mind. You must wear the bodice of one dress with the skirt of another, so that she will think that you have several.'

'And what,' inquired Guido, 'am I supposed to change into? An "Eton"? Leone's First Communion jacket?'

'Cease chatting, children. It is time we went to the station.'

'What! *All* of us?'

'Certainly not! She will become acquainted with us by degrees.'

'You mean Guido on Tuesday, Amerigo on Wednesday, and Mario on Thursday?'

'Don't be silly, you will all meet her at luncheon. The car will not hold more than three with comfort, as you very well know; then, there is the luggage.'

Gina's square country face suddenly appeared round the Moorish curtain. 'È pronta la macchina.'

'Signora Contessa,' prompted the Countess.

'Signora Contessa,' amended Gina.

The car, a hired Fiat (Papa Papagalli had, of course, a car of his own, seldom seen by the family), was impressive in many ways. First, its height: other cars only came to its shoulder, so to speak; secondly, the display of artificial flowers in its two cut-glass vases; thirdly, the dignity and gloom of the interior, which had earned it the nickname of 'il bigliardo,' the billiard-room.

Il bigliardo took them to the station in its unhurried manner. Mamma pestered the porters about any possible delay in the arrival of the Paris train, whilst her offspring licked torpedo-shaped sweets, adhering in some mysterious manner to a straw.

At last, the train was signalled: Mamma ordered an interruption in the sweet-licking. All three were standing at attention when the train drew up with the prolonged hiss peculiar to continental expresses.

Vica and Guido had a bet on as to which would identify Elizabeth first; Vica lost; she had plumped unhesitatingly for Francie and was bearing down on her, when Elizabeth suddenly stepped out of the train, unorthodox, hatless, her golden hair like a nimbus about her head. Vica and Guido gave an involuntary gasp as the light fell full on her face, but whereas theirs was sheer gratification, Mamma's gasp, on the other hand, was one of sheer dismay. Short of locking up her sons. . . .

A rod of stippled light reached from between the slats in the shutters, across the mosaic floor; it dipped on Elizabeth's bed, alighting finally on her pillow. Bells filled the air with their bronze clamour; they jostled and contradicted one another in their morning altercation; now and then, a stronger deeper note, like a fateful stride, broke into their confusion, imposing its rhythm, rebuking the din.

Somewhere, on the banks of the Arno, a donkey brayed with extraordinary insistence; the baker's boy on his morning round sang a popular refrain with precocious passion:

'Stretti, stretti, al tuo sen' ognor
La Spagnuola sa amar così, bocc'a bocca la nott'e il dì.'

Hooked by the luminous fishing rod, Elizabeth stirred uneasily, opened one aquamarine eye. 'Where am I? In the train? No' – she missed its rhythm. 'At home?' Her bed was softer. This one was like an ironing-board. With a considerable effort, she tweaked her mind out of unconsciousness. 'Italy!' Of course, she was in Italy; Florence, all alone in a strange house, surrounded by dentists. No Francie, no Mummy, no Madamzell, no anyone. For fully half a minute she allowed herself to luxuriate in self-pity. It was inhuman of Mummy to have sent her to a strange country, without under-standing one word of the lingo. Suppose she fell ill? A lot they cared, the heartless crew . . . Poor little exile, poor little Liza. . . . The boy and girl who came to meet me at the station, I'm bound to admit they were unusually good-looking, especially the sister, rather like a photograph in Father's study of Karsavina as "Thamar." Moreover, she spoke English, now I come to think of it, rather peculiar English, but English, nevertheless,' she giggled, 'no doubt her English will improve by leaps and bounds. Poor darling Mummy, once again she is doomed to be frustrated!'

There came a knock at the door, Liza, turning on the light by the bed, said 'Come in!' in that brusque capable voice that was so out of keeping with her physique. Enter Gina, bearing an enormous tray. She nearly upset it on the bed. To her surprise Liza was confronted with a poached egg; several slices of raw ham (prosciutto di Parma); a cutlet; with great difficulty she mastered a desire to laugh. If this was an Italian breakfast, so much the better! She began to tuck into it with relish. Gina backing towards the door muttered something about a 'bagno.' 'Bagno?' That must mean a bath. 'Yes, by all means, bagno,' Elizabeth nodded emphatically, 'and caldo too, it can't be too caldo.'

Once she had finished her breakfast, she felt much better.

It was rather a lark, really, staying with an Italian dentist! Who would have thought dentist's children could be so good-looking? She wondered if she would hear the muffled screams of the patients. But he was the Pope's dentist, wasn't he? A Pope's dentist would go to the Pope, not the Pope to the dentist, surely? But perhaps he had other patients? Again there came a knock at the door. A scarcely perceptible pause, then Vica entered. Without a trace of self-consciousness, she crossed to the window, opened the shutters, flopped down on Elizabeth's bed.

'Mamma said I was to see if you had well reposed?'

She had been taught her English by the infatuated
Mephisto Macpherson; a natural gift for languages, which she
shared with her brothers, was to bring her much enjoyment
in life.

'Very well reposed,' answered Elizabeth. The sun had
recognized its child and was playing havoc with her hair.
The two girls, so different, yet completed each other. The
one, so shadowy, so mysterious, with the grape-like curls,
recalling one of Leonardo's androgynous drawings, the other,
all light, all candour. Dusk and Dawn.

'Never have I seen such hair as yours,' Vica marvelled.

'Haven't you? Well, it's very useful,' smiled Elizabeth,
meaning that she could count on her hair to break the ice.

'No,' there was a note of awe in Vica's voice. 'Nor such
eyes, all light and no pupil, like a young astore.'

'What is an astore?'

'A bird, I know not how you say, except in French, an
épervier, an *oiseau de proie.*'

'A bird of prey! I've never been told that before,' said
Elizabeth smugly, 'I must make a note of that one.'

'It was difficult to keep Ugo out,' Vica remarked at a
tangent.

'Who is Ugo?'

'My brother, one of my brothers.'

'Have you many brothers?'

'Five, you will see them all at *colazione.*'

Elizabeth gave one of her schoolboy guffaws: 'Mummy
told Father you had only two baby brothers, twins; are they
all as good-looking as Guido?'

'No, though some people admire Leone more, he is larger,
stronger. Mario and Ugo are also sympathetic, but poor
Amerigo is – *come si dice?* – a dwarf.'

'A dwarf! How dreadful!'

Elizabeth had all the healthy person's horror for the
deformed, the abnormal. As a child, she had been taken to a
circus with a 'dwarf number,' and had shrieked so loudly, that

she had had to be taken out. Now she shuddered at the thought of stumbling over the little creature in a dark passage. Vica, with her customary shrewdness guessed what was passing through the girl's mind.

'No, you will not often meet him. He is very sensitive, so *vuol fare bella figura*, he tries to show off. He will perhaps be here to-day, as he will want to see you, though Mamma hopes not. You must pretend not to notice anything, promise?'

'I promise.'

'I hope,' continued Vica earnestly, 'that they will not all fall in love with you. I would not mind so much about Ugo or Leone, but of Guido and Mario, I would be jealous.'

'I see. Hands off Guido and Mario then.' Liza was much amused. Was this candour deliberate, or to be imputed to the restrictions of her English vocabulary?

'You see,' explained Vica laboriously, in a voice that was like a muted 'cello, 'my brothers have always preferred me to anyone. I hoped you would be nice, but not beautiful.'

'And your brothers hoped I would be beautiful, but not nice?'

Vica nodded. '*Appunto*,' she said.

'But perhaps I am nice as well as beautiful?' Liz suggested. Vica shook her head gloomily.

'O no, that is impossible,' she sighed.

Suddenly there came an ear-splitting whistle from the street below. Galvanized, Vica put two fingers in her mouth, and emitted a whistle no less piercing.

'È Ugo,' she explained, 'I must go, he is getting impatient.'

The Contessa was passing an inspection of her sons, they were drawn up in front of her, dazzling as to teeth, fragrant as to hair. She couldn't help thinking what a handsome chorus they would make, the smugglers in *Carmen*, for instance. Only one was missing: Amerigo, but perhaps that was just as well. . . .

Mademoiselle Crispin, sewing away, in a corner of the room, looked on with silent disapproval. The infinite adaptability of the Italians filled her with disgust. In France, she thought, the English girl would have to conform to *our* standards, not us to hers.

'Are you satisfied, Mamma?' demanded one tenor and three baritones.

'Yes, but Guido's hair is a shade too long, and Ugo's handkerchief looks a shade too feminine.'

'Of *course* it looks feminine,' Ugo pouted, 'I stole it from a lady.'

'I should hardly have thought it was necessary to *steal*,' observed Mamma fondly. Ugo was her favourite.

'Will we do?' inquired the sons in chorus.

'Yes, but try to look more natural.'

'How *can* we look natural, Mamma, if you want us to behave like Milords inglese.'

'I'm sure no Milord inglese has such a handsome family, your father. . . .' At that moment, the Moorish curtain was slowly drawn aside, and all eyes were focussed on Amerigo; Amerigo the refractory, the only one who hadn't wanted to play, and who was now dressed as a music-hall version of a British tourist. His plump, squat body was clothed in an outrageous check suit, and knickerbockers of a cut that suggested cycling bloomers; he carried a rumpled umbrella in one hand, and was drawing at an enormous pipe with the other. A long drooping blond moustache was gummed to his upper lip. The brothers were torn between the desire to give way to their merriment and to keep in with Mamma this day of all days. It was she who found her voice first:

'Amerigo, how *dare* you? Do you want to render your mother and your brothers ridiculous? Do you want to bring discredit on your family? Should our guest catch a glimpse of you in this get-up, she will certainly take the next train back to England!'

The dwarf shrugged his check shoulders:

'Macchè! She will think she *is* back in England, and the
journey will seem superfluous. My costume is intended to
nip all Nordic nostalgia in the bud.'

'Will you go and change immediately, before our guest . . . '
the Countess broke off in dismay, the curtain had been noiselessly thrust aside, and there, in their midst, stood Elizabeth.
She took one look at Amerigo and burst into uncontrollable
laughter, it was dreadful, she couldn't stop. This Sancho Panza
of a person dressed in checks with the round blue face and
blond moustache – the pipe and the gamp! Charlie Chaplin,
at his best, could not hope to compete. She collapsed onto a
chair, laughing helplessly. The beautiful brothers, anxious to
be on the right side, were not slow to take their cue. They
could now give vent to their suppressed glee and pointed
fingers of derision at the delinquent, who stood there, trans-
fixed. He was doomed, stricken beyond recall. For the rest of
his life he would be in love with Elizabeth.

Mademoiselle Crispin's bedroom was the confessional of
the Papagalli family. Despite the high ceiling on which were
depicted eagles carrying scrolls, it contrived to look curiously
un-Italian, though it could only boast of one piece of French
furniture, a Louis XV *coiffeuse*, small, compact, with feet as
elegant as any gazelle's. Nobody knew how it had found its
way into 'la Crispa's' bedroom, or into the Papagalli household for that matter. Then there were the hats, just begun,
in process of being made; completed. These were the
Frenchwoman's recreation, her violin d'Ingres, so to speak,
snatched from the more onerous duty of dressing the
Papagalli ladies. Anybody would have guessed they were not
Italian hats. No self-respecting Italian hat is ever impertinent,
ironical, arrogant, provocative.

All Crispin's repressed Gallicism had taken refuge in the
hats, expressing moods rather than modes; they were stamped
nevertheless with the indelible mark of France. The room

was full of mute repartees. There was also a four-inch replica of Joan of Arc's highly gilt statue in the Rue de Rivoli and a large flyblown photograph of the Château d'Amboise. She was at work on one of her hats, a thing positively bristling with defiance, when Mario burst in without knocking, flung himself on the ground at her feet, pressing down her bent head with its widening rose du Barri parting (cruelly known to the family as 'l'autostrada') until it nestled against his shoulder.

'Crispina cara, I can hardly wait to hear your impressions! What a morning, what a beauty! Povero Rigo, che disgraziato! How could he have put himself in such a position! He was ridiculous enough already!'

She drew herself up; integrity was not compatible with Mario's nestling head.

'I'm afraid I thought you were all terrible.' The high-heeled French voice deflated each sonorous Italian syllable. 'If his joke was in bad taste, your subsequently turning him into a butt for your sallies, was in even worse. After all, it is not his fault if he is only four foot eleven!'

'But, Crispa, nobody could have helped making fun of the poor little toad. Why, he was staring at Elizabeth as though she were the blessed Virgin!'

'So were you all. Why shouldn't Rigo?'

'But, Crispa, Rigo is an abortion, no doubt he could find some contadina to marry him, but how dare he cast his eyes on Elisabetta?'

'Mon cher enfant,' said Crispa, lapsing in her exasperation, into French, 'comme tu es simpliste! Do you imagine in your primitive Italian way, that it is necessary to be an Adonis in order to appeal to women? What do you make of Stendhal, Voltaire, Benjamin Constant, do you suppose *they* never had any success with women?'

Mario shrugged his fine shoulders. 'They were French, French women are notoriously unexacting in matters of physique, whereas *we* Italians –' he tapped his magnificent chest.

'It's time you travelled, mon cher. The life you lead here is very bad for you.'

Mario's flawless brow puckered. 'Are you quoting il Babbo? He said something to that effect the last time he was here.'

'Your father is a wise man in many ways. He would not want his sons to make fools of themselves avec cette petite Anglaise qui n'est pas pour vous,' rapped Crispin giving a vicious stab at the hat she was trimming.

'And why not, pray? Are we not young, handsome, *ben educati*, rich?'

Crispa's shrug was infinitely wounding. 'No doubt you are all these things, but she is differently orientated – how shall I put it? She looks on you as a necessary stage in her education. She will be very charming – demonstrative, even – but her life is not here. She belongs to another world.'

'You mean, she is *snob*,' suggested Mario, frowning.

'Not necessarily. But I know these English. There were lots of English tourists on the Loire, where my mother kept a small hotel. They were very polite, even friendly, but, inside, they think we foreigners are no better than natives, niggers,' she amplified, wrinkling her kitten's nose. '*Je connais le genre*. She has probably been brought up in a house the size of the Palazzo Pitti with dozens of servants, and waited on like a princess.'

'You mean,' translated Mario, 'that her parents are *pezzi grossi*, immensely rich?'

'On the contrary, they are probably not rich at all. For all that, they may live in feudal splendour, like the Strozzi or the Corsini.'

'*Diamine!*' Mario was impressed. The old Italian nobility and the middle-classes were separated, in those days, by nothing short of an abyss. He suddenly slapped his thigh. 'But this lady Caracole may have letters of introduction, for all we know. Through her we might get to know them!'

'Quite possibly, she may have letters of introduction,' Crispa reflected. The utilitarian aspect of Mario appalled her.

So young and yet so astute! 'But even if she has,' it was better to throw a cold douche at once over these aspirations, 'the invitations would not necessarily include you.'

'Not unless she asked to have us invited. That's easy!'

'Mario, tu me fais peur!' said Crispa with genuine concern.

'Aha! you see!' He rubbed his hands with glee. 'And don't forget we have the Pope on our side.'

'That, in the eyes of the English, would scarcely constitute an asset.'

'I only meant,' returned Mario with hauteur, 'that she might like to have an audience with the Pope.'

Elizabeth to her Mother

Darling Mummy

I have with difficulty restrained myself from sending you a facetious telegram: 'Not twins, quads, male, well developed, all over 18,' it ran, *but*, I reflected, it would not be kind as you have no means of checking up on me, until that old Princess comes nosing around. Comfort yourself with the twin-honoured cliché, there's safety in numbers. I'm never alone with any of them. Their sister sees to that. She is very possessive about them and has made them into a kind of team, or syndicate: they are allowed to admire me collectively, but not individually. The most attractive is Guido (Vica's favourite) the best-looking Ugo, the gayest Mario, the most athletic Leone, and the funniest Amerigo, who is a dwarf (funny how frightened I was of dwarfs as a child), or practically, he is as broad as he's long, and wears frightfully flashy clothes, like a bookmaker. He plays the guitar like an angel and has a lovely dusky voice. His brothers are obviously very much ashamed of him and never cease making fun of his clothes and his figure. He is, incidentally, very amusing, though he can't speak a word of English; what's more, he does the most marvellous conjuring tricks. I should like to have him for a jester.

When he thinks nobody is looking, he gazes at me with
the doting eyes of a dog.

You have no idea how ghastly this apartment is,
Mummy darling. I am perpetually bruising myself against
the furniture, which is surely the most angular that was
ever made. Everything is simply hideous, the pictures
are all of skinny old hermits gazing at skulls or ominous-
looking landscapes with a tiny figure scuttling across them
as fast as it can.

The bathroom reminds me of a disaffected chapel, so
high it is and bald-looking. The bath itself is small, narrow,
and somehow, scratchy. How I miss the nursery bathroom
at home, with its soggy carpet and smell of scorching
flannel!

The food here is copious, flabby and easily masticated;
in fact, Italian cooking seems to be designed for people
with no teeth, one would have thought that a successful
dentist would offer one almost *impregnable* food, as an
advertisement of what his teeth can do!

As a matter of fact, Conte Papagalli is rather a sweet old
boy. He came on a flying visit from Rome. He is the only
member of the family who dares to be natural. Yesterday,
in the middle of luncheon, he coyly produced a small
morocco box – the sort that usually contains jewellery
– which he opened with a flourish, and inside was an
exquisite ratelier, perfect in every respect. I longed to
ask if it was H.H.'s, but didn't dare. The governess is the
dead spit of Zelly; except that she is primmer, more self-
contained. I want you to do something for me without
telling anyone. You know what millions of ties Father has,
put away, and which he never wears. Well, I want you to
send me at least half a dozen, it's for the Brothers who
wear the most awful fancy affairs and long to look British.
Do, this just to please your devoted

                          Liz

P.S. Couldn't Charles come here for the holidays? He

would inevitably fall for Vica, who is frighteningly beautiful like a runaway horse.

The ferocious day, striped white and black, like a zebra,
was declining at length, as though loath to let go. A nimbus
of dust hung over the bridges, never free of the shuffle of
feet. At the angle of the Ponte Vecchio, Beppino, the blind
guitarist, scratched at his instrument with the frenzy of one
affected with erysipelas, raising his moonstone eyes to the
Heavens, whenever he heard a foreign language spoken.

The bells had begun their evening pounding. As usual the
day would be beaten to death. A long glittering canoe like
some diaphanous water insect shot from under the arches
of the Ponte Vecchio. It was Leone, the athlete of Casa
Papagalli taking his evening row. Elbows on the parapet of
the bridge, Vica and Ugo watched him.

'Are there male naiads?' Vica speculated. 'If there are,
Leone must be one of them.'

'Since you're so fond of mythological associations, Vica
mia, you might at least acknowledge my pretensions to being
a centaur.'

'I tire of you and your pretensions,' said Vica smoothly,
'you must learn to become more objective.' Ugo paled. This
was the harshest thing his sister had ever said to him.

'But, but – '

'Zitto. I know what I am saying, Ugoccione mio. You are
charming, but provincial. I did not realize this until I saw you
with Elisabetta. You try too hard to adapt yourself, you are
too forthcoming, too flexible. It is better to be a Leone than
a cameleone,' she added with a chuckle.

'*Meno male.*' Ugo sighed with relief. 'I thought you were
really angry with me.'

She nudged a little nearer.

'Of course not, but listen, tesoro: Leone at least has the
courage to be Leone, that is to say, a handsome brainless
brute, whereas you try to behave as you imagine young

Englishmen of Elisabetta's age and class would behave; the result is, you are ludicrous. I love you, but you are ludicrous. You must change.'

'But how,' there were tears in his eyes, 'only tell me how?'

Vica gave him a comprehensive look as though she were about to measure him for a suit.

'Be more natural, do not say "What ho!" every time you meet her. Something tells me that What ho! is an obsolete expression, anyway. Do not shake hands with her in such a manner that one hears the poor girl's bones crack, kiss her hand.'

'But the English never kiss the hand,' he objected.

'Are you English? She naturally expects you, as an Italian, to kiss her hand. It must be a nice change.'

'*Bene*. Which of us, if any, has discovered the right formula according to you?' inquired Ugo with some bitterness.

'Rigo – '

'*What!*' Ugo could not believe his ears. Vica realized that she was being cruel, but it was salutary.

'Rigo,' she reiterated, 'because he is natural. He is vulgar, exuberant, clownish, inventive. He has but to enter the room for Elisabetta to split her sides with laughter. He plays the guitar, he gesticulates, he does conjuring tricks. He is exactly what Elisabetta expected and hoped Italians would be like.'

'*Santissima madonna!* This is the end! If Rigo is the embodiment of masculine charm, I may as well throw myself into the Arno at once!'

'Don't be silly, Ugo, use your eyes. Who does Elisabetta elect to sit next to at meals? Neither you nor Guido, who are attractive enough, in all conscience. No. She sits near Rigo because he makes her laugh.'

'Naturally. He is a freak.'

'Nobody asked you to be a freak. Content yourself with being an Italian. Pay her compliments, buy her flowers, sing serenades under her window, in short, do all the things you feel tempted to do!'

'Mmà! If it's as easy as that!'

His cares fell from him as a shed garment. He seized his sister by the waist, and they mingled with the dusty crowd of loiterers, pressing their noses against the windows of the small, yet bulky shops, full of jewellery, that savoured more of Clarkson's than of Cartier. Silver-gilt peacocks spread out tails clotted with rubies and sapphires; curiously Wagnerian-looking bracelets, silver, embossed with turquoises, were on the lookout for some passing Wotan; there were branches of coral, like the antlers of some aquatic stag; baroque and seed pearls; chasubles; ikons; old and wicked-looking Spanish combs, inclined more to torture than to coquetry, all these, and more, made the hearts of Vica and Ugo beat with excitement and covetousness.

'When I am rich, Vica, I will give you that necklace set with stones the colour of owl's eyes.'

'And I will give you that huge pearl stud like a blister.'

'O, Vica, look! That must be the dagger, that Lorenzaccio used to kill Alessandro – '

It was stifling in the 'Buca.'

A stench composed of several ingredients, cheese, garlic, sweat, tobacco, was almost tangible, but nobody minded, or even noticed. Smoked hams hung from the rafters, Bologna sausages and chaplets of onions; Chianti had been split on the sawdust which put one in mind of a Spanish arena, after the passage of the horses. The lighting was fitful, treacherous, becoming. The diners fantastically illuminated, resembled a picture by Lenain; among them was Rigo, a trifle tipsy, the blunt bull-curls stuck to his glistening forehead. He pushed a drawing he had just done on the back of the menu over to his best friend, Fortunato Sambuco, the wine merchant.

'There! It's about as like her as an advertisement in a

railway station resembles a Ghirlandajo, I am no artist.' With despair, he added a few flourishes, stretching across his friend.

Fortunato examined the drawing critically, holding it at arm's length.

'A beauty, certainly, but not my type. Too aloof, too stand-offish. *Ci manca qualche cosa.* I would not feel at my ease with this person.'

Rigo pulled a wry face. 'Neither do I, but I pretend, I go through all my antics. All of them. She laughs like an angel. No, she doesn't. She laughs like a jolly sailor. Ho ho! Her laugh is so unexpected. So is her voice, for that matter gruff and impersonal, the reverse of Vica's.'

'Ah! *Ecco una donna!*' Fortunato blew a kiss in the air. 'The other day she came into my *bottega*, you should have seen my *impiegati*. They were *sbalorditi*, dazzled. She wanted a bottle of Strega for a party your mother was giving, I gave her as many bottles as she could carry. I would have given her the shop.'

'She knows that quite well. That's why she came herself instead of sending Gina.'

Fortunato, who was picking his teeth exhaustively, regarded his friend with some suspicion.

'One would think you were jealous of your sister,' he muttered. Rigo shrugged.

'I, jealous? *Sei pazzo!* She cares not for me, nor I for her, though I perceive her points. We are not duped by one another. Curiously enough she is the only member of my family who appreciates me, perhaps because she is the most intelligent. We respect each other.'

'Strange. Respect is the last sentiment I would associate with your sister. As for your brothers. . . . ' The other two guests so far absorbed in a political controversy suddenly whipped round as though they had been stung.

'Brothers, did you say *brothers?*' one shrilled. 'There's only one set of brothers in this town, the Papagalli, and the sooner they clear out of it the better! I do not insult our friend by including him in the family. No doubt he himself shares our views.'

'Come! Come! Dindo,' interposed the wine merchant, 'we are attracting attention. It is not Rigo's fault that he belongs to this . . . this fatuous fraternity. He is the first to acknowledge their absurdities.'

'No one would ever have heard of them,' growled the rebuked one, 'if the Pope had had better teeth. . . . '

'*Zito, Zitto, per carità!*' Fortunato glanced fearfully around, though most of the diners had left, there's no knowing who may be listening. 'The person I am sorry for is your mother, Rigo. I remember hearing her sing when I was a little boy. Un bel di vedremo,' he hummed. 'She was then *un bel pezzo di donna*, a fine figure of a woman.'

'Poor Mamma! It turned her head becoming a Countess, it turned all their heads except il Babbo, who is an artist in his way. If there is a muse of dentistry, she is his mistress.'

The others were inclined to agree.

'Si,' nodded Fortunato, still picking his teeth, '*hai ragione.* He does not give himself airs, your father. The other day he strolled into the bottega and had a glass of Marsala over the counter, as natural as could be . . . just like old times.'

'They will want to make grand marriages, no doubt,' scoffed Callisto Fagioletti, the apothecary, who resembled Erasmus, 'members of the aristocracy, I shouldn't be surprised, Counts, Princes. I must say, Rigo, it would suit your sister to be a Princess, Donna Ludovica . . .' he raised his glass to the light. 'One can understand social aspirations in a woman.'

'O my sister is nothing so simple. She is a romantic in her way. If she thought she looked her best as a nun, she would take the veil. She is ambitious for us, very anxious we should make a success of ourselves. I will say that for her. She approves of me because I have taken the only line she considers suitable to one of my . . . physique. The court buffoon. A Velasquez. Perfect.' He clapped softly. His pals began to feel uncomfortable. Rigo, in this Pagliacci mood, was out of place. They wished he would return to his usual vein of salacious anecdote, inimitable mimicry.

'A little music,' Fortunato insinuated, 'a little music is what we need to soothe our savage breast.' Rigo's guitar was very popular and now that they had the place to themselves . . . Feeling that he had somehow let them down, Rigo immediately acceded to their request.

'*Volentieri*. I will fetch my guitar which I left with my coat.'

He returned a few minutes later with the instrument that was his most cherished possession. Tenderly he bent over it, as though seeking its consent. His friends grunted contentedly. This was a great treat. Rigo had a fine, if untrained, baritone; he was shy about singing, the discrepancy between his voice and his physique he found shocking, he would have liked to sing hidden. Shyly, slyly, he glanced up at his audience, he knew they expected the latest popular song: 'Stretti, stretti' – or better still, 'Nostalgia.'

With a malicious twinkle, he said: 'The words of the song I am going to sing are by Lorenzo de Medici, the music is by – me! *Ascoltate*!

> Quant'è bella giovinezza
> Che si sfugge tuttavia.
> Chi vuol esser lieto, sia,
> Di doman' non c'è certezza . . .
> Di doman' non c'è certezza . . .

The lovely song mounted in the air like smoke, where it lingered as though loathe to dissolve . . .

> Di doman' non c'è certezza . . .

His friends, receptive, enlightened, listened, entranced. So this was the real Rigo, a poet, a lover. They assessed his chances running their eyes over the preposterous clothes, the disproportionately large head, the round lustrous, slightly prominent eyes, like cherries in brandy.

Mmà! Women have fallen in love with less than he. The
blonde miss was a dark horse. These blonde misses were
well known to throw discretion to the winds, once they set
foot in Italy.

The same word passed through three minds, simultaneously, philosophical, fatalistic, the eternal refuge of the
Italian: *Pazienza....*

CHAPTER FOUR
The Princess

AT three o'clock every afternoon, a profound, a consecrated silence descended upon the Palazzo Arrivamale. At ten minutes to three, precisely, a small red-headed figure would be seen flitting purposefully down the passages, through the drawing-rooms, through the sala, down the grand staircase, through the offices, even into the kitchens.

It was Valka, Princess Arrivamale's maid-companion, who took it upon herself to paralyse the nerve centres of the house as a prelude to her mistress's siesta. Woe betide the luckless footman or *cameriera* if her or she should split the silence by a song.

Valka was omnipresent, Valka was behind every pillar, Valka lurked down every passage. Like a small freckled fury, she would spring out on them, hissing, vituperative. . . .

The etymology of the word 'Valka' was a curious one. Her real name was Walker, Ivy Doris Walker. She had been for many years the companion of a Russian Countess, a survivor of the once flourishing, now practically extinct, Russian colony in Florence. When she was not engaged in telling her own fortune with a pack of cards as greasy as that of any gipsy, the Countess was to be found in the kitchen, a cigarette-holder the length of a conductor's baton jutting from the corner of her mouth, stirring a horrid concoction made out of *frutti di mare*, which, she alleged, was as good as any caviar.

'Prijivalka' is the Russian term for that ambigous creature, half lady companion, half poor relation, who figures in every Russian novel. The Italian pronunciation of Walker is, of course, Valka; it fitted in beautifully with her vocation of prijivalka, hence the diminutive adopted by the Countess and her friends.

Indeed, it is doubtful whether the Walker family (of Orpington, Kent) would have recognized the original Ivy in the frail, though formidable flail, the domestic Savonarola, she had become since she had entered the service of Princess Arrivamale. It was her justifiable boast that she had saved the contentedly robbed Countess from ruin. The Countess regarded this as quite a normal state of affairs, was, indeed, prepared to let it go on indefinitely. Ivy Walker was temporarily engaged (her own maid was on holiday), but there was nothing temporary about Ivy.

In less than a week she had triumphantly proved to the Countess that all her staff was dishonest and that she, Ivy Walker, was indispensable. Wearily, the Countess gave in. The servants gave notice one after the other; and were replaced by serfs, who knew an Ivan the Terrible when they saw one.

In another sphere, and with a different upbringing, Miss Walker might have been a Christabel Pankhurst, or even a Lady Hester Stanhope.

There was certainly something intrepid, pioneerish, about her: she knew not the meaning of the word fear.

The Countess eventually died, tired out by hygiene and accuracy. Valka, by that time, had become a byword; her name was synonym for integrity: 'as honest as Valka' . . . The Countess left her the money she had saved her during her lifetime, and a collection of Fabergé objects. Would Valka retire? This question was discussed in many a Florentine salon. . . . Would Valka rent a small seemly apartment, there to end her days surrounded by jade animals and cigarette cases? Not she. Valka was accustomed to running a large and (preferably) undisciplined household, to cracking her knout, to lording it over the lesser fry.

Moreover, she was a snob.

She had been for five years the confidant of a countess. What was to prevent her from becoming the protégée of a princess? She was prompt in answering Principessa Arrivamale's advertisement in the Nazione, prompt and pressing. She did not immediately realize that in the Princess she had met her Waterloo. The latter was little, brittle; she resembled a black little ant. From her mother, who had been a Spanish duchess in her own right, she had inherited eyes that were like deep pools of melancholy, superb teeth, exquisite tiny hands, legs scarcely thicker than a grass-hopper's; from her Venetian father, a sinuous, humorous mouth, a straight arrogant nose; malice, wit; a vitality unabated by her sixty years.

She was not in the least impressed by Valka, or her references. She engaged her in a sporting spirit, as one buys a horse reputed unmountable (Valka's reputation had, of course, preceded her), determined to get the better of her; also, because she wanted to keep up her English.

If the Princess was not impressed, Valka was. The poor Countess' muskovite massiveness, clumsy jewels, tarnished samovars, paled into significance before the ambassadorial *portiere*, marble staircase, frescoed galleries, papal portraits, armorial tapestries of the Palazzo Arrivamale.

Everything about the Princess was exciting; that husky all-too-rapid voice, the tattoo she beat on the table, the final ultimatum: 'I give a hundred lire a month; take it, or leave it.'

Valka took it. It was half of what she was in the habit of asking.

She left the palace feeling more like Ivy Walker than she had done for years.

*

Now the Palace slumbered, or feigned to slumber. The fountain in the *cortile* dribbled, unchecked; a small green lizard was clamped like a brooch to its rim. Bluebottles buzzed impatiently against the closed shutters, endeavouring to get in, or out. A brilliant butterfly, like a fragment of stained glass, palpitated, trapped in a lozenge of light on the mosaic floor of the Princess' bedroom. She was not asleep in spite of all Valka's precautions. She slept but seldom; to do so involved such strategy, such preparations, such isolation of this plan and that, that it became too much trouble.

She was too lazy to sleep.

If it amused Valka for her to do her sleeping beauty act, she saw no objection; occasionally, she would give Valka the treat of saying she had made a perfect siesta, occasionally, but not to-day. She was half amused, half irritated by a letter she had received from her English friend, Sylvia Canterdown, which had arrived that morning, and which she hadn't had time to read until now, by the light of her bedside lamp. . . . Really the English were too extraordinary, nice, but un-civilized, without a notion of *ce qui se fait et ce qui ne se fait pas*! Fancy sending one's seventeen-year-old daughter to stay with a dentist, with four fully-fledged sons! Not content with this, Sylvia Canterdown must needs ask *her*, la Principessa Arrivamale, née Duquesa de Sotomejor, *nerissima*, but stay: the man was the Pope's dentist, that, as far as she could make out, was his only redeeming feature? . . . Still, one does not call on a dentist, except to make an appointment. Had Sylvia taken leave of her senses? True, she never had much. Luz recalled with affectionate contempt, poor Sylvia's irruption into salons, scattering bibelots right and left, all feet and teeth, but with lovely hair, like spun gold. No doubt the child was pretty! She sighed. She would have liked Sylvia to marry her brother, Alfonso.

Let's face it, Alfonso was not, well, not quite as other boys. O, not cretinous, Heavens, no! A case of arrested development. At twenty he had the mentality of a boy of ten, that is to say on his *good* days. Of course, her parents, despite their vagueness, would never have given their consent. The English were categorical about some things. So unworldly. Alfonso was a *parti* not to be sneezed at. O well . . . The poor boy was dead. *Alea jacta est.* He was killed bird-nesting; fell from a tree. She recalled how Marcantonio, her husband, had actually seemed relieved; the only remarks he had ever made in bad taste had been at poor Alfonso's expense. You see, there was madness in the Sotomejor family, two generations back. . . .

Marcantonio, was an astronomer, 'tipo Galileo,' a savant, an original. They were universally known as '*l' astronome et le gastronome.*' They got on very well. She had had many lovers in her crepitating Spanish manner. As for Marcantonio, he was only interested in young girls, mere children; preferably the daughters of his *contadini.* He was very kind to them and always gave them generous dowries; in fact, he was much in demand as a *dépuceleur.* The Princess was all for these rustic affairs, as, officially, at least, she was able to boast the most faithful of husbands. . . .

The title and lands would go to Marcantonio's nephew, Gian Galeazzo de' Pardi, who was calling on his aunt this afternoon. She felt a thrill of pleasurable anticipation. Gigi was all that Marcantonio had never been: handsome, spirited, deliciously impertinent, subtle, unscrupulous. And what a figure! Like an *espada*, that so handsome *espada* who always stood poised with his *bandilleras* high over the bull's head, to show off his figure to the fullest advantage. Not Belmonte, that other one, Pepito, Chiquito? Never mind, she would remember later. She turned on her lamp again. The hands of the little enamel clock pointed to half-past four. What was Valka thinking of? She knew she took at least an hour to dress, rejecting this dress and that. Really, the woman was insupportable! It was easy to see she had been with a Russian, no idea of punctuality, it served her right for having a 'Bohemian' maid!

At last! At last! Valka's quick light step was heard crossing the squeaky parquet floor of her *cabinet de toilette*. With infinite precautions she opened the communicating door. A voice like a whip, lashed out from the bed. 'Valka! Are you mad? It is now nearly twenty-five minutes to five!'

'But I always call you at half-past four, Princess. If I am three minutes late . . . '

'Do not argue, you know I am expecting il Signorino at five-thirty. Get me dressed at once!'

Dear! Dear! Valka felt as though she were treading on eggs. It was up to her to put the Princess in a good temper within the next five minutes. As she threw open the shutters, she cast around for a palliative. The vast room appeared in all its macabre grandeur. The walls were hung with a bilious seventeenth-century damask, it matched the complexion of the misanthropic family portraits, their straight arrogant noses possessively pointed to their parentage with the one on the bed. Realistic Spanish renderings of the gory ends of Saint Margaret and Saint Cecilia were placed so that they were the first pictures that caught the eye on waking.

By the Princess' *table de nuit* stood an almost lifesize photograph of her brother on his deathbed, stressing his rather unfortunate resemblance to Gian Gastone de' Medici. This was not all. A high perpendicular prie-Dieu, worked in hideous wools by a chanoinesse aunt of Marcantonio's and which was never dusted, let alone moved, appeared to conduct this symphony in metaphorical 'blues'. Sacrosanct, it was the bane of Valka's existence; many were the passing swipes it got from her duster.

On one side of the immense bed lay the diminutive form of the Princess, clad in white crepe-de-chine pyjamas.

'Supposing you wore the Chanel check,' suggested Valka in what she hoped was her most ingratiating voice. 'The Signorina said you didn't look a day over thirty in it.'

'Mmm, it might do,' replied her mistress, slightly mollified, but she was not going to let off Valka so lightly. Sylvia

Canterdown's letter still had to be discussed. 'Perhaps you can tell me, my good Valka, why all your compatriots are mad, mad as hatters? What do you make of this?' She tossed Valka Lady Canterdown's letter. To Valka it was so much gibberish. She was unversed in the ways of the British aristocracy; her only experience of life in a British family had not been a pleasant one; she had accompanied a terrifying old lady, subject to epileptic fits, to the Riviera some twenty years ago. Thence she had drifted to Italy – Italy and the revelation of Life. . . . Meanwhile her present employer was impatiently awaiting her diagnosis: 'Well?' demanded the Princess, drumming on the table.

'It seems a very nice letter,' faltered Valka, at a loss.

'It does not occur to you odd, that Lady Canterdown should bid me call on a dentist?'

'Yes, no, indeed, your Highness cannot possibly call on a dentist' stammered Valka, falling headlong into the trap.

'*Of course*, I shall call on the dentist,' thundered the Princess, bringing her tiny fist down on the table, 'it is the least one can do for an old friend! I thought the English made such a fetish of friendship?' she added, scathingly: 'perhaps not, in *your class. In ogni maniera*, I shall call on the dentist to-morrow.

Having confounded Valka, she suddenly felt in a very good humour.

'Now I will dress, and you need not look as though Attila and *all* the Huns had passed over your negligible corpse. You must learn to become more resilient. How do I look with this gardenia in my hair?'

Gian Galeazzo de' Pardi waited in the Venetian saloon. He lit cigarette after cigarette, taking only a puff or two at each. Never relaxed, never still, it was as good an occupation as another. He was for ever on the qui vive; ever prepared, ever ready to parry sting with sting.

Though feminine, he was not effeminate; he could be

spectacularly brave, provided it was a solo performance, and
that the spotlight was focussed on him. Though fiendish to
his equals, he was a kind and considerate landlord, much
beloved by his *contadini*, who were as proud of his elegance
as though he were a successful and 'representative' relation.
His good looks were proverbial. He had been painted,
sculpted, caricatured, photographed. He was conscious of
his good looks, conscious, but critical; no slackening
escaped detection, no wrinkle passed unchallenged. He
was the severe guardian of his physique, impatient of excess,
contemptuous of over-indulgence – like a boxer, ever in
training.

For the last five years, his love affairs had been strictly
rationed (he was getting on for forty); they were more
awards to beauty, fashion, charm, than the undisciplined
plungings of a runaway heart. Once or twice in his lifetime,
he had been seriously in love, but this was to be deplored;
one grows either too thin, or too fat, too bohemian or too
luxurious, too grim or too gay. The person he was probably
fondest of was la Zia, the Princess. He never took so much
trouble as with her, she was his most fervent admirer, his
most fastidious critic.

When she entered the room, with her usual *haute école*
step, he tossed a freshly-lit cigarette away, rushed to meet
her, kissing first both cheeks, then both hands. '*Zia cara*!
How happy I am to see you! You do not know how I have
missed you when I was in Paris. Not one of these women
have your quality, your chic, your brio; you make them
appear like kitchenmaids.'

'*Enjôleur, va*!' She lightly tapped his virile though
discreetly powdered cheek. 'Come, sit by me, and relate all
the latest *potins*. Are Gabrielle and Louis René still a model
couple?'

'Yes and no. Officially no, unofficially yes. They so adore
each other that they fear to look bourgeois, so that in
public they go out of their way to be rude to each other,

though I suspect that she dines with him, veiled, *en cabinet particulier.*'

'*Gigi, tu m'enchantes*' (speaking French was one of their many affectations). 'How jealous I shall be the day you get married!'

'*Zia cara*, I shall never marry.'

'But you must, *mon petit*, you must. It is essential you should have an heir.'

He shrugged; he knew it was inevitable; in point of fact, he had allotted himself but another year of celibacy.

'Find me someone as attractive as yourself, *ma tante.*'

For a moment his eyes held her, pinned her down, she was his . . . A delicious tremor shook her thin shoulders; to carry it off, she lit a cigarette.

'My dear boy, there are heaps of young ladies, *qui ne demanderaient pas mieux.*'

'I dislike young ladies. They either reek of the convent or are more enterprising than tarts. There is never a *juste milieu.*'

'Your uncle says . . . '

'That I ought to marry a nice chubby country girl, who will give me plenty of children, and not a moment's anxiety.'

'Well, I think there is a lot to be said for your uncle's point of view. After all, you don't want to be jealous of your wife.'

'*D'accord.* One does not marry in order to be jealous, if one can help it. Cara Zia, we see, as usual, eye to eye. The topic of my marriage is like an old family dog, to which one accords a perfunctory pat from time to time. Let us consider the pat as given. Now we can talk of something which really amuses us. When I was in Paris, guess who I saw, as young as ever. An old friend of yours.'

'Not Carlotta?'

'Precisely. How old would you say she was?'

'At least as old as she says I am.'

'Bravo. As witty as ever, *ma petite tante*. Well, Carlotta has taken up a French *industriel*, young, but with a huge posterior. They say he is amusing – '

'Beauty is not everything.'

'It *is* with Carlotta, she can practically dispense with conversation.'

Et patati et patata.

In the Venetian salotino, the shadows began to lengthen; the mirrors that looked as though they should be operated on for cataract, became less particular as to what, and whom, they reflected. Aunt and nephew were too absorbed in their indiscretions to notice the two charming, silently tittering Longhi ladies who, mask in hand, sat just behind them and drank in every word they uttered. . . .

'Goodness gracious! One would think the Queen was coming to tea!' exclaimed Elizabeth on entering the drawing-room, where the entire family, with the exception of Rigo, were busying themselves over preparations for receiving Princess Arrivamale. Mario was arranging the flowers (which he did to perfection). Vica was trying out a new coiffure in front of the looking-glass (the one in her bedroom was cracked); Ugo was grouping the chairs; Guido, squirting lavender water from a cut-glass spray; to Leone, was allotted the more virile task of spanking the rugs out on the balcony; as for Mamma, armed with the *plumeau* inseparable from French farce, she went around flicking imaginary dust from the uncompromising furniture. (Crispa, meanwhile, was putting the last touches to Gina's revised appearance in her bedroom.)

'I'm sure she wouldn't have come, if she had thought she would give so much trouble,' deplored Elizabeth, uncomprehending.

'Mmà!' Mamma tossed her head, 'it is not everyone who has the honour of receiving the Principessa Arrivamale,' she said in the execrable French which was her only means of communicating with Elizabeth.

'Mais elle doit être une très vieille dame, elle doit être soixante, si elle est un jour,' Elizabeth countered in a French equally vile. ('What is sixty if the heart is young,' murmured Mamma, fluffing her side curls) . . . 'about the same age as Mummy I should think,' continued Elizabeth in English, which Mamma understood but could not speak. 'They knew each other when they were girls. She said the Princess was tiny, and black, and very, very active. I expect she'd be amazed if she saw you all milling about like an army of ants.'

'You forget: la Principessa is one of the doyennes of Florentine aristocracy. Really, my child, you might be a *contadina*. No, a *contadina* would know better!'

Then, at long last, the scales fell from Elizabeth's eyes. Of course, these people were snobs, she had always known it. Their anglophilia was all part of their snobbishness. That's why Ugo exclaimed: 'What ho!' whenever he met her, and which she had taken to mean she resembled a Watteau; that's why they were so pleased with father's old ties, that's why Leone pretended to practise approach shots with the poker . . .

O dear! What a pity. The only one who wasn't a snob was poor little Rigo. *That's why he isn't here.*

Roused to indignation, Elizabeth inquired with the innocence she no longer possessed: 'And where is Rigo? What task have you set him?'

'O Rigo is out for the day,' supplied Vica airily, patting a rebellious curl into place, 'he does not like social functions, he prefers to play *tresette* with his queer little friends.'

'Why doesn't he ask them here, I'd like to meet them,' insisted Elizabeth, her Anglo-Saxon love of lost causes asserting itself more strongly.

'I do not think you would, really. They are not very attractive, you know. They smell of garlic and they pick their teeth,' came the languid reply, as she essayed a gardenia behind her ear.

'I think it would be rather fun to meet people who do whatever comes into their head,' said Elizabeth doggedly. Her tone sounded so rebellious that Vica looked round sharply. This was something quite new. For a moment she was at a loss, but only for a moment. Of course, *i fratellini* had overdone it, as she never tired telling them, their anglomania had made them ridiculous. As for Rigo, he had struck the right note from the beginning. She was convinced she had always been on Rigo's side, which was true, in a sense, but she had lacked the official confirmation. Swiftly, she came and sat by Elizabeth, taking her square, curiously serviceable hand, in her own narrow gothic one. '*Hai ragione, cara*, Rigo is – how you say, a *festa* of fun, but I scarcely think he would be a success with la Principessa, do you? He is too rough, too *turbulente*. We did not *ask* him to go out, we just said we were expecting an old lady to tea, *basta*! Rigo likes not old ladies!'

Elizabeth grunted, unappeased. Her discovery had distressed her. She liked the Papagallis *en bloc*, admired their looks, was amused by them. She was '*en coquetterie*' with Leone, who was really too magnificent, but coquetry is not the right word to use in connection with Elizabeth. She was not oblique enough for coquetry; if she liked you, she openly proclaimed her liking. Let us say, rather, that in view of her quite open admiration for Leone, he felt authorized to do what he could to make her fall in love with him. Unfortunately the only language in which he could express himself was the language of flowers; he had already coaxed a thousand lires out of his mother for the purpose of furthering his floral suit. Every morning his sister gave him an English lesson. This suited Vica. It was necessary that Elizabeth should fall in love with one of the brothers. Leone was the one she could most easily dispense with. She was astute enough to realize that Elizabeth had, so to speak, debunked her family, astute enough to cut her losses and let in the air. (Lest it should seem improbable that anyone as young as Vica should be so perspicacious, let it be recalled that Vica was nearly twenty-one and that an Italian girl of twenty-one is at least equal to an English girl of twenty-five).

'Cara Elisabetta,' she soothed in her hypnotic contralto, 'surely you had realized what an absurd family we are? Since Pappà became a papal count we all suffer from what Crispa calls '*la folie des grandeurs*' – all except Pappà, who lives in a world of his own – but the rest of us! Why, I never play the same part twice! One day I am Lucrezia Borgia, another day I am Isabella d'Este. Have you never seen me as Floria Tosca?' So saying she snatched a few lilies out of the hands of the passing Mario, allowed them to droop over one arm, placed a large flat basket at an audacious angle on the top of her head, strutted a few yards with prima donna-like aplomb and burst into: 'Vissi d'arte, Vissi d'amore – ' which she sang in a voice soggy with throaty passion. Of course, Elizabeth burst out laughing, which was what she was intended to do.

'There, you see!' exulted Vica, replacing lilies and basket, 'I told you I was versatile!'

Abruptly, the front door bell rang, strident, peremptory.

'Mamma mia! la Principessa!'

She flew to the looking-glass. The family who had also heard the front door bell, were now rushing about like scene shifters, just before the curtain goes up.

The front door was at the end of a long dark passage. Fully a minute elapsed before the drawing-room door was thrown open, and Gina, overcome by all the recommendations lavished on her, announced in an inaudible voice: 'La Principessa Arrivamale.'

A diminutive figure, black and brilliant, like a live coal, came quickly into the room.

Everything about her scintillated, eyes, teeth, ear-rings. Her face was not so much a face as a facet. But what she saw was at least as arresting as what *they* saw: Vica and Elizabeth stood side by side. The Princess gasped involuntarily, she had seldom seen two such beautiful creatures; one so fortunately fair, mythically fair, the other so dark, so beautifully designed, so *apposite*, an allegory representing what? But these poetic impressions were quickly dispelled by considerations of a more practical nature: Gigi must marry this dazzling child. As she shook hand after hand, reason upon reason rallied to her cause, beauty, birth, fortune, prestige. Sylvia must be made to realize that it would be in no way derogatory for her daughter to marry the future Prince Arrivamale. The dentist's brood were certainly a handsome lot. They were doubtless all in love with Elizabeth. It was to be hoped she had arrived in time, but *had* she? A realist, the Princess was aware of the shock the first impact of Italy must be on the senses of one so young and so beautiful. The Anglo-Saxon is only too prone to shed his inhibitions once he is on the other side of the Alps. She also knew that in England, it was not considered disgraceful to have one or two *novios* before settling down. Would one of these spectacular young men dare propose *à l'anglaise* to Elizabeth, who, in her ignorance, would not immediately transpose them into terms of English middle-class climbers? Everywhere her gaze was met by eyes above their station. What a chance for the dentist's sons! They would be fools not to profit by it. While she sipped her excessively nasty tea and exchanged platitudes with the Countess her connoisseur's glance took in every detail of their anatomy. How would Gigi compare with their extreme youth, their luxuriance of hair and leanness of limb? The answer came, pat enough. At Elizabeth's age one was more attracted by maturity than by inexperience. Gigi's technique was proverbial throughout Europe. Had he not refused Mrs. van Push's millions, the hand of a semi-royal Princess? Her gaze strayed from the brothers to the more enigmatic features of Vica; she realized with one of her infallible intuitions that here was someone to be reckoned with. The girl proved her intelligence by seating herself impulsively on a stool at the Princess's feet and by saying in that voice that caught you unawares, 'All my life I have wondered what kind of person lived in the Palazzo Arrivamale. Please do not think me impertinent if I say I hoped it would be someone like you.'

The Princess peered down into eyes that seemed to

contain a foreground and a middle distance, the first, green;
the second, gold. It would never do if Gian Galeazzo gained
admission into eyes such as these; mercifully, he was
momentarily sated with his own countrywomen. 'You must
come and see my Palace from the inside,' she found herself
saying. Hardly were the words out of her mouth than she
regretted them, but, she reasoned, I can scarcely ask one
girl without the other, besides, Gigi, in common with most
of our compatriots, prefers the nordic type. Moreover, he is
no fool. He would never dream of marrying the daughter of
a dentist, however attractive.

Elizabeth is not self-conscious, neither does she show off,
noted the Princess with approval. A kind of gruff humour,
more boyish than feminine, invested all she said. She had a
brother, Luz* recollected: so much the better, she was not an
oie blanche.

'Tell me, my dear, how old is your brother now?'

'Charles? Oh, he's getting on for twenty-three.'

'And no prospect of marriage?'

'For Charles? Goodness, no! He is a perfect baby, years
younger than me mentally.'

'I was forgetting how young Englishmen are for their age.
You see, it is such a long time since I was in your country.'

'Mummy often used to talk about you. She used to say:
'What a – I mean, how very amusing you were.'

Luz twinkled. 'Yes, I used to go and stay at your grandparents' villa at Cannes, when I was a little girl. I used to
make your mother play *corridas*, bull-fights. She was always
the picador's horse. *I* was the picador.'

Elizabeth burst out laughing.

'Poor dear Mummy, she *would* be.'

'When we were in our 'teens,' continued the Princess with
relish, 'I used to send anonymous letters to your odious old
grandfather, written in red ink, to the effect that there was a

*The name should be pronounced LOOTH.

plot to assassinate him. He got so nervous that he never went out after dark.'

Here was a person after Elizabeth's own heart; how refreshing it was to converse with someone with a sense of humour!

'Weren't you and Mummy both in love with the same young man at one time?' she prompted.

The Princess looked dubious for a moment. 'We . . . ll, the young man was in love with your mother: I tried to get him away from her.'

'And did you succeed?'

'Yes and no. Yes, in the sense that he was more amused by me; no, in the sense that he wanted to marry your mother.'

'Was Mummy very pretty?'

'Very. She had hair like you, but she was on a larger (she nearly added, clumsier scale) – she played the harp and I the castanets.'

There was more of Elizabeth's gusty laughter. 'O dear, how funny! The Harp and the Castanets, fable, like "la Cigale et la Fourmi" . . . ' She was suddenly conscious of the mute, aggrieved, family circle, who could make nothing of this dialogue on terms of equality between an elderly *grande dame* and a raw schoolgirl. This was surely not how a person of seventeen should behave to la Principessa Arrivamale, even if she *had* been *en pension* with her mother, but far from taking offence, she appeared to be enjoying herself. The Papagallis felt out of it, that is to say, all but Vica, who was listening with rapt attention. This was the lesson she had need of. How to be at ease with the great, how to put the great at their ease. She perceived she had always been on the right track: deference without servility. The brothers were beginning to think that the Princess would take her leave with nothing accomplished, when, from the next room, known as '*lo studio*,' where no one ever studied, came the first tender tentative pluckings of a guitar, then, pian piano, Rigo's velvet voice singing a song which seemed strangely out of keeping with his personality, something about 'Giovinezza' and 'certezza.' At the first words of the song, the Princess put up her finger to impose silence. As the invisible singer finished singing, she sprang to her feet: 'Who is this hidden artist? I want to see him, please bring him in.'

Poor Contessa! This was the final betrayal, the defeat of all her hopes; manfully, she strove to keep back her tears: 'Go,' she almost sobbed to Guido, 'go and fetch your brother.' With pathetic dignity she turned to the Princess. 'It is my son, Principessa, he is very shy, because he is small, unlike his brothers, you will see.'

Vica, sardonically humorous, flung open the 'studio' door. 'Va, mascalzone,' she hissed, 'go then, saboteur of the family's aspirations, you are wanted.' Even *she* did not think Rigo could get away with this.

The Princess was expecting yet another Papagallino in pseudo-British clothes. She was hard put to keep a straight face, when a mannikin almost as broad as he was long, dressed in a check suit, a purple shirt, open at the neck, and sandals, came towards her, lugging his guitar, as though it were a recalcitrant child.

'Come, *piccinina*, say how do you do to the lady, she won't eat you. Don't slouch.'

This was the sort of joke that appealed to the Princess. She laughed outright.

Rigo, seeing that it was a success, kept it up. He settled the guitar on his knee, improvised the kind of patter one exchanges with a marionette. He had had no intention of spoiling the party, no idea that his music *en sourdine* would culminate in a show-down. He often used '*lo studio*' to practise in. Surely it was better to brazen it out, now that the harm was done, judging from his brothers' expressions?

This was the second time, they were thinking, that Rigo had let them down, the second time he had stolen their thunder. *Pazienza*, he would lose nothing by waiting.

At length, as though tired out with laughing, the Princess rose to go. Elizabeth, delighted with her protégé, patted him on the head.

'Elizabeth must bring you to see me,' cooed the Princess, as he bent over her hand (they were much the same height, though the Princess, of course, wore high heels). 'Sunday, I shall be at home. You must bring your guitar, I long to hear more of your songs. I shall expect the three of you' – her nod included Vica – 'Countess,' she turned to her dumb-founded hostess – '*Grazie infinite* – such a delightful party – your son is most talented.' A collective bow was all the beautiful brothers got.

Tiny and formidable, familiar and inaccessible, the Princess, with a final scrabble in the air to Elizabeth, hurried out.

Valka had been in the library for at least twenty minutes, hunting high and low, for what her irascible mistress termed the English 'Gotha.' It did not occur to her literal mind that what the Princess wanted was Debrett. She had been gazing at its faded pink bulk for quite a long time, not daring to return empty-handed, the main thing was to bring some-thing in English. Perhaps the fat pink tome would pass for a plausible error? She peered more closely at the title: Peerage, Baronetage, Knightage. Could it be that? Tremulous but hopeful, she bore it aloft to the Princess' *cabinet de toilette*. 'There is no English Gotha. I thought this might, perhaps, do instead?'

'What is that but the English Gotha, *mujer poco ilustrada*?' scoffed her mistress (nothing, she knew, unnerved Valka more than to be apostrophized in Spanish).

'The English Gotha, my poor ignorant, goes under the name of Debrett. This particular volume belonged to my mother, who, like all Spaniards was a snob, and a fanatic about "*places à table*." Read what it says about Canterdown, Earl of. I have mislaid my spectacles.'

Valka was by no means familiar with the English Gotha, and after floundering about for a few minutes in the Baronetage, she was no nearer her goal.

'Give *me* the book,' commanded the Princess, in the tone in which Lady Macbeth says: 'Give me the dagger.' Squinting through her lorgnette she found it at once. 'Here, silly, but I can't read the rest, the print is too small.' With that she plumped the heavy volume on Valka's lap, lit a cigarette and waited. Valka read, in a reverent voice, with highly accentuate suburban aspirates:

CHRISTOPHER CHARLES CARACOLE, C.V.O., 9th Earl and 11th Baronet; b. June 1st, 1870; ed. at Wellington; Lieut.-Col. Royal Horse Guards (Reserve); European War, 1914-1918 (despatches, Legion of Honour). Sometime an A.D.C. to H.M.; has orders of Crown of Italy and Rising Sun of Japan; M.V.O. 1901; C.V.O. 1918; m. Lady Sylvia Trude, dau. of the 5th Earl of Random, and has issue.

SON LIVING

CHARLES CHRISTOPHER (Viscount Risingdale), b. Jan. 6th, 1900.

DAUGHTER LIVING

LADY ELIZABETH FRANCES GERTRUDE, b. May 22nd, 1906.

'A very old family, I'm sure,' was Valka's summing up, 'and highly thought of in the country, I'll be bound! *My* home was not far from Knole, Lord Sackville's seat, one of our stately homes, so to speak. My auntie took me over there, when I was ever so tiny, she was a friend of the housekeeper's. I can only remember two things,' she added complacently, 'the way my pore little legs almost gave out, and the smell of moth ball.'

But the Princess was not interested in Valka's reminiscences:

'It is indicated that Elizabeth should marry the Signorino. Æsthetically how pleasing, he so dark, she so fair. . . . '

Her pointed chin cupped in a claw-like hand, she gazed into the future: she saw a couple of curly blond Anglo-Italian babies, romping in a luscious green park, with Gian Galeazzo and Elizabeth fondly looking on, and conscious that la Zia was the author of their happiness. . . .

Valka, too, had her vision: Valka on a gracious visit to England with the Princess; Valka lording it over the British housekeeper's room.

'Yes, we *are* pleased to see the young people so happy. Of course it was the Princess' idea. The Princess and I . . . '

She planned to take the English Gotha up to her bedroom before replacing it in the library. It was high time she got acquainted with the aristocracy of her own country.

The trio aroused considerable interest on their way to call at Palazzo Arrivamale. The flashy little man, who had only just escaped being a dwarf, flanked by two such ravishing young ladies, caused a good deal of staring, and not a few obscene comments. The Florentines are chary of neither. The young ladies pretended not to notice; as for Rigo, it was the happiest day of his life. He was actually escorting his beloved on a visit to the most hermetic palace in Florence. An inverted Cinderella, he had been preferred to his beautiful brothers. The beautiful brothers remained by the fireside, whereas he . . . it was impossible to repress a skip!

It needed the Cyclopean portals of the Palazzo Arrivamale to put a little seemly awe into his bubbly heart. The great door clanged behind them. They found themselves in another world, in a world of golden green penumbra, placid fountains, Olympian statues. A world where Time yawned, and stood still.

Vica felt suddenly appeased, as though all her half-formulated wishes had been granted, as though she had

been idly fingering a book and had suddenly come across
her own name. She resembled some marvelling nymph, with
her dilated nostrils and parted lips. . . .

As for Elizabeth, her reactions were quite different. She
exclaimed: 'Who would have thought this gloomy old palace
could be so nice inside?' Poor Rigo, deprived of speech, could
only grin slavishly. As in a dream, the three followed the
puzzled footman up the marble staircase with the Correggio
ceiling, through drawing-room after drawing-room, past
statue after statue, until finally they reached the Venetian
boudoir, where the Princess and her nephew waited. Gian
Galeazzo towered beside her, curiously disarmed. He had all
his countrymen's immediate response to beauty; he had
expected one assault on his senses, not two. *La Zia* had said:
the dentist's daughter is very good-looking, certainly not
banale, but wait until you see Elizabeth! An aubade or a
nocturne, light or shade, *l'allegra* or *la pensierosa*? He drew
his imagination up with a jerk, this would never do. The
dentist's daughter was ruled out. The future Prince Arrivamale
does not wed the dentist's daughter, he takes her as his
mistress. That wouldn't do either. It was time he settled down.
This was a unique opportunity, as la Zia had pointed out so
forcibly. No dentist's daughter, however alluring, could be
permitted to interfere with it. Besides, she would keep. Once
he was comfortably married, the father of a son and heir . . .
Chi lo sa? . . . Gian Galeazzo selected his manner as he would
have selected a foil. *Empressé* but not obsequious; a tempered
gaiety, faintly tinged with irony; a suggestion of ardour kept
under control.

Elizabeth thought: What a handsome man, I'm sure he
fancies himself, like all Italians. Pity! He's got a lovely voice,
I like the way his hair is beginning to grow grey at the
temples . . . what actor does he remind me of?

Vica's thoughts were less speculative: This explains why
I have never really been interested in anyone. Instinctively I
was keeping myself for this man. What poise, what assurance!

How coltish he makes my brothers seem, this is what they ought to look like, only we had no pattern. . . .

The Princess was an uneasy spectator, she fully realized the danger of showing Vica to Gigi. Still, a love affair is one thing, matrimony another.

Gian Galeazzo had, in common with most of his compatriots, a 'sense of the family,' which would surely not allow him to deviate from a course which, they both agreed, was inevitable. It never entered her head for a moment that Elizabeth herself might have something to say in the matter. The only possible objection might come from her parents. Of course, Elizabeth would have to become a Roman Catholic, that went without saying; but Sylvia, she reminded herself, had always been as putty in her hands; she was so vague that a change of religion might be easily assimilated if properly prepared . . . Tea was brought in. It was probably the first time, the Princess accurately guessed, that Rigo had participated in so delicate a meal. For him, it was unadulterated anguish. At home they only had tea when there was company; and when there was company there was no Rigo. He sat with the cup precariously balanced on his pudgy knees, clasping it with both hands, occasionally ducking his head almost to the level of the cup. The Princess was charming to him; he was meant to create a diversion. He did. Gian Galeazzo's questions were both skilful and stimulating. To his amazement, in spite of the cup, Rigo found himself being funny.

Gigi and his aunt roared with indiscriminate laughter at everything he said. Presently he was solicited to sing; as though la Scala itself waited on his moods. As he sang, Vica noted, pondered, deduced. . . .

Unbelievable as it might seem, Rigo did not look out of place! No doubt there had always been a buffoon who regaled the Arrivamales with songs and sallies, no doubt he would have been a *persona grata*, the only member of that cowed and whispering household who was allowed to speak his mind! The privilege of the freak. Freaks are international, emancipated, irresponsible, like gipsies. It is chic to be a freak. The Arrivamales had always had a freak on the premises. No wonder they had taken to Rigo, no wonder Rigo had 'fitted in.' He had his niche, like the *portiere* in the *cortile*. What about her brothers? Would they fit in too? No, came the inflexible reply, they would not. Not in their present state of wobbly fetishism, torn between plus-fours and sandals, between serenades and jazz. It is of no use trying to be fashionable if you are not quite clear as to what the fashion is. This Gian Galeazzo did not have to follow the fashion, he *was* the fashion, people copied *him*. He was talking to her now, she was so busy admiring him that she did not listen to the words. His interrogative '*È vero?*' brought her to her senses.

'Of course, of course,' she hastened to assure him, 'ha ragione.'

'You were not listening,' he smiled into her eyes, 'you did not hear a word I said.' Vica's mobile features suddenly took on that fugitive, *surrounded* look, that became her better than any other (nothing is more beautiful than Vica at bay, Guido was in the habit of saying).

'No,' she confessed, 'I was thinking.'

Gian Galeazzo moved a little closer. 'Will you not tell me your thoughts?'

'Certainly: I was wishing my brothers resembled you!'

'But my aunt tells me your brothers are superb!'

'She is right, but you would make them look all wrong.' This, he realized, was praise indeed, how intelligent not to fob him off with banal compliments.

'Your brothers have at least the advantage of being much younger than me, why, I might almost be your father –'

'A very young father!'

'Anyway, I am glad, I –' They exchanged glances that were like summer lightning.

'Gigi, I want you to show Elizabeth the house.'

The Princess's voice flicked him lightly but firmly. The
aparté with Vica had lasted quite long enough, it was clear.
'I must have a talk with this young lady,' she said, drawing
Vica down on the sofa beside her. 'Rigo,' she addressed him
with the lofty familiarity he found so engaging, 'go and play
your guitar in the next room; leave the door open, it will
be a delightful accompaniment to our conversation.' The
fathomless black eyes she had inherited from generations of
Montemejors followed the retreating pair. She lit a cigarette.
It immediately became an annexation.

'How well they match one another, do they not, child? He
so dark, she so fair . . . An ideal couple.' Her eyes bored into
Vica's through the smoke.

'I intend my nephew to marry Elizabeth.' It was kinder, she
decided, to dispel any ambiguity at once. Vica felt as though
she had received a blow in the pit of the stomach. She was
incapable of saying a word. The Princess, of course, saw this:
Gian Galeazzo, she thought with involuntary pride, is indeed
a quick worker! It would have been crueller, far, to allow the
slightest hope to burgeon.

'Listen, my child,' she flung a skinny arm about the girl's
shoulders, 'I am more alive to my nephew's charm than
anyone. Gian Galeazzo is no sinecure. In a way, I pity the
woman who marries him, but Englishwomen are fortunately
placid, unimaginative, they do not suffer torments of jealousy,
Elizabeth will not suffer as you and I would, for instance.
I have selected Elizabeth for one purpose, one purpose only:
to become his wife, and to bear his children. Why she more
than another? I will tell you. Because my nephew may love
whom he likes and where he likes, but twenty generations of
Arrivamales compel him to choose his wife and the mother
of his children in a certain restricted sphere – how boring
this sounds, but marriage *is* boring! – where they can meet
on terms of equality; where they have the same education,
background, traditions, where in all the social problems that
can arise in life they are likely to have the same reactions.'

'But why,' faltered poor Vica, summoning all her courage, 'must it be a foreigner?'

'*Precisely*, now I am going to say something difficult: the same environment, habits, associations, are more likely to produce a harmonious relationship than the marriage of two people of the same nationality who have been entirely brought up in entirely different circumstances. Let us transpose: Elizabeth in England has been brought up, *grosso modo*, in the same way as Gian Galeazzo in Italy. Aristocracy is international, Elizabeth and Gian Galeazzo, in spite of belonging to different nationalities, speak the same language. *Now* do you understand?'

'I think so,' Vica's reply was almost inaudible.

Heavens! thought the Princess, with some concern, it must have been the *coup de foudre*! I must cheer her up, poor child.

'Now, you are a very fortunate young woman. No, do not shrug: if you will pay attention you will see that I am not so stupid. To begin with, you are very beautiful. *Zitto!* You are thinking, what is the use of being beautiful if . . . all the use in the world! Some day, not immediately, perhaps, we must get you married.' Vica made a violent, inarticulate gesture. 'Give me time to think; there is no immediate hurry. I will help you if you will let me. I can be very helpful. To begin with you must try not to hate Elizabeth. If you cannot help it, you must not show it. It would be vulgar and . . . unless. You must endeavour to do what people least expect, it makes them look such fools! In the meantime, I mean to give a ball, you will bring your brothers, *all* of them, *their* future, at any rate, is in your hands.' This was a shot at a venture, she saw at once that it had been an aspiration. Vica's face quickened, as though brushed by the wind.

'That is kind of you, Princess,' impulsively, she put out her hand, it was immediately grasped in a small vice-like grip. The girl was no fool. Once married to some honest 'fonctionaire,' she would go far.

'Listen, child, if you do not attempt to interfere with my scheme, I will be your friend. Naturally, I rely on you not to mention this to Elizabeth. It is *our* secret.' She gave poor Vica a wink of complicity, that was balm to her wounded pride. . . .

The evening had been excruciating: Mamma's indefatigable questions: What was the Princess wearing? How many footmen were there in the hall? Did the marchese speak English? What did he wear? from the brothers; Elizabeth's insensitive comments: 'I must say he looks the part, he's frightfully good-looking, but I could wish he had more sense of humour,' Rigo's rhapsodies about the Princess: 'Ecco una grande dama!' All this, and more, had made Vica increasingly conscious of the chasm which separated their world from hers.

She saw, only too clearly, what the Princess had meant when she said that the same upbringing is more important than the same nationality. All the precautions, the pre-liminaries, *travaux d'approche*, that were necessary in order to bridge the gulf between the Arrivamales and the Papagallis became superfluous, to be cast aside. When they had returned from the inspection of the Palace, Elizabeth and Gian Galeazzo gave one the impression they had known each other all their lives.

On the other hand, there was none of that undercurrent of emotion there had been in Vica's abortive *tête-à-tête* with him. Should she attribute this to the purity of his intentions with regard to Elizabeth, or to a certain rawness on the part of the latter? Apart from this, in many ways, Elizabeth was not grown up, in Vica's estimate. She had no intuition, little taste. She roared with laughter at Rigo's circus jokes, she possessed the code of humour of a schoolboy, did not as much as suspect the poetic licence accorded to a pretty woman. . . .

Unanalytical, uncritical, she took everything as a matter of course, her beauty, health, riches, and now, Gian Galeazzo!

Everything fell into her lap without the slightest exertion on her part, whereas I, thought Vica bitterly, shall always have to sing for my supper!

Let us get this straight: I am the daughter of a dentist – better far, if I were the daughter of an executioner! . . . I am surrounded by a bevy of beautiful, if burlesque, brothers. I live in a hideous, a hideously respectable apartment – I had not realized *how* hideous till to-day. My particular brand of looks do not get a chance. They require fountains, perspectives, a *teatro di verdura*. Handsome common young men will make love to me; one day I shall be compelled to marry one of them, or else, an elderly rich friend of Papa's, one of his *milanese*.

Elizabeth will marry Gian Galeazzo, without being really in love with him, because he is decorative and suitable, and it is rather exciting to marry an Italian. Perhaps, once or twice a year, I and my abashed husband will be invited to the Palazzo Arrivamale. We shall go there just often enough to revive my regrets, my nostalgia for the kind of life I should have led and for which Nature intended me. I shall be like Emma Bovary: all my life I shall be haunted by a *valseur* and a chandelier. . . .

Gian Galeazzo, I could make you so happy, you would never be bored with me. For you, I would turn into Scheherazade, for you I would make up stories always stopped on the threshold, so that your curiosity would never be satisfied. For you, I would vary a little each day, never quite the same, never completely different, like the woman in the sonnet, so that you would never feel too certain of me. For you, I . . . '

A man's voice was wafted up from the street. He sang the usual refrain ending in 'amor' and 'dolor' with the ardour of discovery. No wonder poor Vica buried her face in her pillow and sobbed. . . .

Elizabeth to her Brother

Crunch, you swine, this is the second letter I have written you during the last month without receiving the shadow of a reply. For all you know, your innocent little sister may have been abducted by the time this reaches you, but I'm afraid there's not a chance. It's terribly above board. Figure to yourself, as Zelly says, I have an Italian suitor, no, I didn't say admirer, I said *suitor*. A highly suitable suitor, frightfully good-looking with a widow's peak and going grey on the temples, but it's more like powdered hair. Of course, he is not at all young; he must be getting on for thirty-five if he's a day, but I'm not all that partial to my own contemporaries. I get quite enough of them here, the competition is overwhelming. Now, Crunch, I am going to be honest. If there had only been one of them, I might have succumbed, but four variations on the same theme somehow kill all incentive to misbehave. It becomes funny, like people having triplets, giving birth to a son is a serious event, but having triplets is farcical. That is just what the Papagallis are, poor sweets! All except Rigo who is officially farcical and inwardly tragic. But I was forgetting Vica. She isn't funny, she is the unknown quantity in this family. . . . But to return to my suitor. The name is Arrivamale which means the reverse of Welcome. Henceforth, I shall call him 'Welcome,' for luck! Well, 'Welcome,' or rather his uncle, whose heir he is, owns several places (all rather morose, judging from the photographs). I must say, I like the Florentine palazzo, in some curious way it reminds me of Test, which, after all, contains masses of Italian pictures and furniture. (Do you remember how furious Aunt Alice was when we attempted to clean the Tintoretto with Vim?) He (Welcome) shows me all the photographs of his future possessions in the most blatant way, remarking what a becoming background they would make for me! (He himself, I am bound to say, looks exactly

as though he had stepped out of one of the ancestral
frames.) He and his old aunt, Crunch, I can't wait to tell
you about his old aunt . . . have worked all this out
together. The aunt, if you please, was a childhood friend of
Mummy's, don't you remember the snapshot in Mummy's
album of a lady on horseback with a sombrero and a
bolero (my Spanish, I hate to confess, is better, far, than
my Italian). Well, that is she. She now looks like one of
Zelly's *épingles neiges*, brittle, black, and pointed. In spite
of her age, she is as tireless as a cricket. Her entourage
seem to love and dread her. I took to her the first time I
saw her. . . . She's so funny! If she insists on my marrying
her nephew, I wouldn't dare refuse. You had better find
out what Mummy and Father's reaction to an Italian son-in-
law would be in any case. I already know what yours are.
I can see your frown of deepening disgust, and, of course,
I can guess the reason: *Peter*. You are horrified because
you think I am letting him down. I suppose I am, in a way,
but we never came to any agreement, I mean, I never
made him any promise. Ask him, if you don't believe me.
I am devoted to Peter, but he has never attempted to make
love to me, he has never put anything into words, and ever
since I have been here, he has only written me two
extremely grumpy letters.

May I quote one of Zelly's favourite axioms: *On ne
prend pas les mouches avec du vinaigre!* Italians are not
so niggardly.

Anyhow, why don't you come and see for yourself? Please
do, Crunch darling, I really do need a second opinion.

Your loving
Liza.

Miss Walker was preparing to go to church. She was Valka
every day of the week, but she became Miss Walker on
Sunday. Sunday was dedicated to her God, her country, her
correspondence and her Friend.

With some complacency, she now pinned a large malachite anchor (a gift of the late Countess) to her thin bosom. She was ready. No matter the season, no matter the weather, she carried an umbrella. It was part of her dominical equipment and somehow made her feel one with the Royal family. Down the marble stair across the *cortile*, she tripped. The great door clanged behind her.

As the reverberations echoed through the house, they produced various repercussions: the youngest and most irrepressible footman slid down the banisters; the chef took a deep draught from a bottle of Chianti which he kept always at hand; the majordomo, who was in the act of cleaning the silver, lit a *toscana*.

Meanwhile, Miss Walker, crisp and cool in the morning glare, sped along the Lung'arno, as uncompromisingly British as the day she stepped out of the train twenty years ago. She wore the same gold pince-nez; her flowered muslin looked as though it had been designed for the vicarage garden-party . . .

Her entry into the English church, in the Via Maggio, caused quite a stir. Everybody, except a few transitory tourists, knew that she was the companion (maiding was a profession she no longer admitted to) to the Princess who lived in the great red palace on the Lung'arno Corsini. Miss Walker was treated with deference by the usher, as an equal by most of her co-worshippers. She took her place in a row of kneeling scanty *nuques* so parochial, so typically Anglo-Saxon, as to make you fancy you heard the chirp of a robin during the pause for finding the hymn, or the gentle patter of rain on the porch. . . .

The British colony of Florence!

Who may hope to do justice to its bedraggled gallantry, obstinate ideals? The ancient flower-maidens, wedded to Florence since they first saw the light, nearly half a century ago, making do on a miserable pittance, cutting down everything except their tea! Year by year, as they grow older, their hats get younger, more floral, more desperately girlish: 'Roses flowering on the head of three score years and ten.' Their eyes, too, refuse to age. Inveterately, incorruptibly blue, they are all that is left over from what was once, no doubt, a fresh and rounded face.

Reared on Ruskin and Vernon Lee, their faithful ecstasies have never subsided, they continue to admire what they were told to admire when first they came to learn, or to teach. What do they know of Italy, who only Florence know? They have not ventured far afield: Pisa, Venice, Assisi ('Dear Saint Francis! I always think there is something so *English* in his love of birds!') a few sacred days in Rome, with the uneasy feeling that they are reincarnations of the early Christian Martyrs; perchance, a daring dash to Naples ('Why is it that there is something improper about Naples? Maybe it's because the men stare so'), then back again, with O! what relief! to Florence. Back to Pineider's, back to the English Church, back to cosy Giacosa's. It really seems like home. . . .

Here, at least, they are treated with amused affection by the 'natives'; every indigent Florentine family keeps a tame 'Mees,' like some curious pet. The ever-increasing children are taken to see her, as they would be shown a giraffe in the Zoo. They gape at her with the comfortable awe of the oasis for the desert. Never have they seen anything so flat, so barren, so limitless. . . . In return for their stupor they get toys, sweets she can ill afford, raptures in her letters home about 'the *bambini*, for all the world like Verocchio *putti*'!

Sometimes letters would arrive bearing the postmark of Bournemouth or Sevenoaks. For a few minutes, the voluntarily exiled blue eye is reclaimed by the memory of a certain herbaceous border in June, or a windy walk on the pier, then she catches sight of the ubiquitous Duomo from her window, and all else is blotted out. She sinks back reassured. Yes, it was worth it!

Miss Walker found herself sandwiched between two ladies in very different circumstances from those we have just described. One, Mrs. Tripple-Armstrong, owned an historical villa at Settignano, and the other was Miss Winifred Tuck, *the* Miss Tuck who made those papier maché Venetian trays, that were all the rage at that Italianate period.

Both ladies were well off, and on fairly good terms, though Miss Tuck alleged that Mrs. 'Tipple'-Armstrong was anything but a teetotaller and Mrs. Armstrong covertly accused Miss Tuck of being an opportunist and a time-server. As it was, age and success had rounded their angles; their clothes fitted them; they wore the uglier, more expensive Ponte Vecchio jewellery, adequate stays, hats devoid of pathos.

Mrs. Tripple-Armstrong, did she but know it, had been Miss Walker's ideal. Before affronting the Florentine aristocracy, she had once been to the Villa Pomona to apply for a situation. Unfortunately, Mrs. Armstrong was already 'suited,' but Ivy would never forget the English butler, the glimpse of starched linen and properly-cleaned silver, nor the pile of illustrated papers, and curiously English-looking garden . . . for Ivy was British to the core and, in her heart of hearts, despised all foreigners. Even now, when confronted with Mrs. Tripple-Armstrong's stately bulk, she could not entirely stifle the feeling that she had passed over to the enemy.

She knew that she would never rise above a Nod, a benevolent Nod, if you like, but a Nod nevertheless, not to be confounded with the Wave of the Hand, such as was accorded many other churchgoers.

This particular Sunday, Ivy Walker felt she was at last getting even with Mrs. Armstrong. Once '*il signorino*' had married Lady Elizabeth Caracole we could afford to look down on Mrs. Armstrong and all her ways. No doubt, as a leading member of the British colony, she would be invited to the wedding; once we have married into the British peerage we can safely dispense with her nods and her patronage.

Ah, thought Ivy, clutching her prayer book, you little know. . . .

It was not long before she was joined by her Friend, an infinitely subdued, mousey satellite, who sat in the last pew but one, and thought of Ivy as a would-be candidate for Hollywood might think of Greta Garbo. She was never referred to as anything but 'my Friend.' There was never any need to explain her, she was so nebulous and needy, poor little creature!

Once a week, on Sunday, she was allowed to gather up the crumbs from the rich man's table and would be seen leaving Palazzo Arrivamale with her string bag stuffed with the remains of the Gargantuan tea that was always served in Ivy's 'workroom.'

To-day, as they sat over their cups, voluptuously stirring the sugar and daintily trifling with a chocolate biscuit, Miss Walker was leading up to her big news: 'Whoever do you think we had to lunch to-day, *and* to dinner last night, never out of the house, so to speak?'

She paused, her Friend made the noise that was expected of her, she conversed almost entirely in onomatopœia, hence her charm for Miss Walker who had no use for dialogue.

'Mm – well, as you'll never guess I might as well tell you: Lady Elizabeth Caracole (How could she know it was pronounced Crackle?) only daughter of the 9th Earl of Canterdown, one of the biggest landowners in England, *and* a friend of Royalty, it seems. Well, this Countess of Canter-down used to know my Lady, the Princess, that is to say, when they were children. They were ever such pals, grew up together, so to speak. Lady Elizabeth was sent to Florence to learn the language, I wish you could see her, she's as pretty as a picture. You've often heard me talk of the "Heir to the throne," Marquis de' Pardi, well, we've wanted him to marry and settle down for many a long day, and now Miss Right has come along, ha! ha! I shouldn't be surprised if they announced their engagement on the night of the ball.'

The Friend made an inarticulate noise, meant to denote surprise, incredulity.

'What! Haven't I told you about the ball?'

Miss Walker poured herself out another cup of tea. 'Well, we are giving a ball, if you please, on the night of the 22nd. People are coming from all over the place, Rome, Naples, Milan, even Paris, it seems. You see, the Princess has relations in every country. Why, Lord Risingdale, Lady Elizabeth's brother, is even coming all the way from England! I tell you what. There's no reason, no reason at all, why you shouldn't come round after the Princess is dressed, and see them go into dinner. We've only got to look over the banisters. Why, you'd hardly think . . . ' But no one will ever know what Ada would hardly have thought, for at that moment the Princess' bell rang. Miss Walker dropped the Tuscan version of a *chou à la crème* she was about to convey to her mouth. 'My! Whatever can she be wanting at this hour? She never rings before five on Sunday. You stay here, Ada, I'll be back in a minute.'

She rushed down the precipitous backstair which communicated with the Princess' *cabinet de toilette*. Here, a scene of devastation met her gaze. Her mistress was standing ankle-deep, in a sea of paper: bills, love-letters, cheque books, programmes, newspaper cuttings – the accumulated rubbish of years.

'Where in hell,' stormed the Princess, 'where in hell, *hija de puta*, have you hidden the snapshot of Lady Canterdown and myself that was taken at Biarritz in 1910 and which I propose to present to my future niece?'

Miss Walker was Valka again with a vengeance.

Vica had a curious and individual talent for drawing which brought her a feeling of security and detachment. Not unlike the irresponsible itinerary of the planchette pencil, it supplied the answer to many a question, sometimes unexpressed. The drawings were portraits of people she knew, surrounded by accessories which gave a clue to their character. At the moment she was engaged in drawing the Princess, wrapped in a picador's *capa*. She was encircled by miscellaneous objects: a castle; a roll of parchment; hearts; a skull. In one hand she held the statuette of a saint, which saint? St. Terese of Avila, of course. She also had been a tyrant and a *grande dame*, and in the other? The draughtsman hesitated. In the other? A pair of castanets. Vica held it at arm's length, satisfied. It was, she thought, very odd that she should have obeyed the Princess' instructions to the letter. At first she had been sorely tempted to try to get Gian Galeazzo away from Elizabeth, then two excellent reasons for not doing so intervened. Primo: it became apparent to her already experienced eye, that Gian Galeazzo, though eager and flattered, was not really in love with Elizabeth, the marriage formed part of his duties as future head of the family, no doubt it was a pleasant duty, but had Elizabeth been plain instead of pretty, so numerous were her other assets, that, Vica was convinced, he would have gone through with it just the same. Then there was la Zia; had she succeeded in luring Gigi away from Elizabeth, she would have made two enemies, first Gigi himself, who, in the long run, would never have forgiven her for having sabotaged a plan which brought fresh lustre to his name. Then la Zia – Vica shuddered to think what inquisitions, what far-reaching spells would be devised in the secret silent palace. In other words, it spelt the social ruin of the Papagallis. No, no. The Princess had promised to befriend her, her and her brothers, henceforth they would all be under her patronage, but the word stuck in Vica's gullet. Why should they need patronage? Were they not young, handsome, gifted? Why should they have to labour to acquire all the things that fell into Elizabeth's lap like ripe plums? Why? Vica's topaze eyes blazed. She dug her pencil into the Princess' stomach. She was damned if she would be patronized by any Princess. She would beat the Princess at her own game: '*Pazienza!*'

Charles Risingdale was on his way to fetch his sister home. He was more perturbed than he would have cared to admit;

he blamed his parents: crazy to send a girl who looked like
a film star to Italy, alone, unprotected. Asking for trouble.
Well, they were getting what they deserved, and *better* than
they deserved. At least the fellow wasn't one of the dentist's
sons. No doubt Liz would cut up rough, she had a nasty
temper when roused. The fact that she said she required his
opinion was, in itself, reassuring; this was not the language
of love. It all depended on how far they had gone. Of
course, he said nothing about bringing her home in his
telegram. He had merely said he was at a loose end, and
could do with a fortnight in the sun. Elizabeth's reply had
been enthusiastic. She would book him a room at the
Grand Hotel, and now he was in the train, sweeping through
the Tuscan landscape, over which hung a crescent moon
like a perilously poised scimitar. He was not insensible to
the shimmering poplars, the semi-colon of cypress and
umbrella pine, which seemed to occur in perfectly-timed
rotation. When the train paused, he heard the croaking of
frogs: he leant out to breathe the syringa-laden air. Poor old
Liz! It wasn't fair to expose her to a night like this . . .
No wonder . . . Prato. Another half hour. This fellow who
shared his sleeper was already in the corridor, sorting out his
luggage.

   Charles hadn't been to Italy since he had been to stay with
an old Anglo-Italian relative, in Florence, to recuperate from
scarlet fever at the age of sixteen. He did not remember
much about the place except the Cupola of the Duomo,
which he had scandalized his cousin by referring to as 'that
hump.' Must do some sightseeing (his taste belonged to the
I-don't-know-much-about-pictures-but-I-know-what-I-like
category). No doubt Liz will trundle me round the picture
galleries. Damn nice kid, Liz, loyal, discreet as a man, with
no end of a sense of humour. More energy in her little finger
than in my whole body! I'll be hanged if I see her throw
herself away on some oily dago. Poor old Peter! He'd be in
the hell of a stew if he knew what was going on. He must

never know. We'll make a funny story of it, when it has all
blown over. It may even make things easier for him, in the
sense that it would help Mummy and Father to get over the
eldest son period. Surely, they would rather Liz married an
honest-to-God Englishman than a macaroni, even if he *is*
a prince? Still, it was difficult to fit Peter into the family
vernacular: Elizabeth is marrying such a clever young man,
my dear, he did brilliantly at Cambridge and *personally* I
think he may have a great political future . . . No doubt, that
would do, but they could not add confidentially: 'You know
his mother was a de Vere, one of the *Norfolk* de Veres,'
neither, Charles reflected, could they go through the enjoy-
able process of what the family called 'looking him up,'
which, to the uninitiated, sounded like a projected call on
someone and which simply meant, hounding down the
unfortunate creature in Debrett. . . .

The train began to slow down, Charles moved laboriously
down the corridor: at length the platform streamed into view.
He thrust his head out of the window, raking the crowd for
Elizabeth. Was it, could it . . . Yes, of course, it was her, arm
in arm with a tall dark girl. My word, she's a good-looker,
and no mistake!

Charles pushed past several irate ladies, jumped down on
to the platform. Elizabeth came running towards him. They
hugged each other with mutual appreciation.

Then: 'This,' said Elizabeth, disentangling herself, 'is Vica,
of whom you've heard so much!'

In after years, Vica always looked back on her first meeting
with Charles with amused affection. He was so young, so
pink, so golden, his hair really resembled a new guinea. It
was plain sailing from the outset. He never gave her a
moment's trouble. It was a foregone conclusion, he would fall
in love with Vica. He did. He had never met anyone like Vica,
so boyishly familiar in public, treating him as she treated her
own brothers, so mysteriously aloof in private. Her slightest

gesture became significant, her most superficial glance, an omen. He had always been a bird-watcher, now he became a Vica-watcher. It wasn't so very different. Of course, he did not immediately realize that he was undone. What should have denounced the accident that had befallen him was the way he handled the 'talks with Liz.' Instead of treating the whole affair as a joke, which was what he had intended, and which he knew by experience was the best way to deal with Elizabeth, he found himself asking anxiously about her 'symptoms,' whether her Italian lover's most trivial utterance seemed fraught with meaning, if she had become super-stitious, hyper-sensitive, self-critical. . . .

'What in the world has come over you, Crunch? Have you been dabbling in Freud?'

He shifted uneasily under her gaze. 'No, no, I only wondered, that's all.'

'Well, I must say, I never thought you would be so objective; I thought you would give me hell.'

Poor Charles felt doubly guilty, guilty towards his friend, guilty towards his family. He tried to appease his conscience, by saying lamely: 'I didn't know Gigi, did I? I can't help seeing he is a very decent fellow – for a foreigner.'

'Am I right in supposing that your attitude toward foreigners has undergone a change, since you have become acquainted with Vica?' his sister queried with some malice.

'How like a woman!' returned her brother sourly, 'quite the little detective, aren't you? *Cherchez la femme*, and all that.'

'You were always very bad at repartee, Crunch, I shouldn't take it too much to heart if I were you. Vica, I'm sure, finds you very good practice.' She neatly dodged a cushion that came hurtling across the room, dropped Charles an ironic curtsey, and withdrew.

All the same, she did not at all relish the idea of Vica as a possible sister-in-law. She no longer had any illusions about the Papagallis, least of all about Vica; she'd be damned if she would stand by and watch Charles being used as a stepping-stone by this unscrupulous, if philanthropic, person. She had seen her brother through several *béguins*, but something warned her that this was different. Who could have guessed that Charles, who was the most insular person in the world, would take the Papagallis to his heart?

Needless to say, the brothers were mad about him, they copied his coiffure, his walk, his drawl (a difficult feat in Italian). Plagiarism in its most blatant form was practised by all, except Rigo, who continued to wear his check suit and to breathe garlic impartially over the dinner-table. . . .

Curled in the fork of a tree, Charles was engaged in his favourite pastime of watching Vica. Apparently unconscious of his presence, she drew in her usual horizontal position, stretched on the grass. As a matter of fact, she was drawing Charles. A young man in shorts, with a helmet on his head. Charles, by wriggling forward a few inches was able to look, as it were, over Vica's shoulder. He nearly fell off his perch for surprise, when he saw her place an oar in one of the young man's hands, and a spear in the other, 'Who the devil – ' he burst out.

'It is you,' said Vica without looking up, which meant, of course, that she had realized his presence all the time.

'You see,' she amplified, 'the helmet and the spear mean that you have the soul of a crusader, in other words, that you would fly to the aid of the oppressed, in fact, any lost cause, and the shorts, not to mention the oar, mean that *lo sport*, games, play a large part in your life. It is a symbolical portrait.'

Charles scrambled out of the tree, and threw himself down beside the artist.

'You have made me very good-looking,' he remarked in a gratified tone.

'But you *are* very good-looking,' she gravely assured him, 'like a kind of child's drawing of Elizabeth, with all the details left out, but no man could be as good looking as Elizabeth.

It would be unbearable, unless he were an archangel, and archangels are not exactly men.' Charles listened, entranced. He had become a voice addict, a Vica voice addict. It was fatal. There was no known cure. He blurted: 'Your voice is my favourite drug, not that I know much about drugs.'

'That,' drawled Vica, 'I take as a very pretty compliment. My first compliment from an Englishman, I shall always treasure it.'

'Oh come, you've had heaps, I never stop paying you compliments.'

'They were not so noticeable, this one was perfect, a solitaire, to be worn by itself . . . I shall,' she frowned at her drawing, 'do you in water-colouring, because your hair does not show in this. *Basta.*' She pushed it away.

'I say, Vica, you'll turn my head if you go on like that, and you may not like the result.'

'What result?' Vica enquired, opening her topaz eyes very wide. She was lying on her back with her hands crossed behind her head, Charles hung over her dizzily. It was like looking down into a rock-pool.

'Your eyelashes stick out like the petals of a daisy,' he said thickly, his head swam, he was lost. Down he plunged, his face meeting Vica's with the impact of a fall. It was more like a blow than a kiss, she sat up, rubbing her lips.

'Charles, you have hurt me, you are *brutale.*' He flung his arms round her, all contrition. 'Darling, you are right, I am a brute. I must have bruised your darling mouth. Can you forgive me? I worship you, Vica. I'm mad about you. Will you marry me at once, as soon as it can be arranged? Please, Vica, say yes, O please – '

Vica had no intention of saying anything but yes, for several reasons. Charles was as appetizing as new mown hay, she had made a fetish of his fairness. She was not in love with him as she could have been in love with Gian Galeazzo. There was not, there never could be that deep complicity of the spirit, that sharing of tastes and distastes; she found him more disarming than charming, he was an excellent foil, an endearing slave, moreover, didn't Charles spell liberation, social security, pride rehabilitated, the launching of Guido, of the others? Most of all, didn't he supply her with the ideal Reprisal, the snub to end snubs? She hugged herself to think of the disdained dentist's daughter becoming Gigi's sister-in-law, on equal terms with the Princess and all she represented. Aloud she said: '*Carissimo*, whenever you like, the sooner the better, but I have one condition to make: you must promise not to tell a soul, not even Elizabeth, until the night of the ball. That is the day after to-morrow, so it should not be difficult.'

CHAPTER FIVE
The Ball: I

VALKA was in her element.

Like a general the night before the attack, she surveyed her forces, assessing each unit, endeavouring to forestall eleventh-hour contingencies. '*Ascoltate* Bandini,' she interpolated the majordomo in her fluent detestable Italian, 'we have made a list of possible chucks and possible substitutes. We have written out the cards and the menus. In short, we have seen to everything, what about you?'

Bandini gave her a look which could have caused any less leathery heart to quail. He loathed Valka with a sinister subterranean loathing, as unventilated as the catacombs, but none the less deadly. He was a Neapolitan, and many were the secret devices he employed to bring Valka to a really sticky end. He had examined all of them, but had a sustained *penchant* for leprosy. He had in his possession a rag, which, he had been assured, had formed part of a leper's clothing and which was powerless to convey the disease to anyone but the appointed victim. Many's the time it had been pressed into Valka's hand, when she had asked for something 'to clean her odds and ends with.' He could wish the effects were a little more expeditious, *ma pazienza*! That innocent-looking blister on her fourth finger, for instance? He couldn't take his eyes off it.

'*Stia tranquilla, Signorina*,' he assured her, smiling with restored confidence in his rag. 'Everything has been done. Let me show you the flowers in the ballroom, I think the Princess will be pleased.' Followed by the budding leper, he entered the sala, where giant azaleas in tubs, venerable and flame-coloured, had been placed in each corner of the immense room. Garlands of roses linked pillar to pillar, the eye lost itself in the altitudes of the magnificent ceiling, where titanic torsos were kneaded together; they swayed, wrestled, staggered, one almost heard the muscles crack, the panting of their compressed and hairy chests. Everything, pictures, statues, was on the heroic scale, more adapted to gregarious Goliaths than to ordinary human beings.

The sallow, stocky butler, and the red-haired wisp of Albion, ricochetted from mirror to mirror, they seemed to belong to some inferior creation.

Laughing *contadini*, the colour of terracotta, were arranging the flowers from Gian Galeazzo's villa at Bellosguardo. The presence of Valka meant nothing to them, her legend was confined to the town; immune, unabashed, they wove their garlands, now bursting into snatches of song, now trying the effect of flowers in their own hair. Their pleasure was disinterested, they wanted their Signorino to be happy, each contributed his quota of natural courtesy and grace.

Amadeo Papagallo, conte di Cippolare, shook the mothballs out of his 'tails' with undisguised distaste.

He loathed parties, *all* parties with the exception of an occasional meal with old cronies, in their shirtsleeves, in some rustic *osteria*, where you could sprawl over the table, and it was not considered bad form to pick your teeth. He had cajoled, threatened, prevaricated. All to no purpose. Artimisia was adamant. 'It is the chance of a lifetime,' she proclaimed. 'No one but a fool would neglect such an opportunity.'

'Opportunity for *what*?' he asked warily.

'Opportunity for mixing with the highest society, the society that sets the tone, whose photographs grace the illustrated papers, le monde où l'on s'amuse' (only she pronounced it '*amousse*').

'It may amuse you, but it does not amuse me. Why must an elderly dentist, corpulent, inæsthetic, glum, be dragged to a party, where he knows no one, where nobody knows him, when he could be comfortably at home in his shirtsleeves, compiling a thesis on pyorrhœa? To think you have dragged me back to Florence on a spurious telegram, for *this*!' He raised his arms to the Heavens.

'What could I do? Had I told you the real reason you would not have come. I think, Amadeo, that you are the most selfish man I ever met, I think that you do not deserve to have a wife who does not make you horns, in spite of the not-so-unattractive men who pay court to her!'

Amadeo sighed. He knew this was his cue. It was more than his life was worth to confess complete absence of jealousy. How often had it been rubbed into him, that a man without jealousy was not a man? Not for nothing was her favourite opera Carmen. She longed for violence, desertions, '*À la montagne si tu m'aimais, à la montagne tu me suivrais.*'

But she had never been able to make Amadeo desert anything, not even his damned old dentures.

Meanwhile, she waited. He realized that something must be done, done quickly.

'Listen, Arte,' he panted, struggling with his collar-stud, 'it is not because I conceal my sentiments beneath a phlegmatic exterior, that I am not human, that I am not as other men.'

'Yes, Amadeo?' she prompted hopefully.

'It is not,' he plodded on, 'because I do not strike or beat you, that I am less vulnerable to the pangs of jealousy. Were you to forget you are my wife – ' he paused, menacing.

'Yes, Amadeo, yes?' she trilled.

He cleared his throat: ' – you are my wife – ' Where had

he got to? O yes – 'I would have exactly the same reactions as a man twenty years younger!' This was wonderful, her evening was made, she would spare him – up to a point. 'So far, *caro*, you have been lucky.' She admired at arm's length, the large diamond ring he had once given her, through half-closed lids: ' – *so far* – '

She would leave it, at that. Just a tiny seed of doubt, which might, or might not, be allowed to take root. *Vedremo.*

Charles Risingdale was, above all, a tolerant, uncritical person. He took life easily, shunned introspection, was ready to believe the best of everyone.

The least snobbish of human beings, he thought it was a huge joke to be marrying the daughter of a dentist, 'as funny as though I were marrying the daughter of a conjurer and you came out of an opera hat, between the dove and the guinea-pig,' he confided to his betrothed, who did not perhaps, think this quite as funny as he did, but who with characteristic adaptability pandered to this view, wise enough to know that burlesque was preferable to the slightly comical.

'I say, I suppose your father puts tiaras, not crowns, on the Pope's teeth? Does he wear an overall, or a surplice, when he attends his Holiness?'

'You must ask Pappà, after all, both Popes and dentists look their best in white!'

'Darling, is that why you are going to wear white to-night; because you are the Pope's dentist's daughter?' etc. . . . etc. . . . etc. . . .

It was all quite effortless. From time to time a cloud would momentarily obscure his beatitude.

'I say, Vica, I wish you would let me tell Liz, I have always told her everything.'

'Surely you can wait until to-night, Carlino?'

'Why are you so dead set on telling her *after* the ball?'

'Not after, *during*. We will tell the Princess and Elizabeth *during* the ball.'

'O, but why, it sounds so official, I would much rather tell her when we are alone.'

Vica's spectacular and obliging face immediately registered the stern watchfulness of the Recording Angel. 'But your promise, Charles? Do your promises count for nothing?'

He sighed gustily, 'O well, have it your own way.'

Vica let him have a whiff of the waywardness he found so attractive. 'But no. It was just a whim on my part. It was to be the climax of the ball, the reward, the *apoteoso*, but no matter, I care not. Why tell anyone for that matter, why be engaged? Is it not nice to keep it secret, to be, *come si dice*, on the threshold, and not to go any further? A glimpse is more exciting than contemplation.'

Charles, who had been listening, motionless, with dismay, shook off the sweet nightmare. 'Vica! You must be mad! You can't back out now! Don't you *want* to marry me, darling?' Distraught he caught both her hands, practically shook her, raked her innocent face for denial.

'But of course, only I thought *you* did not want to,' she smiled blamelessly. He hugged her as though she had been shipwrecked.

'O my darling, my darling; what a clumsy fool I am! Of course, we will announce our engagement when and where you please!'

Casa Papagalli, always a melodramatic household, had never so strongly resembled a provincial theatre on a first night. 'Properties' littered the furniture, half-naked people flitted from room to room, the telephone rang almost uninterruptedly, the leading lady (Vica) could not be approached. She had been closeted with the *jeune premier*, Guido, for over an hour.

Let us peep through the keyhole. Guido is striding up and down smoking cigarette after cigarette.

'But you will go to live in England!' he mutters. 'What will
become of me?'

'Amore, I cannot take you with me. Besides, you will be
"lancé," by then. The most sought-after young man in
Florence.'

He suddenly whirled, threw himself at his sister's feet. 'I
know, I know, all that you are doing for me, but I cannot
live without you, Vica. You have always been my interpreter,
without you I am lost, I shall do everything wrong.'

'O no, you won't,' she held his head to her heart, 'besides,
I won't leave you for long, tesoro, you will come to stay with
us in England.'

He shook off her hand. 'I don't know that I want to, I – I
can't help being jealous – though, I admit, not as jealous as
I would have been if it had been Gian Galeazzo.' He gazed
up into her face with the obstinate adoration of a child. 'I
wonder, if it is worth it? After all, we are happy here; you
don't know anything about England.'

'No, but I can guess. It won't be exciting, but it will be
safe. I can rest on my laurels – for a bit. Guido, you *know*
we both agreed that something must be done. We don't want
to vegetate here for the rest of our lives.'

'Charles – you will love him more than me.'

All Vica's sapience, potency, possessiveness was condensed into one word: '*Imbecile.*'

'I want your candid opinion of my dress.'

'Pretty good, I should say, but I don't know a thing about
women's clothes.' Elizabeth was complacently posturing in
front of the looking-glass.

'You seem to notice Vica's quick enough.'

'Vica isn't my sister.'

He suddenly felt a swine, flung his arm round his sister's
neck, gave her a resounding kiss on the cheek. 'You're the
top, Liz, if that is any comfort to you.'

She regarded him with suspicion. 'Crunch, it's unlike you

to be so demonstrative, you're keeping something from me, your embrace denotes a guilty conscience, rather than brotherly affection. You had much better come clean.'

The temptation to tell her *now* was hard to resist. He lit a cigarette, walked over to the window, looked out on the shimmering city. 'Never mind,' he temporized, turning round, 'it's only for the time being.'

'What is?' A knock at the door, before anyone had time to say 'come in,' a resplendent being entered. It was Ugo. A bride could not have been more self-conscious. 'I hearda voices, I comea ina,' he said in his incorrigible hurdy-gurdy English.

'Turn round,' commanded Elizabeth. He did as he was told.

'You'll do. I must say his "tails" fit better than yours, Charles.'

Ugo's happiness knew no bounds. He felt like embracing everyone, including Charles, but he knew this would be un-English, and was content to fling an arm about his idol's shoulders. 'I tinka I musta confess,' he exulted, flashing his incomparable teeth at them, 'I copia your coata, I takea my little *sarto* to see it when you were *uscito, ecco,*' he held a lapel in either hand, '*il resultato!*'

'How typical,' teased Elizabeth, 'to improve on the original!'

'*Elisabetta, tesoro,* how can you be so unkinda to your little Ugoccione who woulda die to give you a moment's *piacere!*' Seizing her round the waist, he pirouetted wildly round the room, singing: 'Caracoli, carocola,' to the time of 'Funicoli, funicola.' She broke away, laughing. 'Sorry, Ugoccione, but it won't work. You have eyes for no one but yourself. If ever there was a Narcissus –'

'Narcissus,' echoed a deep voice, 'who is being called names?' Vica, unnoticed, had entered the room. All three gaped.

The treacherous quality of her beauty – she was never beautiful once and for all – was like a hold-up. She seemed

to be able to turn it on and off, at will; dimmed all day, to-
night it blazed forth, every candle lit. Her dress was not so
much a dress (all her life she was to snub Fashion), as an
accomplice. Her whole appearance suggested the triumphant
flowering of a conspiracy. Charles, crimson, speechless,
could do nothing but stare. Elizabeth, the least impressed of
the three, was the first to break the silence: 'I must say, you
have brought it off this time, Vica,' she said magnanimously.
'You look like something out of the ballet, the débutante in
the Spectre de la Rose, for instance.'

Charles found his tongue, at last. 'I – I think she looks more
like that photograph of the Empress Elizabeth, in the album
we have at home,' he stammered. His sister flashed a quick
look at him. With a jolt, she realized how much in love he
was. I wonder if he has proposed to her yet, if he hasn't, he
will, this evening, probably. What a fool I was to let him come
here! A flirtation was to be expected, I never thought it would
end up in this Tristan and Yseult business. Anyhow, now
it's too late to do anything about it, what a curious exchange,
I for Italy, Vica for England, like a figure in the Lancers.
Visiting. The visits of Vica. How many more countries will
she visit, in a bridal capacity? Now I'm being bitchy, why
shouldn't she be as much in love with Charles as he is with
her? But she knew instinctively that this was not the case.

Count Papagallo was waiting for his womenfolk to
assemble. He had taken refuge with the only member of the
household on whose sympathy he knew he could count:
Mademoiselle Crispin, who, strange to relate, had not shared
in the collective delirium. Cautious, on the qui vive, her
eternal French reflex: '*Nous sommes trahis*!' well in sight, to
use her own idiom, *elle laissait venir*, she bided her time.
Realistic, level-headed, she was the only person in that
immoderate household who saw things as they were, and not
as they would like them to be. Although she had identified
herself with the Papagallis she was by no means convinced

that the mere fact of being invited to a ball, in a great house, was sufficient to launch them on their social career. She had watched with ironical reserve the seduction of Charles. '*Le mieux est l'ennemi du bien*' was an axiom that was constantly on her lips. Enamoured with respectability (her brief lapse from the paths of virtue had only served to settle her more firmly in the saddle of a reliable mount) she was not in favour of the metamorphosis of Vica, whose divined programme filled her with misgivings. '*Elle finira mal, cette petite,*' she was in the habit of confiding to her pillow. Elizabeth was quite another matter. It was fitting and natural, that she should become the wife of the Marchese de' Pardi, she would be merely acquiescing to what her upbringing and environment demanded of her. As for the boys – the future, no doubt, would demonstrate how overweening were their pretensions; why could they not be content with devoted parents, perfect health, a comfortable, respected home?

With genuine commiseration, she listened to the grievances of her patron. In order to escape from the turmoil they were installed in the so-called 'studio,' surrounded by books no one ever read, and furniture no one ever dusted.

'Look at me, Crispa. Am I not ridiculous? All dolled up in clothes which, though my own, somehow looked hired. The hired husband, because Arte thinks it is becoming to show herself with a husband. Who will speak to me at this party? The footman who thanks me for my cloakroom tip. I feel more at home at the Vatican, where at least, I have my entrée. God knows I have been a good husband and a good father. True, I have spoiled Vica. How could I help it? She is so beautiful. She now moves or would like to move, in another world. Everyone makes fun of my friends. Can you be surprised that I do not regard this house as my home? I am happier, far, in my little pied-à-terre in the Via del Babuino, with my work and my books of reference. The Holy Father – ' At this juncture, yells of: Amadeo! Pappà! tore the musty silence. Papagalli leapt guiltily to his feet,

Mademoiselle Crispin followed him into the hall, where his entire family, plus Charles and Elizabeth, were assembled. Parrot cries assailed him on every side: 'Pappà! Your tie is all crooked. Pappà! You must brush your hair. Amadeo, pull down your waistcoat!'

He was overwhelmed, engulfed. He had to pass through a barrage of brushes and 'last touches.'

The door slammed at last.

Gina had gone to the Palazzo to watch the guests arrive. Mademoiselle Crispin was left alone.

Nostalgia for France, such as she had seldom known, overcame her.

Once more she was back in the maternal hostellerie. Once again she was playing on the banks of the Loire, that turgid river, broad and pale, leisurely in appearance, but treacherous in character with half-drowned islands supporting uneasy willows. Chalky châteaux trailed their gardens to its brink; vineyards producing the wittiest vintages of France, Vouvray, Anjou, Saumur, garnished its slopes . . . She dined *sous la tonnelle*, with Monsieur le Maire, her mother, the chemist. Their thick bubbly glasses clinked . . . She longed for shrewd, malicious conversation, parochial projects; a shrug; a wink; a sigh . . .

'*Accidenti!*' exclaimed Gian Galeazzo throwing his third white tie into the wastepaper basket. An adroit man, he was all fingers and thumbs this evening. Lack of experience, he muttered, reaching for another, but he was not referring to the tie. He had never proposed to anyone seriously in his life, and he viewed the coming evening with a lack of self-confidence which was new to him. The right note, it was so important to strike the right note. Elizabeth had a disconcerting habit of looking him straight in the eye, as it were, daring him to tell a lie. Even now, he didn't know quite how he stood with her, how much she was a victim of her youth, Italy, the spring? He had kissed her more than once; skilfully, not too passionately. She had appeared to like it, but that was nothing to go by, he had kissed dozens of English girls, they had all liked it, and had seemed to attach little or no importance to the gesture. Where did they consider love-making began and flirtation ceased? How much passion was compatible with matrimony? How long would Elizabeth expect him to remain faithful to her?

Once married, it was quite on the cards that he would fall mildly in love with her (Pygmalion had ever been his favourite part). For a year or two it was even possible that he might remain faithful without any effort, especially if she produced a son and heir. Like most Italians, he was anxious to have children, he knew he had it in him to become a tender and attentive parent. The children could not fail to be handsome.

Like all vain men, he was much influenced by his friends' verdict on the girl he was about to propose to, their admiring cries, echoed pleasantly in his ears: '*Che bellezza! ma è un sogno di bellezza!*'

Having at last achieved a presentable bow, he stood back from the mirror, regarding himself critically. He was, as we know, thirty-eight, he did not look a day over thirty-five, in spite of the smear of grey on his temples. His lean angular features gave him an air of domination he was far from feeling; he longed, rather wistfully, for a word of encouragement from la Zia, who knew so much about English women. . . . *Ma!*

With a final dab of pearl-grey powder on his freshly-shaven chin, he turned on his heel and left the room.

The long and intricate process of dressing was over. The Princess had now reached the part of the evening's ritual she most enjoyed: placing the cards on the dinner table. While submitting to the dictates of protocol, she was able nevertheless to distribute rewards and punishments; promoting Y, abasing Z. It gave her a delicious sensation

of power. Now, accompanied by Valka, carrying a flat
basket, she circled round the dinner table. There were
two, to be accurate, one presided over by herself and her
husband; the other, the 'young' table, under the auspices of
Gian Galeazzo. It was essential that this evening he should
appear younger than he really was. 'I told you,' she pointed
out, 'that it was useless to put the Comtesse d'Étanches
on the Prince's left. He hates clever women; especially
French ones. Whom else have we got? He's bound to be
bored, anyway! The duchess is on his right, that goes
without saying, let me see . . . ' She put up her lorgnette,
holding the list of guests as far away as possible. 'But of
course! I was forgetting old Anna, Anna San Pulciano. She
arrived from Rome this morning with her hairdresser. Don't
be silly, Valka. I know she's American, but she's married
to a Roman prince. I suppose the d'Étanches ought, as a
foreigner, to go first, the French are so touchy, but Anna
being the doyenne of the dinner and a princess into the
bargain (Poor Anna, it would be terrible if anyone were to
discover she is only seventy-five, which merely means the
old age pension. Well, of course, it's dowdy to be seventy-
five, and chic to be ninety!) What other foreigners have we
got? Septimus Asche, but he is more Florentine than the
Florentines. We will put him next to the Duchess, he loves
duchesses, and she loves speaking English. Then, there's
Elena Ravitali – she can go to the "young" table, which will
flatter her immensely. She had an affair with Gigi, but she
can be relied upon to behave. *Must* I have the Duke,
Valka, *must* I, *must* I? Don't be so absurd, of course I must!
Surely you should know *that* by now (I wonder what this
table would be like if I left it to you?) O dear, he's so deaf,
and his false teeth click like castanets. And as an antidote
to dotage, whom? I should like to have Juanito, but he is
my cousin; as he hardly ever comes to Florence they
will not immediately realize he is my cousin, anyway he is
a foreigner; as such, he is entitled to one of the first places.

Then there's Bebecita, on whom shall I inflict her? (Why is
it that all infinitely dreary women with long upper lips and
no sense of humour have names like Bijou, or Chiffon, or
Bebecita?) The Duke shall have Bebecita on his right. She
shall be his punishment for being so old and deaf. Now we
come to the more attractive elements . . . Titi Tantalo? Where
shall we put him? Haven't we got a pretty woman at our
table? What about Paola Capodimonte? She's pretty enough,
in all conscience (I wonder if she has slept with Titi yet?).'
She put the card on the table as though she were confer-
ring a decoration. The monologue continued, Valka, only
interested in genealogies, royalties, and diseases, paid little
attention to the Princess' indiscretions. 'It all goes in at one
ear and out the other,' she would truthfully say to Ada.

On the Princess' instigation Valka had invited the Duchess'
'Mees' and ex-governess to her children, to spend the
evening. While she enjoyed showing off the splendours of
Palazzo Arrivamale, it cannot be truthfully said that the
Duchess' 'Mees' was anything but antipathetic to Valka.
She was, as it were, a step higher in the social hierarchy; she
had taught, whereas Valka had waited; she had intellectual
pretensions, Valka had none.

Now, ensconced between the Duchess' 'Mees' and her
mousey satellite, Valka leant over the marble balustrade,
waiting to see the guests troop into dinner. Her Friend was
too awed to utter a word. Not so the Duchess of Aquaviva's
'Mees': 'Aym shaw you must enjaw living in this scrumptious
peless, Miss Walker, though of course, aws is, if anything, on
a grander scale.'

The tortured syllables, stunted and distorted, struggled to
escape from Miss Quince's mutilating lips. It was horrible what
she did to the English language, clipping and compressing it
into an unhappy topiary of burlesque shapes. To Valka,
however, it sounded incomparably elegant and beyond her
means.

'Yes,' she acknowledged, 'it does sorter bolster one up to live in a place like this.'

'The Duchess says it is bawnd to affect the character. Ay mean that we maight faynd ourselves behaving in the manner of the perryodd,' she added with a vicious stab at the last syllable.

'You mean,' preserved Valka, who had a literal mind, 'that we might carry on like those disrespectable old bodies with mugs?' She pointed to a Teniers' 'Kermesse' hanging on the wall behind her. Miss Quince smiled with condescension: 'Deah me, noh. That would be Dotch, would it not? The Duchess had the Italian Renaissance in maynd, ay fancy. Borgia and suchlike.' Valka was beginning to feel outclassed: 'Oh, that would be popes, wouldn't it? I must say I don't hold with popes, if they were anything like as bad as they were painted.'

'*May deah* Miss Walker, there were popes *and* popes. Ay would remaynd you that the Duchess has three in her ancestry.'

'Well . . . we've had two saints in ours, surely a saint is as good as a pope,' snapped Valka, vicarious family pride up in arms.

'Aym saying nothing against saints, Miss Walker,' retorted Miss Quince with some heat, 'but most people would prefer a nice clean white pope to one of those lousy old saints, covered with sores and vermin!' She was so indignant that a whole sentence had escaped castration.

'There's no call to be personal. Miss Quince. It's a good job the Princess can't hear you. Anyway, there's no accounting for tastes. What I say is – ' At this juncture, a mounting though muffled rumour came from below. Doors were thrown open; the rumour, no longer hushed, split up into a score of shrill asides; it all sounded extraordinarily artificial, like 'noises-off.' Black and white, arm in arm, the wound-up, scintillating couples streamed into the dining-room.

In order to give a collective
impression of the dinner, a
specimen of each individual
dialogue must, as accurately
as possible, be submitted:

———

Angelo Carnucci)	(Comtesse Yzquierda Y Derecha
(	)
Princess San)	(Duke
Pulciano (	)
)	(
Prince (	) Princess
)	(
Duchess (	) Juan Yzquiedsa Y Derecha
)	(
Septimus Asche (	) Comtesse D'Étanches
)	(
Paola di (	) Titi Tantalo
Capodimonte)	(

———

Princess to Duke: Maria Teresa is looking very well to-
night.

Duke [*screening his ear*]: Scusi?

Princess [*crescendo*]: I said your wife is looking very well to-
night.

Duke: Yes, fancy! They say she is with her hairdresser. That
is why her hair is always so well done nowadays.

Princess [*bawling in his ear*]: I was not referring to Anna,
I was referring to Maria Teresa.

Duke: *Disgraziata*! I don't know what the world is coming
to. She has no shame, that woman. . . .

Princess [*turning in despair to* Juanito]: *Juanito, mi*

corazon, I cannot cope with that old man. He must try Bebecita, she is very patient.

JUANITO: *Per forza*, as you say in Italy. It requires a lot of patience to be married to me! [*He grins, showing impeccable teeth.*]

PRINCESS: *Siempre lo mismo!* But I should hate you to change. After all, it is something to be married to the best-looking man in Madrid!

JUANITO: *Querida*, after ten years' matrimony, a tactful wife no longer notices if her husband is plain or handsome. Speaking of marriage, your English protégée is *muy guapa*. I knew the father, I have seen him play golf in Madrid, an excellent family, no mésalliance that I know of. Does la pequeña also play golf?

PRINCESS: You and your golf! I must confess I have become less Anglophile since I left Madrid.

JUANITO: You are wrong, Luz. It is admirable for the figure.

PRINCESS: Golf or Anglophilia?

JUANITO: It is the same thing. Look at Jimmy, how well-preserved he is, he plays eighteen holes a day. When are you going to have a decent golf-course in this so-archaic village?

PRINCESS: It's all very well for you to laugh at us, but æsthetically you will admit that Madrid cannot hold a candle to Florence!

JUANITO: Who wants to live in a museum? There's altogether too much beauty in Italy, that's why Italians are so effeminate.

PRINCESS [*tapping him lightly with her fan*]: I am half Italian, my dear, and I know which side of the family I get my brains from. Though we may be feminine, we are not effeminate. Unmitigated virility is apt to be rather a bore in the long run. At least you will acknowledge, there is no lack of pretty women in the Florence you so much despise!

JUANITO: Indeed no! La pequeña rubia at the end of the table is just my type.

PRINCESS [*raising her lorgnette*]: Paola Capodimonte? Yes, she
is very pretty, in an obvious way. Tell me, what do you
think of the girl sitting next to Gigi?

JUANITO: Too dark for my taste, too pale. I'll admit she's
striking in a way, she will develop into what the French
call *une femme à histoires*, if she has not done so already.

PRINCESS [*lightly*]: Quien sabe? I am interested in this girl,
I think she should have an interesting career.

JUANITO [*sententiously*]: There is only one kind of career
open to a pretty woman.

PRINCESS: How Spanish, how old-fashioned. My dear, it is
time you turned your attentions to the Duchess. Look at
her! She's as happy as a king; she adores airing her
English.

JUANITO has to wait at least a minute before a slight pause
in the dialogue permits infiltration.

JUANITO [*with aplomb*]: You know, Duchessa, I speak
English as well as your neighbour.

The DUCHESS, a faded but enthusiastic blonde, has indeed
often been mistaken for an Englishwoman. She is notoriously
charitable and as stuffed with good intentions as a girl guide.
Now, baring her plausibly English teeth, she turns, all optimism,
to her left-hand neighbour:

DUCHESS: But I'm *sure* you do! Spaniards are such good
linguists; are they not, Mr. Asche?

MR. ASCHE has been a resident in Florence for longer than
anyone can remember. His yellowish, almost fleshless face
resembles an old white kid glove which has been sent many
times to the cleaners. Each time it returns a trifle more
shrunken. Cultured, urbane, of an almost frightening suavity,
he owns a magnificent collection of *settecento* drawings,
which he enjoys showing to newcomers. He is even prouder
of his 'd'Annunzioesque' Italian which he speaks without a
trace of foreign accent. Unfortunately, the DUCHESS is equally
proud of her English. A terrible tussle between the two poly-
glots has just taken place, each speaking each other's idiom

with equal authority and determination. In the end, gallantry
has compelled Septimus Asche to retire, leaving Britannia in
the field.

DUCHESS [*recklessly*]: I was just saying to Mr. Asche that I love
everything about England, *especially* the food!

MR. ASCHE [*raising celebrated episcopal hands to the
heavens*]: Duchessa, what new heresy is this?

DUCHESS [*who likes to think she is a regular madcap*]: But
I do, I do! I even like your *smashed* potatoes!

ASCHE [*mournfully*]: In that case, there is no hope.

DUCHESS [*rushing on*]: I find there is something so pure, so
naïve, about your English cooking, which makes me feel
young again. That's it, nursery food, not for grown-up
people. [*Ardently.*] Do you sketch, I feel sure you sketch,
Yzquierda?

JUANITO [*raising his eyebrows*]: I am afraid not. I am not
interested in art. Do you play golf, Duchessa?

DUCHESS: I have watched play, but I am not, what you
call in Spanish, an affectionate.* Now, my daughter [*they
continue in this train,* MR. ASCHE *is now free to resume his
Italian. He leans across the table, addressing his* vis-à-vis,
PAOLA CAPODIMONTE, *that is, when he can get a word in
edgeways*].

ASCHE: *Ben tornato, Contessa.* My spies tell me you have
been in Paris, but I need no spies to tell me that that
exquisite creation is signed by Chanel.

PAOLA [*she is resentful at having her tête-à-tête with* TITI
interrupted, snaps]: It is by Lanvin.

Meanwhile TITI has turned to his other neighbour Madame
d'ÉTANCHES, a woman whose clothes, conventional to the
point of austerity, are at variance with her unorthodox face.
She has the green oblique eye of the adventuress set in small
demure features; they can only be the result of an error in
assemblage, but they dared you to turn them out; the cuckoo

---

*Aficionada.

in the nest. Tɪᴛɪ was uncertain how to approach her: was she as dull as her clothes or as nonconformist as her eyes?

He chose a middle course, a national compliment.

'How picturesque French dressmakers make Italian dresses appear!'

She gave him a rapid look, which assessed his appearances, potentialities, limitations. 'Meaning that I look dowdy?' The irresponsible eyes danced.

Tᴀɴᴛᴀʟᴏ: Meaning, on the contrary, that you make our Florentine ladies look overdressed.

She was intelligent, quick. Good. He could afford to relax: secure in his good looks, charm, and deserved reputation of wit, he was, he thought, more than a match for her.

'I don't agree,' she was saying, 'Italian women are far more beautiful than French women. It would not suit them to wear literal, discreet clothes. Their clothes have to play up to their faces. My compatriots are not really beautiful, so they try to be chic. *Le chic est un pis aller*, but they are good at making the most of their small capital; your attention is immediately drawn to their one asset: if a woman has pretty ears, she will contrive that the first and foremost thing you will notice is her ears, if it be her arms, you will be sure they will be displayed to the fullest advantage. Tenez,' she added, in a matter-of-fact voice, which successfully neutralized the audacity of her next remark, 'I'll be prepared to wager you haven't noticed I have a nose like a thumb and an indifferent complexion.'

Titi, off his guard, completely taken aback, experienced the tingling sensation of one who, stepping into an apparently ordinary bath, discovers the water is effervescent. 'You mean that I have only noticed your eyes,' he floundered.

'Precisely,' her voice was scornful. 'That's why I wear no jewels. I don't need them. If I wore jewels, *ils feraient une concurrence déloyale à mes yeux, mon seul atout.*' Now he knew where he stood. This was merely a novel rendering of 'l'Invitation à la Valse.'

'Indeed, they are remarkable, so unexpected, so – '

'I have made my point, now I want to talk about something else. This, I take it, is a *diner de fiancailles avant la lettre? La jeune fille anglaise* (*there's* a beauty, if you like) is going to marry the young man who resembles a portrait by Bellini?'

Titi nodded. 'They will make a handsome couple,' he acknowledged, dismissing them. He looked upon the topic as a setback. It was quite a new experience to be told what he was to talk about; this singular young woman did not appear to realize he was a spoilt darling of Florentine society. The sooner she did, the better.

'I doubt if it will be a success,' the maddening creature went on. 'We Latins are bad mixers. Take a Franco-Italian marriage, they are relatively rare, but a French husband married to an Italian wife immediately adopts a patronizing, governessy attitude, which, were I an Italian, I would find particularly galling. In fact, France is not so much a *sœur latin as la belle-sœur latine*, and there is, as you know, the world of difference between a sister and a sister-in-law!'

Titi burst out laughing. He could not help being amused by her independence, vivacity. 'It is easy to see, Madame, that you belong to a country that is ruled by your sex.'

'Yet,' her eyes challenged him, 'you Italians do not seem exactly indifferent to women.'

'It is different,' he conceded, 'we adore women, but our women have never thought themselves our equals, in any sphere, they beguile our leisure, they charm us, we worship them, but a conversation such as we are having now would be unthinkable with my compatriots. I follow where you lead, you rap out your instructions, Sit up! Beg! Trust! Paid for!'

'With the difference that you haven't been paid!' The exhausting eyes seemed to give out sparks. She was enjoying herself. She did not yet know what she was going to do with this attractive, over-confident young man.

'But surely it must be a welcome change from the beautiful

young women who sit and wilt at your feet, and throw you looks of cold fury,' she lowered her voice, 'like those flung at you by your left-hand neighbour, because you happen to be having an animated conversation with an intelligent, but by no means beautiful, foreigner.'

This was indeed the case. Paola Capodimonte was outraged. *Il y avait de quoi.* Titi was supposedly having no eyes for no one but her, and here he was obviously fascinated by a plainish French woman, in a banal dress, with not even a jewel to carry it off. Conscious of his indignity he said: 'I realize I am monopolizing you to a scandalous degree, our host has been waiting to talk to you for the last five minutes. I shall look forward to dancing with you later.'

The Prince's rumbling, slightly asthmatic bass makes itself heard as he bends dutifully across the table, anxious to atone for the fact that Mme. d'Étanches is not really in her 'right' place.

'*Je sais que vous arrivez de Rome*, Madame, what were your impressions?' he inquired heavily, expecting the usual flow of clichés.

'My impressions of Rome?' she repeated, 'something grandiose and sinister, as old as time, as old as the Sphinx. The Colosseum, like the Sphinx, sinks ever deeper into the greedy earth. I was alternately repelled and fascinated.'

The Prince raised his eyebrows. 'You did much sightseeing?'

'As much as my engagements would permit, but I admit I soon got bored with your superb, malicious, more or less illiterate patrician ladies, I threw my engagements to the winds, then I began to enjoy myself.'

The Prince's social prejudices suddenly collapsed. 'Ah, Madame,' he said warmly, 'I sympathize with you, I never could bear Rome myself, because of the "monde." *Je suis un ours, moi.* I hate parties, potins, puerility. I have been dreading this one for weeks, now if I were to tell you –' they never drew breath until the end of dinner.

Meanwhile, Princess San Pulciano, who was the epitome of all that the Prince most detested, was having as scurrilous a conversation as she could wish with Angelo Carnucci, a bearded ageing satyr of so warm a heart, so genial a disposition, that it was impossible not to overlook his most outrageous escapades.

The Princess, one of those international octogenerian American bullies, looked not a day under ninety; she had a mind compared to which the proverbial cesspool was a Grecian urn filled with rose petals. Invariably dressed as Mary, Queen of Scots, *en deuil blanc*, the white cobwebby draperies suited her haggard Cassandra-like countenance to perfection: 'And would you believe it,' she was saying with relish, 'she was compelled to *sack* the canary!'

'But why, Princess?' inquired Angelo.

'Well, in Rome, you know, we haven't quite yet got over that Léda story.'

Angelo threw back his handsome head, and laughed until he choked. 'Oh Princess,' he gasped, 'you will be the death of me yet.'

'Why, of course!' she exulted, slapping him on the back with considerable vigour, 'you're such a little innocent. Now, supposing I were to tell you all I know about the people sitting round this table but you'll say you know already – still, there's plenty of food for thought in this party – *fresh* food, I mean. You see that handsome young man, rather too well dressed, sitting at Gigi's table? Well, he's Luz's latest!'

'*What!*'

'Yes, I know it on the best authority. He is the son of a dentist, she's mad about him. Apparently, she slips out of the Palace in a mantilla, when everyone has gone to bed. . . . '

'Princess, I simply don't believe you!'

'And why not? Heavens knows, Luz is no prude, he's just her type.'

'Yes, but you forget, she has a great sense of decorum, she's the last person in the world to indulge in a scandalous love affair on the eve of marrying her nephew to one of the most sought-after young ladies in England: *noblesse oblige*. I do not say she may not be attracted by this young man, he is good-looking enough, in all conscience, but I am prepared to bet you anything you like that, for the moment, there is nothing between them.'

'Have it your own way,' retorted the Princess sulkily, 'since when have you become a squire of dames, and old dames at that, Angelo Carnucci?'

Whereupon she began shouting across the table to her *vis à-vis* the Duke who, considering that he had done more than his duty by Bebecita, was doing justice to an excellent dinner.

Angelo, on the other hand, was conscious that he had barely addressed a word to Bebecita. Bracing himself to a further effort, he said: 'Do you find Florence very much changed, since you were last here, Contessa?'

She raised her faithful, mournful eyes: 'Changed? O no, not changed. Just the same, just as frivolous. Just as many silly fatuous young women. (For her, one realized, there would always be a super abundance of silly fatuous young women.)

'M . . . m . . . m . . . ' muttered Angelo, in whose opinion there could not be too many, 'I see what you mean, but surely in Madrid?'

She nodded sombrely, 'Yes, but there one knows where one is, here one doesn't.' (Poor creature, thought the kind-hearted Angelo, what a terrible life she must lead, like that frumpish, frustrated English Queen, who was so jealous of her Spanish husband, Maria Sanguinosa, wasn't it?')

A fanatical gleam came into Bebecita's bloodhound eyes.

'But God will punish them,' she barked suddenly. 'The Day of Reckoning is at hand!'

Angelo, shocked and startled, looked nervously round to see if she had been overheard, but by this time everyone, with the exception of the deaf Duke, was shouting at the pitch of their voices.

'I think, Contessa,' he soothed, 'I think you take life too seriously.'

The animation of the other table was slightly different in quality.

There was more indiscriminate laughter, less stocktaking. The younger table was not in the least interested in the older table, and never bestowed on it so much as a glance, with the exception of Gian Galeazzo, who, in need of reassurance, now and again, stole a rather wistful look in the direction of his aunt who gratified him with a wink, whenever he was lucky enough to catch her eye. He was not really enjoying herself. For perhaps the first time in his life, he was fully conscious of his thirty-eight years, he needed no one to tell him that, in the estimation of his fellow guests (mostly under twenty-five) he was merely mutton masquerading as lamb. Only in the eyes of two women did he read the response to which he was accustomed, one was Elena Ravitali, his ex-mistress; the other, Vica. Elena plainly recalled the very pleasant hours they had spent together; the sense of decorum she was known to possess, allowed her eyes a latitude she forbade her tongue. She fully realized she was here 'on trust,' she knew better than to alienate la Zia. With Vica it was another matter altogether, it was the first time she had dined with Gian Galeazzo, much against her will, she could not take her eyes of him; the fond platitudes lavished on her by Lord Risingdale fell on careless ears. With an effort she reminded herself she was going to marry him, not Gian Galeazzo, and that this very night, she would have the pleasure of announcing the event to this self-same Gian Galeazzo, who could have married her himself, had he so willed.

Blissfully unconscious of all these subversive undercurrents, Elizabeth was enjoying herself greedily, wholeheartedly, without *arrière-pensée*. She loved, would always love, parties. She was gay as only the extrovert is gay, living for the moment, secure in her beauty, self-possession. She thought everything wonderful, Gigi, the Princess, the Palace, the guests, everything! Very young, she believed the best of life; the old harridan flattered and played up to her. Even in after years, she was to be let down but seldom. At the banquet of life, her place was permanently laid.

CHAPTER SIX
The Ball: II

THE ball was in full swing. It was being a great success: the Prince had already taken up a strategical position, behind a porphyry column, which he relied upon to cover his retreat. Luz had exacted a promise that he would not vanish before midnight. He consulted his old-fashioned turnip watch: it was ten minutes to twelve, with any luck there would not be another ball until – *Caspita!* He was forgetting: a worse, an infinitely more prolonged ordeal loomed ahead: Gian Galeazzo's wedding, with all it entailed of putting up relations from all over Italy. Entertaining an unknown English family (his English was practically non-existent), tradesmen invading the palace, no doubt his beloved observatory converted into a lady's cloakroom!

A wary circular glance assured him that he was safe for the moment: Youth was dancing in the ballroom, the other guests were either playing bridge or scattered about the adjoining salons, the colonnade separated the official part of the house from the private apartments. He was just about to light his *toscano*, when to his surprise and irritation, he saw a bulky bearded figure bearing down on him with many a furtive backwards glance. . . .

Were his pockets bulging with silver spoons, or was he, too, trying to make his escape?

The Prince saw that he was wearing glasses with very thick

pebble lenses and that in another minute he would cannon into him, if he did not step aside.

He did not look like a man who would steal anything, except, perhaps, a stethoscope. He judged him to be either a doctor, or a professor of something or other, but in either case, what on earth was he doing at Luz's ball?

In order to avoid a collision, for again the man was glancing over his shoulder, the Prince addressed him: 'Are you looking for someone? Perhaps I can help you?' The man started as though he had been shot.

'Please forgive me, I did not see you, Signore, I am very shortsighted.'

'I was partially concealed by the column, but you seem anxious. Is there anything I can do for you?'

'Well, as a matter of fact,' he produced a large white handkerchief and began to mop his *bombé* brow. 'I'm trying to get out, I'm not much good at parties.'

The Prince relaxed, 'Neither am I. Why don't we sit down, there's quite a comfortable sofa over there. Can I offer you a *toscano?* He dived in his pocket, produced the companion to his own.

'That is very kind of you, I'm sure, I never thought to meet a *toscano* in a house like this.' The Prince extended a match which lit up two beards, strikingly similar in texture and shape.

'Quite a surprise, isn't it?' The Prince grinned. He liked this man. Encouraged, the other, who was clearly very shy, said: 'It is very beautiful, but I would hate to live in a house like this, wouldn't you?' The stranger's laughter he thought disproportionate to such a banal remark.

'It is all very well as a museum,' he amplified, 'but I could not work in such large rooms.'

'What kind of work do you go in for?' inquired the Prince, with more curiosity than he had experienced for a long time.

'I am a dentist. I know most people think dentists as comical as mothers-in-law, but I love my work.'

'Well,' the Prince sympathized, 'if it is any comfort to you I am an astronomer, which is very nearly as comical, you will admit.'

'For some, perhaps,' assented Papagallo with a twinkle inhaling his *toscano*, 'no doubt you are a friend of the *padrone di casa*, who is also, I believe, an astronomer. I have not met him but I am not sure I would like him, though they say he is not a bad old bastard, if you take him the right way. I am ill at ease with the aristocracy. I slunk in, in the wake of my family and succeeded in shaking hands with no one. Where do you work?'

'I . . . er . . . I have a small observatory.'

'In what part of the town?'

'In . . . er . . . this quarter, quite a nice little place. You must visit me sometime.'

'*Volentieri*. If I may say so, this is the only pleasant interlude in an O! so boring evening. My wife and children were set on coming. I suppose it means a lot to a woman to be invited to a house like this. Unlike us they have no, what the French call *vie intérieure*, poor things, their lives are composed of puerilities.'

'Indeed, indeed, they are,' echoed the Prince with fervour, 'my wife looks upon my researches as sheer waste of time. It is incredible! But that is not all, for instance . . .

Reassured, disarmed, the Prince gave himself up to the joy of communing with a kindred spirit. . . .

In the *cortile*, the fountain let fall curdled monosyllables from its Habsburg lip. The gardenias in their great tubs were out, laying traps for the unwary, who sniffed them *en passant*, not realizing they were more heady than any wine. Music, sufficiently distant to be a discreet accompaniment, or, if need be, an accomplice, waited on the night.

Elizabeth and Gian Galeazzo were sitting the dance out. They would not be disturbed for at least another ten minutes. Gian Galeazzo was resolved to be the climax of this resplendent evening, not just part of a whole, no more important than the gardenias or the music. 'How heavenly it is out here,' Elizabeth sighed voluptuously. 'How happy I am, how I love this place!'

'Yours, yours, everything in it is yours, Elizabeth, including myself.' (Oh dear, he sighed inwardly, how much better this would sound in Italian.)

'You have been frightfully sweet to me, Gigi,' said Elizabeth fondly, with her instinctive Anglo-Saxon preference for the diminutive.

He shrugged, 'What is that, being sweet to you! No, that is not what I want. I want to marry you, *amore*, most beautiful. It is as though this palazzo had been built for you!' He slid an arm about her shoulders. Elizabeth thought: O dear! Now I suppose I must make up my mind. She was quite content with their present relationship and saw no reason why it should receive further promotion. If only she could gain time.

'Surely there is no hurry, Gigi darling, can't we go on like this for a bit longer?'

'Elisabetta, tesoro, you may be happy, I am not. For a man it is different. I was so hoping we might become engaged to-night as a fitting climax to the ball, how you say, *l'apoteoso*,' he floundered, his English was deserting him. The curiously ascetic features suddenly took on the mask of tragedy. He could have served as model for any young mediaeval saint, betrayed, encircled. Elizabeth was dismayed to discover she was the author of so much suffering; she leant over him: 'I had no idea you cared so much.'

Quick to perceive his advantage he pressed: '*Tesoro*, all these weeks I have been playing a part, trying to behave coldly, decorumly – '

To his bewilderment, Elizabeth burst out laughing, flung both arms round his neck, gave him a smacking kiss on the cheek. 'O Gigi, you are sweet! "Decorumly," O you pet! Of course, I will become engaged to you if you really want me to!' She thought: I can always change my mind if it isn't a success. She had once been engaged for a whole afternoon to a boy in a punt. I'm all for trying things, she decided cheerfully, since he seems to set so much store by it.

'My beautiful, my angel,' Gian Galeazzo genuinely exulted, taking her in his arms, 'this is the proudest moment of my life, I cannot wait to announce our engagement to the whole of Florence!'

'Whole of Florence, whole of Florence be damned!' she cried, breaking loose from his embrace, 'you must be mad! What on earth has the whole of Florence to do with us?'

She had risen in her alarm, he put his hands on her shoulders, compelled her to sit down. 'Darling, in my country that is what is expected of us.' Really, English girls were the limit!

'But Mummy doesn't know anything about it, I have barely mentioned you in my letters.'

'Charles knows.'

'Yes, Charles knows you want to marry me, that's all.' Starkly laconic in moments of stress, Elizabeth was not for nothing her father's daughter.

'Of course, had you been Italian,' he said unwisely, 'I should have had to make my demand to your parents first.'

'Precisely,' Elizabeth clutched at the passing straw. 'And, as you haven't, it doesn't count, you couldn't possibly announce our engagement without Mummy's and Father's consent!'

Too late, Gian Galeazzo realized his mistake. He mustn't rush her, it might sabotage the whole affair, 'Of course, I understand,' he appeased, 'I will only ask a little favour; please, may we tell la Zia?'

'Must we?'

'It would make her so happy. She loves me as though I were her son. She will not tell a soul.'

Elizabeth considered. She was conscious of an invisible net being spread about her; on the other hand, she had already acquired the taste for 'largesses,' which is one of the characteristics of the professional beauty. She enjoyed making

people happy, if it was only for a day. 'She'll tell the Prince?'
she wavered.

'Well, no doubt you will tell Charles.'

'I'm bound to tell Charles.'

'Well, then: you see, my darling, it will not go beyond the
immediate family circle, Charles, lo zio, la Zia, *Parola
d'onore*. I will see that it goes no further.'

'O dear, what a pity,' sighed Elizabeth, resting her head
against his arm. 'We were so happy.'

'*Vieni, amore*,' he said, as briskly as he dared, 'we will go
and look for them. The music has stopped, I already see a
couple coming towards us.' Elena Ravitali on the arm of Tito
Tantalo, appeared in the further doorway.

It was only as they left the *cortile*, that Gian Galeazzo
realized, with a pang of superstition, that he had not kissed
his betrothed.

Rigo was installed in a tiny octagonal room, separated from
the Venetian boudoir by a velvet curtain. A fiasco of Chianti,
a pile of sandwiches, and a bottle of *grappa* had been placed
at his elbow, by the orders of the Princess, all of which he had
lavishly partaken. As long as he could be heard, and not seen,
he was quite happy. He liked to think he was contributing to
the success of the party, more than once, his goddess had
peered round the curtain to compliment him on his playing,
naturally he had heard rumours which for his peace of mind
he preferred to ignore: *chi vuol esser lieto, sia*. Besides, something told him Elizabeth was in love with no one. Even the
Princess had thrust her sharp nose in: 'Elizabeth says you play
best on *grappa*, so please do not stint yourself.'

The only obstacle to his enjoyment was the costume the
Princess had insisted on his wearing, a Seicento doublet and
hose, embroidered with the family coat of arms, and which,
strange to say, fitted him like a glove. The coat of arms he
found distasteful, it savoured too much of a livery, which,
indeed, it was, the ancestral livery of the family jester. Rigo

would rather have worn *lo smoking* which he had only recently acquired in honour of Elizabeth. . . .

Well pleased, in spite of everything, with his evening, he was idly picking out a tune on his guitar, when he heard the sound of voices. A peep through the curtains disclosed the Princess, with il Marchese de' Pardi and Elizabeth, hanging on either arm. They looked very excited. He moved nearer to the curtain and began to strum *pian piano*; though he could not understand what they were saying, as they spoke in English.

'Dearest children,' the Princess purred, 'you cannot think how happy this makes me. The moment I set eyes on you, Elizabeth, I thought this is the girl for Gigi, my dear, it was the *coup de foudre*. All his life he had been ransacking the world for you.' Without ceasing to play *pian piano*, Rigo glued his ear to the gap in the curtains.

'Ring, child, for champagne, I want to drink the health of *i promessi sposi*.'

(Nobody noticed that the music had ceased.) Again the door opened: entered Charles Risingdale. Vica's arm was tucked under his own, he looked radiant, Vica befittingly hung back.

'Zia,' he cried, clasping the Princess' hands, 'I may call you that, mayn't I? I can't wait to tell you that Vica and I are engaged. Isn't it splendid, may I kiss you? Without waiting for the permission he flung his arms round her neck.

'How happy I am for both of you,' she said, genuinely moved. 'This is what you call a "double event," you and Gigi, Vica and Charles. Never was a fairy godmother so proud! *Embrassez-vous, mes enfants!* Elizabeth was immediately engulfed in a brotherly hug. So this was Charles' transparent secret. Vica must have made him promise to make the announcement coincide with theirs, the reason would no doubt become clear later. . . .

Vica's lips barely brushed Gian Galeazzo's cheek. He was praying that his thoughts might not become as legible as the signs on Broadway. Rage, indignation, frustration, battled in turn for supremacy.

He felt betrayed, how dared she, the dentist's daughter, flout him thus? He realized that, although he would never have admitted it, he had had, at the back of his mind, a secret, a nameless project, thinly disguised by the term '*pazienza*.'

Meanwhile, Vica was discovering that revenge is dead sea fruit. When, a few minutes later, the Princess, taking her arm, drew her towards the window, murmuring, *sotto voce*, 'Good, clever girl!' it was all she could do to refrain from bursting into tears. . . .

Punctual as a zealous official, the sun rose, tweaking *cupola* and *campanile* out of the morning mist, gilding balconies, galvanizing statues. . . . Complacently it looked down on some of man's loveliest creations, the dome of the Cathedral, the Baptistery, the predatory, hawk-like silhouette of the Palazzo Vecchio, the sprawled beautifully-composed town which hung back from the Arno's escape into the greenest of pastoral landscapes.

Palazzo Arrivamale was an early riser, especially this morning when there was so much to clear away, all the dross and the dregs of the night before, cigarette ends which had burnt themselves into woolly caterpillars, the gardenias shrunken and brown, which had graced the gentlemen's buttonholes, the lipstick-stained napkins, dropped and mis-laid cigarette cases, handkerchiefs, vanity cases. . . .

Cesare, the youngest and most sprightly of Casa Arrivamale footmen, was anxious to 'do' the Venetian *salottino* before Valka, sniffing and suspicious, arrived on the scene. He had just drawn the curtains and flung open the shutters, when he was startled to hear stentorous snores proceeding from the little octagonal room, which was separated from the *salottino* by a thick velvet curtain. At the same time, to his horror, he perceived a broad, still wet stain, of what appeared to be blood, on the rug which protruded from under the curtains. He immediately realized, however, that the conjunction of snores and blood was, on the whole, incompatible.

With a leap he thrust aside the curtain.

A curious sight met his gaze.

The body of a man almost as broad as he was long, in unsuitable, if not obscene, fancy-dress, lay sprawled across the floor. An empty fiasco of Chianti had rolled away from one open outstretched hand, and an equally empty bottle of *grappa* was loosely clasped in the other. Across the lower half of his body, like a faithful dog, lay a guitar.

On hearing the news of Elizabeth's engagement, Rigo had, slowly and silently, drunk himself into a stupor.

CHAPTER SEVEN
Anticlimax

THE most lived-in apartment at Canterdown was a longish, somewhat incoherent sitting-room, known as Mummy's boudoir. Originally two rooms, they had been thrown into one by the previous owner as all four windows framed his favourite views, and neither room was really big enough to be very useful by itself. 'Mummy's boudoir' had none of the cloying femininity usually associated with the term. What it *could* boast was an unusually high standard of untidiness, the chairs which did not contain skeins of wool, contained dogs which were practically un-distinguishable from the skeins of wool.

'One of these days,' Elizabeth was wont to observe, 'Mummy will knit one of the dogs into a muffler.'

There were a number of china ornaments (mostly chipped) and a perfect plethora of Mummy's enthusiastic and eclectic water-colours. The puzzled visitor rapidly reached the conclusion that they constituted a species of architectural cocktail, that could only be the result of many alcoholic ones. For example, the Taj Mahal seemed to take no excep-tion to the fact that it faced the Erectheon; the leaning tower of Pisa had been dexterously woven into the Alhambra, neither of these edifices seemed in the least surprised to find themselves spanned by a disarmingly impartial Pont du Gard. As soon as the eye became accustomed to this pictorial

Esperanto, it was fascinating to count how many apparently irreconcilable monuments figured on the same canvas. Lady Canterdown, though notoriously unobservant, was unable to ignore for long the recurring upward glances of her visitors or their sudden interested scrutiny of the upper half of her face (she does not look as though she drank, was what they were thinking).

'I expect you're wondering what all these tangled monuments mean?' she would inquire happily. 'Well, they're my dream cities. A bit here and a bit there, so much nicer to have them all together, don't you think? All summer in a day, if you know what I mean?'

The perplexed visitor longed to know why, in this homogeneous beautiful house, preference had been given to the only room which was entirely undistinguished, but then, Canterdown was like that. Charles always said you could hardly tell Father's bedroom from the butler's pantry, so full was it of cleaning devices and silver trophies. Never was beauty so snubbed as at Canterdown. Though by no means impervious to beauty abroad, for her own home Lady Canterdown had nothing but a myopic affection.

True, you would be shown the house if you expressed a wish to be shown it. Lady Canterdown, in a fever to get back to her dogs and her garden, would bustle you from room to room, rattling off data at breakneck speed in a disparaging manner. 'That's the chair Charles I was supposed to have sat in on the morning of his execution. This, they say, was Elizabeth's bed – such nonsense I always think – as if she could have found time to stay in so many places!'

On the other hand, were you to evince the slightest interest in her garden, the Song of Solomon was as dry as a lawyer's agreement compared to the lyrical effusions this would suscitate. The house was just a pretext for the garden, Lady Canterdown grudged every minute that was spent indoors. She even contrived to resemble a flower herself: one of those large dishevelled chrysanthemums, doubly dear because on the brink of winter.

Horticultural anecdotes about Lady Canterdown were legion, one of the most endearing being that she was one day indulging in her favourite occupation of showing the garden to a foreign diplomat who had been much impressed by a glimpse of her exceptionally decorative children.

'I must congratulate you, Lady Canterdown, on the beauty of your offspring.'

'Yes,' came the absentminded reply, 'aren't they fine? If you like, I'll send you some cuttings.'

When she was brutally uprooted from her floral preoccupations as was now the case, her mind did not immediately readjust itself, it was like a plant without a prop, it became helpless, etiolated. To whom could she turn for support? She simply did not dare tell her husband. Elizabeth's telegram in one hand, she made a futile attempt to find some writing-paper with the other. If there is such a thing as an apple-pie bed, it would be equally apt to refer to Lady Canterdown's bureau as an apple-pie bureau, than which nothing more frustrating can be conceived.

Each drawer, outwardly innocent, was filled to bursting-point with bills and seed catalogues; these were so tightly wedged that it was impossible to add to, or subtract from, their numbers.

She slammed drawer after drawer with mounting irritation. All the writing-paper had been scribbled on, nothing matched, there were two large blue sheets, and one small white envelope. Almost in tears she opened the blotter. It was as thickly clotted with blots (no one was allowed to touch her Ladyship's bureau) as in any provincial post office. She was about to abandon her project of writing to Elizabeth by return of post, when she caught sight of an unopened envelope addressed to her, and which turned out to be a letter from Peter Speight, asking for news of Elizabeth, whom he accused of not having written for weeks.

Now, Lady Canterdown had always liked Peter. Originally imported by Charles, many were the holidays he had spent beneath their roof. The untidy, shaggy boy, as shy as she was herself, gave her confidence; moreover, he was no mean botanist. Together they would identify the more or less withered wild flowers with which his pockets were stuffed.

Later, when his infatuation for Elizabeth became manifest, Lady Canterdown would endeavour to smoothe his continually ruffled feelings.

Fundamentally, unworldly, at the back of her mind, she entertained a vague hope that he might one day marry Elizabeth. Her husband, she knew, was far from sharing her views on the subject, Peter was just a pal of Charles, a nice boy, but not, well, how do you put it, not quite out of the top drawer. It would, of course, have been nicer if he *had* been, but she realized that Peters did not grow on every bush. With characteristic impulsiveness, she tore off the back page of his letter, on which she composed a telegram summoning him to Canterdown the very next day. The moment she had handed it to Crawle, the butler, she doubted the wisdom of her act. After all the Italian was the nephew of her old friend Luz, so he must be 'all right,' but she only liked people with whom she felt safe. How was it possible to feel safe with an Italian? Besides, she didn't want her precious Liz to marry a foreigner, she was far too young to marry anyone, anyway. If anyone could be relied upon to be a help, Peter could.

As a landscape illuminated by a flash of lightning, she saw with startling suddenness and finality that Elizabeth's marriage to the Italian would not take place.

Peter always enjoyed the drive from the station, the ritual of the lodges, the long beech avenue; finally, the consummate view of the huge amber-coloured house with its slate roof, myriad chimneys. He especially liked Canterdown in winter, when it withdrew into itself, ceasing to pander to the present day – not that it pandered much, for it was as luxurious as it was uncomfortable. One ate out of Queen Anne plate, but the baths – few and far between – were shaped like eclairs, boasted a lid, and had been known to contain more flies than water. He loved the interminable winter nights, when the dissatisfied wind mewed through the keyhole, and gusts of acrid smoke were driven down through the chimney; the imperfect silence when you awoke, as of a conversation hastily lulled, objects being hastily replaced. 'Blow, blow thou winter wind, thou art not so unkind as man's ingratitude.' Why was it he felt so perfectly attuned to winter, to its fatalistic expectation of the worst, then, when the worst came, its rustic heroisms and shouldering of burdens, improvised ingeniousness, constructive despair?

In the meantime, the month was June, and these considerations were out of place . . . he was going to see his dear old friend again, and, above all, he was going to get news of Elizabeth.

'Peter! At last! I haven't been able to do a thing all day, I was counting the minutes until you arrived!' (He couldn't help regretting it was the mother, and not the daughter, who gave him this excessive welcome.)

'Tea? Whisky and soda? Yes, bring a whisky and soda, Crawle.' She added significantly, '*You'll need it.*'

As soon as the man had left the room, she burst out: 'My dear! it's too awful, what do you think has happened: Liz has become engaged to an Italian!'

'The devil she has!' said Peter grimly. He might have known this would happen. He silently cursed the ridiculous education young ladies of the upper classes were subjected to: Begun in Paris, finished in Florence, or was it the other way round? Anyhow, this was finish, right enough.

'Peter, you've *got* to help me.' She held him in her earnest periwinkle gaze.

'How? Of course, I'll help you. What do you want me to do?'

'I want you to go and fetch her home.'

'I thought Charles had already gone to fetch her home.'

'Yes, but you're different.'

'Supposing she refuses to come?'

'She won't refuse, I don't believe she is really in love with this man.'

'Would to God you were right! Of course I'll go, I'll do anything.'

'I knew you would, Peter dear. That's why I sent for you. Christopher mustn't know anything about it. Peter, this is Saturday, you must start, if possible, Monday night, because I told Christopher you were coming for the week-end, and it would look odd if you left to-morrow.'

'I shall probably get kicked out of the office for leaving at such a short notice, but I'm prepared to risk it.'

Lady Canterdown took his large hand covered with blunt golden hairs on her lap. 'Have you got any money, Peter?' she asked anxiously.

'Not what *you* would call money. Only what I earn, it varies between four and five hundred a year, roughly.'

It was on the tip of Lady Canterdown's tongue to say: 'Scarcely more than we give our head-gardener,' but she checked herself just in time. 'Well, that wouldn't matter. Elizabeth has enough for two.'

'D'you mean to say – !'

'O yes I do,' said Lady Canterdown in a reckless drunken voice, as though she had just seen the light, as indeed she had. The words were scarcely out of her mouth, when she found herself caught up in a tweedy hug.

'Lady Canterdown, *darling* Lady Canterdown, I always thought you would kick me out if I proposed to Liz!'

Crawle, returning at this moment with the paraphernalia of drink, cut short this rhapsody. On the silver tray, between the syphon and the decanter, lay a small orange envelope.

'A telegram for you m'Lady.'

Anguish gripped her; she turned to Peter, 'Another

telegram! What can it be!' She opened it with trembling fingers. He watched her poor face turn pink, pucker like a baby's, to his horror, she burst into tears. 'Read, oh read!' she wailed, thrusting the telegram under his nose: 'Charles has also got engaged to an Italian!'

Everyone was out when Peter arrived at the Papagalli apartment: '*I Signori andare campagna per giornata,*' explained Gina in her best pidgin Italian. If the Signore cared to *aspettare?*

No, the Signore would return, he pointed to himself, to the clock, to the figure. Gina found it hard to place this uncouth young man, so hotly dressed for the month of June. A relation of donna Elisabetta *senza dubbio?* He walked down the steep stone stair cursing silently. First and foremost, he must book a room at an hotel, any hotel. '*Albergo,*' was his succinct order to the fiacre-coachman, who assessed him, his suitcase, and probable tip, at a glance. This was no English 'milor' with rich pigskin luggage, rugs, and thermos flasks. No, just an ordinary tourist, hot, tired, dusty. The Hotel-Pension Albion was quite good enough for him. He was driven down narrow streets, septic and sinuous. A synthetic smell composed of fried fish, coffee, leather, cheese, hung about them. Handsome, graceful youths lounged in cavernous doorways, eyeing him with an interest not devoid of irony: tinny churchbells gossiped in a desultory way, without plan or rhythm. . . .

So this is what appealed to Elizabeth, this is what had proved her undoing?

Suddenly they came upon the Mercato with its straw hats, flowers, multi-coloured linens, all bargaining, laughter, vociferation. A crude sun spilt its prodigal rays on the scene, splitting it into stripes, yellow and black, like a tiger – Something in Peter gave in, quietly, without fuss. Why pretend? Of course, he was just as vulnerable as the rest, why attempt to belittle the squandered beauty, the effortless unselfconscious charm of the country, and its inhabitants? He had once been for a walking-tour of the Italian lakes which he had been doing his best to forget, the repressed memory flowered afresh, he had never enjoyed anything so much as that walking tour, the surprises that did not figure in any guide-book, the spontaneous, disinterested curiosity of the native. . . . What was to be gained by taking up an aloof, superior attitude? Don't repress, dilate, he was mysteriously advised, don't disparage, praise. Take stock of your enemy, see how strong, how beautiful he is . . . Then go for his heel of Achilles. Be funny, not grim, turn him into ridicule if you can, a *little*, not too much, for then he might excite pity. . . .

Curiously fortified by this resolution, Peter, on descending from the fiacre, gave the coachman so large a tip, that the latter decided he must be a 'milor' after all.

After having shaved and bathed, he dressed with unusual care. I feel like the wooden horse of Troy, he thought with a grin, all varnish and innocence without, all guns and ammunition within, if need be, I'll kidnap Elizabeth. If only I could modulate the ridiculous beats of my heart, if only I could choke down the ball of apprehension which has risen in my throat. Before starting, he treated himself to a large brandy, neat.

The Papagallis had not long returned when the front door bell rang.

'I wonder who it can be, at this hour, it cannot be Gigi, as we are meeting him at Betti's for dinner,' said someone. They were grouped on the usual perpendicular sofa, Mamma had one of her periodical *prima donna* migraines, and was lying down in her bedroom. Elizabeth was about to go and change for dinner. Ugo went into the hall and returned with a towering stranger. Seeing whom, Elizabeth sprang to her feet with an incredulous cry of delight and flung herself into his arms. It was a well-known fact that the English were mad, and that they had no sense of decorum. Ugo shrugged,

Guido raised his eyebrows, Leone, philosophically, lit a cigarette; Vica sat there shaking her round amused head.

At last, Elizabeth remembered her manners, and pushing Peter in front of her, introduced him as her 'childhood friend.' 'But what a delightful surprise,' drawled Vica, 'he must have dinner with us and meet Gian Galeazzo.' (She was the only member of her family who did not refer to him as Gigi.)

'I say,' Peter sounded very boyish, 'can I really? I should simply love to join you. Will I do as I am?' He pointed at what happened to be his best suit.

'Good gracious, I've never seen you so dolled up in my life,' giggled Elizabeth. 'Don't try to make me believe you're as dapper as this every day. Not if I know my Peter!'

The brothers exchanged perplexed glances, what was, what had been the relationship between these two? It might have been everything, or nothing at all. You couldn't tell with the English. Meanwhile, Elizabeth, taking Peter's arm, had piloted him to the window: 'Before we go any further I must tell you that I am engaged. To an Italian. You will meet him presently. He's a dear. How is it you don't look more surprised, you funny old thing?'

He forced a smile: 'You hadn't written for so long I thought you must be up to some mischief.'

'Well, that was it,' she babbled on, obscurely conscious of indelicacy, but too deeply involved to do anything about it, 'and what's more, Charles is engaged too! To another Italian.' She lowered her voice, 'To that tall girl I have just introduced you to.'

'A regular epidemic!' He could not help his voice sounding grim.

'She's pretty, isn't she? I didn't like the idea much at first,' she continued in the same subdued tone, 'but now I'm getting accustomed to it, I think she's just the person for old Charles. He needs rousing. Now I must fly and change for dinner.' She drew back into the room, 'Vica, look after Peter, will you? Show him what an Italian girl can do.'

*

As far as Peter was concerned the dinner was a success.
Charles was overjoyed to see his friend. It seemed quite
plausible to his unenquiring mind that Peter should be
stopping forty-eight hours in Florence on his way to Rome,
on unspecified business. He was relieved that Peter was
taking Elizabeth's engagement so well. Perhaps absence had
made the heart less fond, perhaps Peter had met some girl
in England. Who knows?

Brother and sister plied him with questions about
Mummy and Father; surely their letter of congratulation was
overdue? Surely he had let them know he was coming to
Florence? No, Peter lied stoutly, he hadn't time, his chief
had only let *him* know at the very last minute, he had barely
had time to pack his grip. Elizabeth looked momentarily
downcast, Charles, more philosophical, said there would
probably be a letter to-morrow. Followed innumerable
inquiries about home, people, things the Papagallis had
never heard of.

The inevitable happened: before long, the dinner was
divided into two camps: on the one side, the suspicious,
frustrated Italians, on the other the intimate, guffawing,
insensitive British. They sat with their elbows on the table,
their heads almost touching, blowing clouds of smoke in
each others' faces.

Gian Galeazzo, who had made one or two unsuccessful
attempts to join in the conversation, moved, unnoticed, to sit
by Vica, '*Ebbene, cara*,' he rasped, 'they don't seem to have
much use for us, our fiancés.'

Vica bowed her head to conceal the gleam of triumph in
her eyes.

'Why should they,' she said innocently, 'they have all
known each other since childhood, apparently. Nothing
creates greater intimacy.'

''Umph,' grunted Gian Galeazzo, 'if you want to see an
Englishman really animated, you must see him with another

Englishman, look at your fiancé,' he added spitefully, 'he might have been living on a desert island for the last month.'

'I like to see people happy,' she replied sweetly. 'Elizabeth positively exudes happiness – to-night.' Gian Galeazzo cast a swift look at her. But no. Butter wouldn't melt in her mouth.

'I cannot see you in England, somehow,' he appeared to ruminate, bent on goading her, exasperated by her indifference, and the turn things were taking. 'I go there often, you know, for my clothes. I am acquainted with their 'vie de château,' tramps in the rain, during which they only converse with their dogs, huge indigestible communal breakfasts, hours drinking alcohol, after dinner, shut up with other men in the dining-room!' He shuddered, then, with feigned commiseration, '*Povera Vica*, I hate to think of your future!'

'But why, "povera Vica," I want to travel, to see life. I'm bored to tears with Florence, I shall welcome the change.'

'Mmà!' He shrugged. '*Tous les goûts sont dans la nature*, as the French say – For a woman it is different,' he resumed, 'after all, everything is a matter of contrast: There will be immense compensations, a beautiful palazzo, wonderful possessions, servants, the privilege of rank.'

'All of which must particularly appeal to the daughter of a dentist,' she flashed; goaded beyond endurance.

'Come, Vica, I was not being personal, I meant all women.'

'But of course, I was joking.' It was as though she sheathed her eyes.

'I look forward to entertaining you and Elizabeth at Canterdown. It is a delightful prospect.'

'*Piacevolissimo.*' His tone was formal. He looked straight in front of him. She thought: You fool! You fool! not to have realized we were made for each other, you and I.

'*Quel giovane*,' he said, nodding moodily in the direction of Peter. 'What do you make of him? He is not unhandsome, in a rustic way. The Scottish *contadini* look just like that. And the jokes he makes! No one over ten would laugh at them in our country!'

'The English are very young, undeveloped. Charles is just the same.'

'Ah, you find that too,' then, maliciously, '*you* will have to live among them, *I* will not.' (Whose fault if I have to, she thought, whose fault?) 'I, personally, find them quite a welcome change, from men who are too complex, too subtle for us poor simple girls,' she countered.

'Is it possible, Vica, that you look upon yourself as a poor simple girl?' he retaliated. 'Why, all the wisdom of the serpent, the sagacity of the Sphinx is in you! You should have a very interesting life. Of course, you are right to marry Charles, you would be a fool if you missed such an opportunity.'

Again her pride was up in arms. 'Meaning that in my position – '

'Meaning nothing at all. My dear girl, you must lose the habit of being so touchy, it is inelegant, like a governess who is always afraid she will be mistaken for a servant.' Her face grew grave. All her life she would remember this insult. He was quick to notice the change in her expression. Impulsively he placed his hand on hers: 'I did not mean to hurt your feelings,' he assured her, 'I only wanted to help you. It does not do to show people you are so vulnerable, people will take a malicious pleasure in seeing you wince.'

'It will not happen again,' she said slowly, 'they will not be given the opportunity.'

Charles and Elizabeth were not in the least surprised when Peter announced his intention of staying on for a few days. His business in Rome could wait, he said. He accompanied the betrothed couples everywhere, sometimes protesting that he felt *de trop*. Elizabeth was more insistent than Charles; when left alone with Gigi, they really hadn't very much to say to each other. She supposed they had already reached the transitional stage between betrothal and matrimony, compliments and intimacy. Gigi's embraces were neither

sufficiently frequent nor sufficiently prolonged to entail a fresh
inventory of her sentiments. Once her thirst for information
about home had abated she no longer addressed all her
remarks to Peter: indeed, she apologized to Gigi for having,
as she put it, 'left him out in the cold' the first evening. He
accepted her apologies; caution was the order of the day:
retaliation could wait. He did not feel sufficiently sure of
his betrothed to risk a scene. *Pazienza* . . . Meanwhile, the
silence of his future in-laws was disquieting, to say the least
of it. Already, a week had elapsed since the night of the ball.
Elizabeth had received an ambiguous telegram from her
mother saying: 'Do nothing till you hear from me,' but they
had not heard. . . . Elizabeth was at first indignant: surely this
was not the way a mother should behave to her darling on
hearing the news of her engagement? She had expected pages
of fond rapture. Gigi was surely everything that should appeal
to her romantic, water-colourful Italianate soul. The silence of
Father was quite another matter, it would take Mummy days
of tactful approach, of secret undermining, before the subject
could even be mentioned. As for Charles' affair it would just
about finish him off, poor old pet. No wonder, taken all in
all, they had heard nothing. Indignation was succeeded by a
covert feeling of guilt. If only Gigi had not rushed her so!
Meanwhile, it was lovely to have Peter to talk to, to confide
in, in the intervals of her rather formal, but certainly traditional,
conversations with Gigi. Besides, he had such a delicious
sense of humour, a way of minimizing the most troublesome
situations. . . . She had, so far, been able to avoid a heart-
to-heart talk with la Zia, but it was becoming increasingly
difficult. . . . What a comfort Peter was, with him one could say
whatever came into one's head. Curious how he had improved
in looks, too. The Italian women made it quite clear what they
thought of him. Of course, he hadn't nearly such regular
features as Gigi, but he was several inches taller, and made
Gigi look, well, not effeminate, of course, but almost too
immaculate, too manicured. . . . Everything Peter did seemed

natural, unpremeditated, as though he were saying it for the first time, she loved his jokes. . . .

Three days after his arrival, the party was walking home after dinner, up the Lung'arno. Elizabeth and Peter were a little ahead of the others: he had such long legs, she almost had to run to keep pace with him. 'I would like a chat with you before I leave,' he suggested in a matter of fact tone.

She caught her breath: 'But you're not leaving yet, surely?'

'Yes, I am: to-morrow. Can I come up with you for a bit? Can you get rid of the others?'

'Of course, they'll quite understand.' When they reached number 43, Elizabeth turned to them abruptly: 'Peter is leaving to-morrow, we want to have a farewell chat, so he is coming up with me,' she gave out in her best 'take it or leave it' manner. Gian Galeazzo bowed ironically.

'One could not receive one's *congé* more emphatically. *Bonsoir, ma belle.* Perhaps you will ring me up in the morning if you have nothing better to do.' Whereupon he turned on his heel, and strode off at a vicious pace. He was furious. Charles made matters worse by running after him. 'I say, old chap, you mustn't mind Elizabeth, she's always been like this – says straight out what she wants, with no consideration for a chap's feelings, means no harm, you know.' Gian Galeazzo eyed him distastefully: 'I do not happen to be any "chap," as you put it. I would remind you that I am your sister's future husband. Pray do not insist. Good night.'

It was clearly no use following him. The crestfallen Charles rejoined Vica. 'I say,' he said, taking her arm for comfort, 'I'm afraid I've added insult to injury. I should have left him alone.'

'Of course,' Vica shrugged. Charles sighed gustily: 'I shall never understand you Latins. You are all so damned touchy. I don't mean you, darling, you're perfect, but Gigi – ' She tried to keep the impatience she felt out of her voice.

'Come, Charles, would you have been pleased had it been you?'

'I dunno. P'raps not. But still, when a feller takes the

trouble to run after you and explain it's all above board, I should have taken his word for it.'

'And spent the rest of the evening hanging about with us?' Vica's laugh was frankly contemptuous. 'Have you *no* pride, you English?'

It was Charles' turn to be offended.

'Damn it, Vica, you've no right to say that. I now know what I should have done in his place, I should have laughed it off, pretended I didn't care. Why show one's feelings?'

'In an official situation, one has official feelings. A man who is engaged to be married has his course marked out for him. He behaves according to protocol. In certain situations his reactions are more or less compulsory.'

'That is precisely what I am gibbing at. It takes away all the romance. Thank God, *our* engagement isn't working out like that, is it, my sweet? Between ourselves, I think Gigi is rather a stick at times.'

'You do not understand him, you never will, you do not even try,' any man less obtuse than Charles, would have been enlightened by the vehemence of her outburst. 'He is a proud man, *vuol fare bella figura*, why should he put up with public insults from your sister?'

'O come now, what did the public consist of? You and me.'

'Nevertheless, in public. Your sister flouts her fiancé in public, she openly prefers another man.'

'Vica, you're talking rubbish: you forget that Peter is my oldest friend. He knew Liza when she was a kid. Why can't you Italians admit platonic friendship?'

'It is not platonic,' she returned with heat, 'it is possible that they do not know it, as you English excel in deceiving yourselves. Where are your eyes? Have you not noticed that your friend is always *apologizing* for being *de trop?* The person who is *de trop* is Gian Galeazzo, not Peter!'

The scales suddenly fell from Charles' eyes. 'By Jove, I believe you're right, now I come to think of it. Peter rushing out here the moment Elizabeth's engaged, never struck me at the time. He said he had business in Rome, but how could he have known she was engaged? Nobody knew except Mummy.'

Vica assumed the air of a young Portia; 'Peter must know your mother, since you are such old friends. Why should not your mother have told him, as he is a friend of the family? It would be only natural.'

'Why not, indeed! – I say, there are no flies on you, my sweet!'

'No flies?' she was puzzled.

'I mean you're very much on the spot, all there – oh damn! I mean you notice a lot that escapes other people,' he achieved at last.

'Ah!'

'All the same,' Charles was doing some strenuous thinking, 'all the same, I don't like it, if what you say is correct, it's unsporting!'

Vica opened her topaz eyes very wide. 'Unsporting?' she repeated as though she heard the word for the first time.

It was Charles' turn to be impatient. Surely the thing was obvious! 'Unsporting of Peter to come rushing out here in the hopes of queering the other fellow's pitch, ousting him as a rival,' he translated stiffly, Vica's laugh struck him as insensitive.

'Do you really,' she inquired with scorn, 'do you really think love cares whether it is *sporting* or not? Do you know what I think? I think your friend has been in love with Elizabeth for years, and that only the imminent danger of losing her is making him behave as he *is* behaving.'

Charles wrinkled his nose. 'I don't like it, I don't like it at all. Then there's Father! I've been worrying about him all day, but there is nothing we can do but wait.' Charles was not made for complication. He ran his fingers through his hair, that was like a canary's rumpled feathers, 'Let's go and sit in the Cascine, I shall feel better when I have kissed you.'

*

Elizabeth and Peter sat confronting one another.

To keep himself in countenance he lit a cigarette.

'Why have you decided to leave so suddenly,' she asked somewhat breathlessly.

'It isn't sudden, I told you I couldn't stay more than a few days.'

'I wish you wouldn't put up that sort of smokescreen between us, I can't see your face.'

He brushed it aside. 'There, is that better?' he smiled.

'You look very Olympian and detached,' she complained.

'What's the good of feeling anything but detached where you're concerned?' he risked.

She chose to ignore this. 'What do you propose to do?'

'Get married.'

'*What!*' she leapt to her feet.

'Why shouldn't I? Isn't that what *you* propose to do?'

'I don't know. I suppose so, I don't know any more,' she floundered, 'who is it, who is it you're marrying? I must know, how could you keep it from me?' Her voice broke. He longed to take her in his arms.

'I had no idea you took such an interest,' he contrived. 'You never told me you intended to get married, at least you never *wrote* and told me.'

'I know, I meant to, but I didn't dare, somehow . . . ' he too had risen, stood towering over her, his hands glued to his sides.

'Didn't *dare?* Why?'

'I felt it was a kind of, kind of desecration.'

'Desecration of what?' he had the strength to demand.

'Of . . . of . . . our friendship,' she faltered. 'O please, Peter, tell me who it is you're marrying?'

She was on the verge of tears. Peter felt he was staking his whole life on the single word he was about to utter: 'You.'

'*Me?* But I don't understand.' In her eyes incredulity and delight met, brimmed, were spilt. She took a step forward, he caught her in his arms, hugging her to him, 'You, my darling, you, you, you, it's you I am going to marry, you silly little goose, I came here on purpose.'

'O, Peter,' she sobbed in his neck, 'I might have known, what a fool I've been.'

'My angel, my beautiful, it's not too late, thank God! I knew in time,' he began kissing her wildly, her hair, eyes, mouth. . . .

It was an unwritten law that the Princess was never, in any circumstance, save in the case of a major catastrophe, to be called till 10. When, accordingly, her nephew burst into her room at 8.30, his reception was what he might have expected. Finding the room in darkness, he did an unpardonable thing, he threw open the shutters, allowing a stream of implacable sunlight to fall across the Princess' bed, and more especially across her averted head which, on the white pillow, resembled a prune. She woke instantly, sat up in bed, her head bristling with curling pins, her eyes snapping with fury. He was irrelevantly reminded of those vicious Tirana brats who would bite your calves if they dared. Curious how, when angry, she could never be mistaken for anything but Spanish. 'Have you taken leave of your senses, my nephew?' she yapped. 'How dare you enter my room unannounced, how dare you throw open the shutters? I can see by the light that it is not my normal waking-hour.'

'I think, Zia, that the circumstance justifies the intrusion.'

'Well, speak, boy, speak, why all this beating about the bush?'

'Late, last night, I received this letter from Elizabeth.' He laid it on the bed; stood back; folded his arms; waited.

'How do you expect me to read without my lorgnette,' she fussed. 'Ah, there it is, entangled with my rosary.' The lorgnette attached to a long gold chain, held in one tiny claw, travelled from line to line with incredible speed. 'But this is impossible,' she gasped, as she came to the end. 'The girl must be mad.'

'Or, merely English,' he said coldly, 'which I erroneously thought meant that however unconventional in appearance, at heart they could be trusted –   Naturally I knew she wasn't in love with me, but it did not occur to me that she was capable of behaving like someone out of a *roman feuilleton*,' he almost spat with vexation.

'And who, in the name of Satan, is this creature?' she demanded, tapping the letter with her lorgnette.

'A childhood friend, a kind of student, huge, uncouth, rustic in appearance, a kind of outsize contadino.'

'Surely her family would never countenance such a marriage, but you never know with the English, you never know when they cease to be ingenuous, sometimes not until they die. Love in a cottage is what they cannot resist; love in a cottage for two years, *et toute une vie de bout de table*,' she muttered.

'Think, Zia, think of the ridicule to which we shall be exposed, unless, of course, you can make her see reason.'

'The *lettres de faire-part* have not yet been sent, thank goodness! We were naturally waiting for her parents' sanction, which has been long in coming. I expected at least a telegram from my old friend Sylvia. It saddens me to think how badly her daughter has been brought up.'

'But, Zia, we are wasting our time in speculation, you must send for Elizabeth at once, and frighten her into doing the right thing.'

'My dear boy, have you not yet learnt that the English do not respond to intimidation? The only thing to do is to appeal to her sense of honour. She gave you her word, her word is her bond, etc. . . . etc. . . . Yes, that is the line to take, I will get up at once, why has not that miserable Valka brought me my chocolate?'

'She does not know you are awake, Zia.'

'True. True. She might have had the sense to guess, though.'

*

Elizabeth was no coward, but she did not attempt to conceal her dread of the interview in store for her and which she had been putting off for days. The one she had had with Gian Galeazzo was only child's play in comparison. Though conscious of her indignity, he had not succeeded in touching her heart. He had never ceased harping on 'the insult to his family,' the ridicule cast on his person, the scandal that must, inevitably, ensue. These accusations occurred in tireless rotation, with the unfortunate result that Elizabeth began to congratulate herself on having escaped from such an egotist. In the blaze of her newly discovered love for Peter, the sensuous little interlude with Gian Galeazzo seemed a poor thing indeed. He had been wished on her by the spring, the moonlight, the gardenias; above all, he had been wished on her by a witch. The Princess had waved her wand, or rather, her lorgnette, and the thing was done. Strange to relate, Elizabeth felt guiltier towards the impresario than towards her fellow actor, for it was really the Princess who had conceived the episode: manipulated by her, Gigi had made the necessary gestures. It was Elizabeth's fault if the play was a flop, moreover, she had grown genuinely fond of the old woman, she admired her wit, her pluck, her *panache*. She would have liked to please the Princess by marrying Gigi.

Feeling very small indeed, and leaving Peter to pace up and down outside, she toiled up the marble staircase. The Princess would no doubt receive her in one of the huge official salons, in order to give a judicial air to the proceedings, and further to intimidate the unhappy delinquent. Her relief can be imagined when she was told that the Princess awaited her in the Venetian *salottino*, as usual. She was standing by the window, as Elizabeth entered, so small, so frail, that the girl's heart smote her.

'You are a brave child,' said the Princess quietly, 'sit there, in that chair, where I can see you, my eyes are getting worse every day. Yes, I repeat, you are a brave child. You must have been tempted to leave without seeing me again.'

Elizabeth, who had been expecting fire and brimstone, was unnerved.

'To tell you the truth, I was, Princess. I don't think I've realized until this minute how badly I've behaved. What *must* you think of me?'

The Princess appeared to reflect. 'It is indisputable that you have behaved badly, according to usual standards, but even worse according to your own,' came the shattering reply. 'Wait. I will tell you why. Because *noblesse oblige*, because one is entitled to expect more from you than from an inferior person. You are *you*, it never entered my head that someone of your standing could break her word: *that is a thing* I could naturally not anticipate. Therefore, I am sorry for you, my child. It must be dreadful to be so disappointed in oneself.'

Elizabeth was beginning to feel a worm.

Encouraged by her dropping head, and certain she had hit on a vulnerable spot, the Princess continued: 'Of course I could say what, no doubt, my nephew has repeated *ad nauseum*. It is a terrible blow to him, to his pride. For a man, naturally, it is very grave. For a man who has been as much loved as Gigi, it is a shock from which he will never recover. You probably think that in his case it was more a question of *amour-propre*, than of *amour*. What you cannot realize is that Gigi is as inexperienced as yourself, that he was playing a part that was entirely new to him, and playing it badly. He was too moved to play it well. He has really never wanted to marry anyone before. What he laid at your feet was a kind of virginity, he had been many things, but never a fiancé. You must remember that in our country it is a very grave step to become engaged. In England, I know, girls slip in and out of engagements like in and out of chemises – no, jumpers – it is a word I have learnt from Valka – but here, it is different, very different.' She paused to light a cigarette also to give Elizabeth time to take in the extent of the damage she had wrought.

'I quite realize that,' the girl's tone was resentful. 'Would

it not have been better if you had explained all this to me
before I got engaged, rather than after? It was like a kind of
conspiracy I couldn't stand up against: the climate, this lovely
house, you, Gigi.'

'I am amused to see you put me first,' remarked the
Princess drily.

'Well, yes; I don't think Gigi would have thought of it
otherwise.'

This brusque, undisciplined girl could hold her own, only
the truth was of avail, it was useless attempting to bluff her.

'Can you blame me if I thought of it first?' Her smile was
disarming. 'When I saw two such attractive young people, with
everything to offer each other, what scheming old person, with
a sense of corps, décor and decorum, would not have behaved
as I did?'

She was rewarded by Elizabeth's abrupt laugh. 'O Princess,
I wish you weren't so funny, it makes me feel a pig.'

The older woman was quick to press her advantage, she
put her hand on Elizabeth's knee. 'Listen, my child. Do not
do anything in a hurry. After all, the engagement is not yet
official. Think it over. Do not see Gigi, or – the other man –
for a few days. There is no harm done, except to Gigi's pride.
No one knows anything definite except ourselves.'

But once again she was confronted by the cliffs of Dover.
'I'm sorry, I hate to refuse, but it's no use. You see, ever
since I was a child, I've been in love with Peter without
knowing it. All I needed was a showdown. The thought of
losing him for ever' – her voice trembled – 'did the trick.
I knew then how much I cared. It is quite impossible for me
to change my mind. I would like you to see Peter,' she
added, with the pathetic belief of the lover in the loved one's
power of persuasion.

The Princess froze. 'That, I think, would be as unconstruc-
tive as it is lacking in taste. I see nothing to be gained by
it.' She drummed on the arm of her chair. There was another
hypothesis: 'Your mother, my old friend,' she submitted,

'would she approve of this *volte-face?* Is the young man a suitable *parti?*

Elizabeth grinned. 'The reverse, I should say. But Mummy doesn't really care about such things, it sounds silly, but all she cares about is my happiness.'

'In that case,' the older woman urged, 'she surely wants you to marry a man of your own milieu, preferably with enough money to keep a young woman who has been brought up as luxuriously as yourself.'

Elizabeth's grin broadened. 'Preferably, but not necessarily, you see, Mummy is completely unworldly.'

'And your Father?' She was at her wits end. There were apparently no limits to the irresponsibility of English parents.

'Father is a bit more practical, but they usually see eye to eye in the long run.'

The Princess gave up.

'Besides, Father would hate me to marry a foreigner.'

Here at last was something tangible, something of utility. The Princess swooped.

'And a Roman Catholic, no doubt?'

Elizabeth considered. 'I expect he would rather I married a Protestant.'

'Ah,' mused the Princess with satisfaction. Anyway, honour was saved, what better explanation could she give for the broken engagement? 'Of course, the Father is one of those insular Englishmen who hate foreigners, and naturally, he could not bear the idea of his daughter marrying a Roman Catholic.' This would do admirably. She was nothing if not a realist; lost causes did not interest her, as soon as it became apparent that there was nothing to be gained by sticking to a mapped-out cause, she was all for abandoning it, and trying something new. Already she blamed Gigi for his clumsiness, lack of psychology. In the meantime, she had played her part to the best of her ability. Now she was at liberty to climb down and mingle with the spectators. This, she proceeded to do. Allowing the twinkle she never banished for long to

return to her eye, she said, in a sprightly voice: 'Now that
you have convinced me that you could not have been happy
with Gigi, you may tell me about the new *novio*. He is good-
looking, yes? A giant, it appears?'

All gratitude, Elizabeth caught the Princess' hands: 'O you
are a wonderful person! I *knew* you would understand. How
glad I am I came! Everything seems quite different now.
Couldn't we send for Peter? He is pacing up and down like
Napoleon on the deck of the *Bellerophon*. I would so love
you to see him.'

'That is quite impossible. You must be mad, child. What
would people say, the servants, my husband, *le monde!*
What would they think if they knew that I received the girl
who has broken off her engagement to my nephew because
she is in love with somebody else, and then I welcome the
somebody else! You are decidedly mad, my child! By the
way, you must promise me something.'

'Of course,' agreed Elizabeth with the recklessness of
youth.

'It is nothing very terrible. I want you to promise me that
you will not marry your Englishman for six months. It makes
us look less ridiculous.'

'Gigi, you mean.'

'Naturally. Promise.'

'Need it be quite as long as that?' the girl pleaded.

'Well, four months then.'

'We are nearly at the end of June. Couldn't we be married
in the middle of October?'

Elizabeth looked so lovely as she said this that the Princess
relented. Memories of her own ebullient youth returned
to her, the passive despair with which she had submitted to
her prearranged marriage to Marcantonio. Impulsively she
cupped Elizabeth's face in her hands, lightly bestowed a
peck on either cheek. 'The middle of October it shall be, but
you must not break your word a second time. For Gigi's
sake, I want people to think that you are marrying a man

you have met after leaving Italy. Even if you have been seen altogether here, it will convey nothing, he will pass for a relation. Gigi is only ridiculous if he appears to have been jilted for another man, *not* if, for reasons of religion, the marriage cannot take place.'

'What a lot of trouble you Italians take to keep up appearances,' marvelled Elizabeth. 'It is not what *is*, but what *seems* to be, that matters.'

'Of course,' shrugged the Princess, '*bisogna fare bella figura*. It is a Latin trait which is by no means the monopoly of Italians. That is why Latin husbands are so much better than English ones. However much they quarrel in private, in public, at least, they are correct. Also in front of their children. Believe me, it does not matter what one does, it is the way one does it.'

Elizabeth pondered this. 'I think I must be very English, but I can't see that it matters all that much. Nobody is taken in.'

'It does not matter so long as people *pretend* to be taken in. It is polite to pretend. When people cease to keep up appearances, as you say, and when other people cease to pretend to be taken in, it will be the end of Society, or, at least, the Latin version of it. Personally, I think it would be a pity, it is our form of *pudeur*, modesty. In England many things shocked me that would not shock you. For instance, the alacrity with which you English let your homes, leaving the most intimate photographs of your family and friends lying about, letting your silver, your linen – Pah! *Fa schifo!* Then the books you write, autobiographies thinly disguised as novels, or not disguised at all. Displaying your sexual idiosyncrasies with the insensibility with which medical students dissect a corpse; it is emotional exhibitionism, no more, no less. But I am forgetting how young you are.' She lit another cigarette and, after a few preliminary puffs: 'Now tell me, this interests me, what attracts you so much in this young man, apart from his looks and the fact that you knew each other as children?'

Love in its initial stages is seldom lucid. Elizabeth, anxious to satisfy her old friend, struggled for expression. 'We think the same things funny, and we like the same kind of person. He has a wonderful way of taking the *sting* out of everything that hurts. I think what I like best about him is that he's so cosy.'

The Princess sat up. 'Cosy? I do not know the word.'

'Why should you? It doesn't exist in Italy. I mean,' she hastily amended, 'you do not feel the need of it here.'

'But what does it mean?'

'O dear, I'm so bad at analysing; it means relaxing, I suppose, not having to show off and make efforts to be amusing if you don't feel like it, saying whatever comes into your head.'

The Princess nodded approvingly: 'I understand. Putting your mind in bedroom slippers. You are a dear child, but you are also very English. I no longer think your marriage with Gigi would have been a success, you would have run away with a handsome woodcutter, and then, poor Gigi would have looked more ridiculous than ever. No,' she sighed, 'it is a good thing you have found out in time.'

'Another thing,' pursued Elizabeth zealous in her search of truth, 'is this. Peter and I both love the country, living in the country.'

'But so, surely, does Gigi? He knows to an oil jar what his estate produces.'

'But that doesn't necessarily mean he loves the country,' said Elizabeth doggedly, 'it means he is interested in what it brings him in, that's quite another matter. He hates the country in winter, when the villa is empty and there are no visitors, he's told me so, he's not thrilled by taming a starving robin, or teaching his dog to retrieve. He doesn't peer and pry for the first snowdrop, or enjoy the lovely feeling of being *en tête-à-tête* with one's most cherished belongings – in short, he does not like the country!'

'Bravo, Elizabeth,' the Princess applauded with her fingertips, 'you are quite eloquent about the things you love. No, according to your standards Gigi does *not* like the country, but what Latin does? We like Nature curbed, combed, disciplined. I am like that myself. I like Nature to be an auxiliary to the house I live in; fountains, statues, gravelled alleys. *J'aime la Nature lorsqu'elle fait le beau!*

'Not just manure and gardening gloves,' muttered Elizabeth.

'What?'

'Nothing, I was merely saying that in England we like Nature unadorned. You must come and stay with us, Princess, if Father gives us a cottage on the estate, for week-ends, only I cannot somehow picture you in a cottage.'

'You are kind to want me, but I have no longer any taste for travel. It is old age. Besides, I could not come, because of Gigi.'

'Of course, I was forgetting.' It suddenly struck Elizabeth that, in all probability she would never see the Princess, or this palace, again. She looked around her with a new interest, wishing to commit the scene to memory; the Princess' yellowish, sickle-like profile, her small neat body against the sumptuous background, the brooding mirrors, frivolous Venetian furniture, gloomy magnificent family portraits –

Her gaze followed Elizabeth's. 'And don't forget the view from that window, it is the one I like best,' she recommended softly. What a way she had of reading people's thoughts.

'You can't think how I shall miss you, Princess. May I write and tell you about everything?'

'Why not? From Liz to Luz. You will give your mother my love, and tell her I regret you are not for us. This has been an unconventional conversation, I had not intended it to be so, but now, I am glad.' The little slip of a woman rose with extraordinary dignity. 'Your *novio* must be getting impatient. You must want to reassure him.' She took the girl's hands, kissed her rapidly on both cheeks.

'Good-bye, *vaya Ud con Dios*,' she said, lapsing into her native Spanish, which she kept for Occasions. Gently but

firmly, she propelled Elizabeth towards the door, cutting
short the girl's thanks; the moment it had closed, her
feminine curiosity getting the better of her, she rushed to the
window that overlooked the Lung'arno. The room was on
the second floor, from which a good view of the street
should be obtainable.

A large young man was pacing up and down below,
his hands crossed behind his back. Hair, clothes, walk, proclaimed him unmistakably British, suddenly, he glanced up at
the window, a glance of exasperation, Liz had said she
wouldn't be more than a quarter of an hour. . . .

The eyes that were like black grapes and the frosty blue
ones met, held each other for a second. She repressed an
insensate, an atavistic desire to throw down a flower, a flower
for the *novio*, drew hastily, guiltily, back into the too retentive
room. When she peeped again, this time from behind the
curtain, he was being joined by Elizabeth, nodding emphatically, she thrust an arm through his, they walked rapidly away
together.

Che guaio, muttered the Princess, *che guaio!*

With a gesture of vexation, she threw away her half-
smoked cigarette. . . .

Peter and Elizabeth, with Charles as chaperone, left
Florence that night.

This decision had not been dictated solely by a sense of
decorum; to Charles, still in ignorance of his Father's reaction
to his engagement, it had seemed an excellent opportunity
to participate in a general 'softening-up process,' in other
words, if Elizabeth's return to the fold could be relied upon
to appease Father, even though it should prove to be the
gilt on the scarcely more palatable pill of her engagement to
Peter, Charles' personal Italian entanglement might appear
less exotic. It was easier to explain Vica verbally than by
letter; given the family habit of understatement, she could
almost be made to sound 'cosy.'

Vica saw them off at the station, Elizabeth and Peter jubilant and facetious, made jokes which Vica internally qualified as 'rustic,' and Charles, who had drunk a good deal more Orvieto than was good for him, was inclined to be maudlin. Vica had played up to their various moods, she was getting very good with the English. . . .

The patient train, which looked as if it were suckling the human clusters clinging to its doors and windows shook them off at last, steamed majestically, conscious of its prestige of Grand Express Européen, out of the station. Feeling slightly dazed, Vica walked slowly up the platform, she passed a Riviera-bound train, which she felt inclined to pat, as though it were a racehorse. Back in the station, posters from all over Europe were spread out like a pack of cards. Choose, pretty lady, choose, try your luck! Normally inaccessible, they offered her bridges and cathedrals, beaches and snow-capped summits; her solicited eye roved from the Dolomites (in blue and white) to Morocco (in ochre and scarlet). Europe was as obsequious as a harem – to whom should she throw her handkerchief? She took a deep breath, a curious feeling of lightness, of irresponsibility, invaded her, she was on a holiday; a wordless content flowed from her thoughtless mind; carefree, incognito, she was the cat that walked by itself.

She was speeding as on wings up the Via Strozzi when she suddenly found herself face to face with Gian Galeazzo. Her impetus would have carried her past him, had he not caught her arm. 'Vica! Whither so fast? You look like the Victory of Samothrace. *Perchè tanta furia?*

'*Non ho furia,*' she felt herself blushing, 'I am not going anywhere in particular.'

'Very well then,' he grasped her arm more firmly, 'you are coming to have a cup of coffee and a chat with me at Gambrino's.

A few steps took them to the crowded clamorous place,

as blindingly white as a new set of false teeth. They sat down, he ordered coffee for two. She noticed then that he was carelessly dressed, unshaven, and that his fingers were stained with nicotine. She waited for him to speak.

'I suppose you have been seeing my ex-fiancée off at the station,' he jeered, 'I am well rid of her. She's mad.' Still Vica said nothing. 'You do not agree that she is mad?'

'No. I think she is impulsive, unconventional, self-centred, but mad, no, that is to say, not according to English standards.'

He shrugged angrily, '*Può darsi*, maybe they are all mad, according to our standards, but to do a thing like that to me, Gian Galeazzo de' Pardi,' he struck his chest, 'it defeats the imagination! When I think of what she is depriving herself!' Not for the first time Vica was staggered by his inordinate, his childish vanity. It put him at her mercy. At the same time, her latent maternal instinct made her long to say: There! there! Is it as bad as all that?

'You would not have been happy together,' she soothed, 'you are too feminine, she, too boyish. It would not have been a success.' He lit a cigarette, offered her one. She accepted it as a game, as a novelty. In those days Italian girls of good family did not smoke in public. She took a self-conscious puff. 'How is it,' he leant forward, 'that you, so young and so inexperienced, understand her so well? Do you know that, *in ogni maniera*, I meant to call on you this evening?'

'*Vero?*' She couldn't help it, if her eyebrows had a mocking tilt. She loved him, but every instinct was on the defensive.

'Yes,' his voice was urgent, 'I have not slept for twenty-four hours, all night I paced up and down my room, one does not insult a de' Pardi with impunity. I thought to myself: how can I get even with this bitch? That was before I received this letter telling me she was in love with the Englishman. If he had been an Italian, I would have called him out, but what can you do with an Englishman? A black eye merely entitles you to a *succès de fou rire*, as the French say. Then I thought of you, Vica.' The hand he laid on hers was beautiful, a hand by Van Dyke. 'Why pretend? I would have fallen in love with you long ago, had I permitted myself to.'

'And why didn't you?' Her heart beat almost to suffocation, distrust was momentarily lulled. She was his for the asking.

'Why? Because I *had* to get married. The girl, the daughter of an old friend of my aunt seemed indicated. My family were unanimous in wishing the marriage. What a fool she made of me! But it is not too late – '

'Not too late for what?'

'Not too late to have my revenge, and you, *carissima*, are to be the means. All you have to do is to behave to your Charles as his sister behaved to me, you are no fonder of him – I have watched you together – than she was of me. No doubt he would suffer, but not for long, he has no imagination. There is no reason why we should not get married as soon as possible – '

'But if you hesitated to marry me before,' she said, disclaiming all pretence of not caring for him, 'how is it that I have suddenly become so eligible?'

Gian Galeazzo rushed headlong to destruction. 'Because the fact of you having been engaged to Charles alters everything. It would be a tremendous feather in my cap if you turned down Charles in order to marry me.'

'I see.' Vica's voice was ominously quiet. 'You could not bring yourself to marry the dentist's daughter, but the woman who could have married an English lord, had she so chosen, becomes an adequate *parti* for a jilted Marchese de' Pardi. It is no longer a mésalliance. Most ingenuous, not to say opportune. I congratulate you on your solution.'

Too late, Gian Galeazzo realized his mistake, he was confronted with a pride that matched his own. 'Vica, Vica, *amore*,' he beseeched, 'do not be angry. Surely it is better to be frank in these matters, you should, on the contrary, respect me for not attempting to hoodwink you. Besides, what does it matter now? The essential thing is that we could still be happy together. Do you at least believe that you have always attracted me, that I have always found you infinitely disturbing, and that it has required the greatest strength of mind not to make love to you?'

This was all too true, and she knew it. Between love and pride, battle was joined. She was, she told herself, in the position of a poor mason, who had once offered his services to a contractor. His offer is rejected. The mason goes away, and brick by brick, by his own unaided efforts, and the sweat of his brow, succeeds in building a house. The rich contractor, passing by, is struck by its air of competence and solidity, he offers to take the mason into business with him, to merge him into the firm. But supposing the mason refuses, supposing he would rather work under his own name, on his own terms, supposing he would rather set up a rival undertaking? Yet was it not better to be two against the world, to collaborate, to share its prizes? She was but a woman, after all, though she already new she was an exceptional one. 'Vica, *amore*,' he pleaded, 'think how happy we can be! As for la Zia, it will appeal to her impish side, you need not worry about your parents, they will be enchanted, I am sure they would rather you made a good marriage in your own country than in a foreign one. As for your brothers, just think what it would mean to them! Why, I will even get them elected for "la Caccia"!'

'That settles it!' Vica brought her fist down on the table, with a violence that caused the other diners, whose interest had already been aroused by the handsome couple, to interrupt their conversation, and endeavour to overhear what she was saying. 'No. I will not marry you, Gian Galeazzo. I would not marry you if you begged me for a hundred years. I could not dream of marrying a man so fatuous, so obsessed by his own importance, so conscious of the honour he would be doing me. You can easily find a suitable substitute, one with the requisite amount of quarterings and an adequate physique. It should not be difficult. I shall now wish you good night,' she concluded, beginning to rise.

He caught her by her wrist: 'Sit down. You cannot make a scene, everyone is looking at us as it is.' Furiously, she obeyed him. He lit a cigarette. 'Very well, have it your own way: *be* as proud as Lucifer. Pride is not a becoming trait in a woman, it will not get you anywhere.'

'Will it not? We shall see. Give me a cigarette if you want me to remain seated.' He offered her his case, held a match to her cigarette, the flame stressed a mouth that was serenely, unfalteringly drawn, the epicene lips of a drawing by Leonardo di Vinci. This put him on a new track.

'Perhaps you will never really belong to anyone,' he speculated harshly, 'perhaps you can only belong to yourself. I hate your self-control, your will of iron. It is not natural in a girl of your age.'

'From now onwards, I will only belong to people on my own terms, as an equal,' she flashed, with what Elizabeth called her 'runaway horse look.'

'When you say "people" you mean me,' he defied her, 'so be it, Vica, what is the use of pretending we hate each other, I love you, you love me. Marry your Englishman, go and live in England, sacrifice your happiness to your pride, I cannot prevent you, but promise me something.'

'I will not promise anything.'

'Allow me to see you in a year, no, two years hence. On your own terms.'

'How can I promise you, how can I tell what will happen between now and then?'

'What do you risk? Nothing. I will behave as you will want me to behave.'

'I will promise nothing. Now, if you have no objection, I want to go home.'

'May I accompany you?'

'If you must; it is only five minutes walk from here, and I am in no mood for conversation.'

He paid for the coffee. Several diners looked up as they
went out, with envy, curiosity, admiration. In no country are
lovers surrounded by so many well-wishers. As they walked
down the dark narrow street, they passed a couple pressed
against the wall, as closely interwoven as a monogram.
Vica, secretly troubled, looked straight in front of her. Gian
Galeazzo did not attempt to make conversation. He cursed
himself for being every kind of a fool, but even now, in his
subconscious, lurked the ineffable word: '*pazienza.*'

As they turned into the Lung'arno, an exclamation broke
from him in spite of himself: '*Che bellezza!*' A crescent moon
was caught in the fleecy clouds, like a fish in a net. On
the opposite bank of the Arno, the old crazy houses leant
over the snaky ripples as though they were linked together
by their infirmities and the things they had witnessed in
common. . . . '*Chi vuol esser lieto, sia,*' he thought, '*di doman
non c'è certezza.*'

When they reached her house, before she had time
to protest, he caught her to him, kissing her lips, which
involuntarily parted. 'Sans adieu,' he whispered in her ear,
the moment she began to struggle he let her go, vanished
noiselessly into the shadows.

'*Un po' di prosciutto?*'
'*Grazie, no.*'
'*Salame?*'
'*No, grazie.*'
'But, Mamma, you must eat *something?*'
'Let her be, can't you see, she is too distressed to eat, figlio
mio.'
'I also am distressed, but I force myself,' mumbled Leone,
stuffing a huge wad of prosciutto into his mouth.
'As for me, I have been pacing the streets all day, I could
not face the empty apartment,' said Guido with a gulp.
'Empty, but for your father and mother and four brothers,'
rectified Papa Papagalli, who had been hastily summoned.

'Yes, I know, I did not mean to be rude, but Mamma understands what I mean.'

The Countess dabbed her red and swollen eyes: 'Yes, indeed, indeed, I do, figlio mio. We resemble the Gods of Walhalla after Freia had departed.' She was partial to these operatic allusions. 'Their consent to Vica's marriage was so sudden, her departure so precipitate – never to hear her lovely voice, never to see her lovely face – ' the Countess broke down.

'Come, come, Arte, pull yourself together, Vica is not dead – '

'Guido has such a tender heart, *vieni qui, tesoro*, he has also imagination which you appear to lack, Amadeo, mercifully for you! You do not picture our darling being whisked through that terrible tunnel!'

'Terrible what?'

'Tunnel. Il Moncenisio: twenty minutes in the stifling dark, I wonder people are not asphyxiated, though *I did* hear of a case . . . '

'You do not even notice you are going through the Moncenisio if you have a good book.'

'I would not say, Amadeo, that you are the most observant of men, but the tunnel is not the only danger, there are others. . . . '

'Let me see: she might get splashed with boiling soup in the wagon-restaurant, she might be garrotted by the wagon-lit conductor, she might – '

'I suppose you think you are being witty, Amadeo. It is not *my* idea of wit. Even *you* will not deny that there are such things as railway accidents, shipwrecks – '

'Seldom are the boats that cross the English Channel shipwrecked.'

'Ah! You admit that it has been known to happen!'

'Artemisia, you are impossible. I merely say all these things to cheer you up. I begin to think you *want* something to happen – ' With incredible agility, the Countess rose, rushed to the other end of the table, placed her hand on her husband's mouth: '*Zitto, per carità!* You will bring misfortune to our child. What possesses you to make such statements. It is a challenge to Fate!'

The Count became apoplectic, spluttered, waved his wife away with his napkin.

'Artemisia, I must insist on being allowed to eat in peace, *mangiare in pace*. Dwell, rather, on the famous British phlegm, which Vica is in process of acquiring, and which your sons flatter themselves they have acquired, though, believe me, they have a long way to go yet.'

The sons in question glared, with collective resentment at their father. Why did he always contrive to deflate them? He had never been popular with his family, he was such a give-away, with his napkin tucked under his chin, his great untidy beard, garlic-infested breath. *Povero Pappà!*

Conversation lapsed, was replaced by a rhythmic sound of mastication, then, in the middle of this relative silence, the front door was heard to open, bang, a shrill irrelevant whistling broke out in the hall, approached, crescendo, the dining-room door, which apparently, blew open.

A gasp went round the table, 'Rigo!'

'Are none of you going to say "*ben tornato*"!' came the impudent, the improper challenge.

The little man, outrageously dressed as usual, bent over his two most fastidious brothers, a podgy hand on either shoulder. 'What! No word of welcome for the Prodigal Son! Or is this a *"veglia funebre"*? Apparently it is. May I draw up a chair, Pappà? I have not lunched and am as hungry as a navvy!' He waddled to the end of the table, imprinted a smacking kiss on his mother's aloof cheek. Fearing an outburst, she said hurriedly: 'Sit next to me, my son, and tell us where you have been. Your Father was asking me only the other day – '

'O what a fib, you know where fibbers go, Mamma,' he blew his father, who was gazing at him with a kind of comical despair, a trapeze artist's kiss, 'I know my place,' he minced, 'I know when little me is not wanted, I thought I would give the scandal time to die down,' he said, cramming spaghetti into his mouth, 'so this little impedimenta to the family ambitions took himself off to Naples, his spiritual home, where he could really let himself go, when he wasn't plucking his guitar, he was pinching pretty girls. *Caspita!* How shocked you all look, but I always forget how easily shocked the British are.'

'Amerigo!' His father's bass voice struck the note of admonishment for which it seemed to have been designed, as impressive as the bronze lowing of '*la vacca.*'*

'If you came home with the sole purpose of being offensive to your family, the sooner you return to Naples the better. Wit is one thing, vulgarity is another.'

The family listened in awe. Il Babbo, it could not be denied, had authority, the authority of the Vatican. It was as though Rigo had been excommunicated.

The meal ended in a stricken silence. Rigo, munching defiantly, half rose as his parents swept out. He made a passing grab at Guido's coat-tails, compelling him to sit down.

'You beastly sycophant,' he hissed, 'have you no entrails? I am the only person in this house who is as miserable as yourself.' Guido raised supercilious eyebrows. 'Why do you suppose I have returned to-day of all days? Because I knew that *they* had left. Do you suppose that I do not find this decorous morgue as detestable as you do? You have lost Vica, I, Elisabetta, I think we are more or less quits!'

'I do not follow you,' said Guido loftily.

'Don't you?' his brother sneered. 'Had you not noticed I was in love with Elisabetta?'

Guido shrugged. 'What was the use?'

Rigo turned on him: '*The use*, you zany? Do you think that love has to be requited to be genuine? On the contrary, it

---

* The big bell of the Cathedral.

thrives on indifference. Do you really suppose I was happy in Naples, drinking myself silly? Where is your imagination? But I had forgotten: it only functions when applied to Vica. What is the use of being in love with your sister, if it comes to that?'

Guido leapt to his feet, pinning him down, he shook the little man until his teeth rattled; 'You filthy dwarf, you disgusting abortion. Dare to repeat that.'

'I repeat, you-are-in-love-with-Vica, though you do not perhaps realize it!'

'Take that, and that – '! Guido boxed first one ear then the other. 'One does not fight with something below the level of the sea,' so saying, he strode from the room.

Rigo waited until his brother was out of earshot, then he took his head in his hands, and sobbed.

His neglected heart, forsaken, isolated, was more lonely than the ace of hearts in the middle of a playing card.

CHAPTER EIGHT
Canterdown

WHEN she awoke, it was raining busily, the landscape and the rain appeared to be making conversation, as though it were raining by appointment; a pre-arranged thing. Innumerable small birds she had never seen, except on spits, dug vehement beaks into lawns, smooth as a well-shaven chin. Now and then a worm would dangle from a beak; it was easy to see the birds were in their element. Did it always rain every day, at the same hour, in order to oblige the birds? Trees, extraordinarily opaque, squatted about like fat cats. The scene, condensed, shut in, had all the intimacy of an interior. Surely rain should be an episode, an intrusion, not taken for granted?

She evoked Florence under the rain, a vertical downpour, fatalistic, spectacular; the streets that looked as though they were made of obsidian; the teeming, squirming figures, like a basket of split eels. There would be an air of outrage, dese-cration; in a country of volcanoes and earthquakes it was surprising it ever did anything so modest as to rain . . .

As the day progressed, she made several discoveries: the most popular word, in the English vocabulary is the word 'cosy': 'I always think there is something cosy about the rain, don't you?' 'Which would you like to look at, *Punch* or *Country Life*? I adore *Country Life*, it's so cosy –'

Then the silence, would she ever get accustomed to it? It

was convex, as taut as a canopy; when the stable clock struck, it made a dent. . . .

It was only after she had been there a few days that she learned to distinguish between the various brands of silence: the silence of the banqueting hall, only used on great occasions, was quite different from the silence of, say, the Yellow Parlour. In the banqueting hall, there reigned a silence that had been, as it were, enforced with difficulty, it was an effort, and a resentful one, as though it were holding its breath, until you got out of the room.

The silence of the Yellow Parlour was subtler, far. It had an attentive, vigilant quality, nothing you said escaped it; it was critical, it drew its own conclusions, where as the Red Drawing Room's silence was sulky, satiated.

It had heard too much, it was as the deaf adder that stoppeth her ears, charm he never so wisely.

To Vica, fresh from the din of Italy, the hootings and tootings, songs and altercations, bells and sirens, there was something uncanny about the silence of Canterdown. She could not realize that it formed part of the even tenor of a gentleman's household, that it is considered ill-bred to raise the voice and that the servants keep themselves to themselves in sequestered and well-defined quarters. She was unfamiliar with the aspirations embodied in the Anglo-Saxon code of good behaviour. To keep a 'stiff upper lip' in face of great emotional stress would have seemed to Vica merely an absurd form of affectation: if you were happy, you sang, if you were sad, you wept.

She hadn't been in Canterdown for forty-eight hours before she had allotted rooms, and possibly professions, to all her brothers. Guido could redecorate her bedroom (for the moment, panelled in plum-pudding oak, it resembled one of the gloomier sacristies), Mario hadn't his equal for arranging flowers; Ugo would be invaluable as a kind of superior majordomo, as for Leone, he was indicated to give the local *jeunesse dorée* lessons in rowing, with a little boxing thrown in as a supplement. Even Rigo with his guitar could bring a whiff of romance into the lives of the so numerous British virgins who seemed all eagerness, frustration.

Thanks to this arrangement, Canterdown could be made into a flourishing Italian colony. Of course, she was careful not to breathe a word of this project to her future in-laws, it would be madness, until she had consolidated her position. A brother would be necessary for the wedding, no doubt: neither Guido nor Mario were indicated; they would create too great a diversion, take up too much of her time. No, Ugo was the one best suited to her requirements, he was less vulnerable to criticism and she herself was less vulnerable to criticism of Ugo. The Canterdowns were by no means ripe for the Papagalli. He mustn't stay more than forty-eight hours. A soupçon of Papagalli sufficed for the present. Meanwhile, one by one the Caracoles fell. Lady Canterdown with her Florentine past, was doomed from the outset. One look at Vica was sufficient. The day after her arrival, she was sitting for her portrait in pastels (an unsuitable medium) to her future mother-in-law. Lord Canterdown, more disposed to be critical, held out for fully forty-eight hours; what Vica didn't achieve with her face, she achieved with her figure; as to her now celebrated voice, it turned out to be an almost superfluous asset, though it rounded off her conquest, so to speak. 'I always thought Italian women screeched like parakeets.'

As to Charles, his infatuation knew no bounds. Elizabeth behaved rather like a jocular brother-in-law: 'I say, old thing, you haven't half brought the family to heel.' Even Peter benefited from the general benevolence. He and Charles spent hours together playing billiards, taking the dogs for a run, etc. Lord Canterdown's verdict was: 'It's nice for Charles to have a companion, when all's said and done, he was always a kind of honorary member of the family.'

Most curious, the toughest nut to crack turned out to be Madamzell: Madamzell on the defensive, Madamzell out to find fault, Madamzell, a fellow Latin.

Vica was never out of the schoolroom. Madamzell and Nana became as thick as thieves.

'I do not say she is an adventuress, but she will 'ave adventures, it sticks out a kilometre.'

Nana, not understanding the words, but grasping the meaning, would nod sagaciously. 'She ain't one of us, though I am not saying anything against her. Charles was always a simpleton.'

The two couples were married the same day in Canterdown Church, surrounded by monuments of dead and gone Caracoles executed in marble, granite – even alabaster. A gaunt crusader with flattened nose and frozen dog between his spurs, lay beneath a florid, periwigged chancellor who looked as though at any minute, he might chuck his attendant angels under the chin. Vica felt somehow more at home with the crusader, he reminded her of a nordic *Guidarello Guidarelli*. . . . As for Charles' grandfather, he was the dead spit of Cavour, she discovered, spectacles and all. . . . She longed to draw Ugo's attention to this . . . With distress, she realized there was to be no incense, no Latin, no chasubles. . . . How was it possible to feel she was really being married?

Hemmed in by a parterre of flowers, hats, starched surplices, apple-cheeked choir boys – all of which she could see out of the corner of her eye – Lady Canterdown's hat, for instance, which had been shown here with great pride, was as eclectic as her water-colours, flowers, feathers, lace, ribbons – her thoughts became more and more irrelevant . . . It was only when the Vicar, smelling strongly of peppermint, bent over her saying in a voice like a stifled yawn: 'Wilt thou have this man to be thy wedded husband?' a question which she had rehearsed with Charles, that she pulled herself together. . . .

Letter from Vica to Guido

Guido mio,

Your letter made me cry, I cannot bear to dwell on your loneliness. . . . If it is any comfort, you may think of me as seldom alone, but even lonelier, in a sense: I will try to explain: you are surrounded by familiar things, familiar minds, people who have the same reflexes as you have. You know in advance how they will react to certain situations; their standards are more or less the same as yours; they eat and drink the same things, have the same aspirations, the same disappointments, whereas here –

Everything has to be translated, transposed, reassimilated. *Mon éducation est à refaire*, as Crispa always warned me it would be. When she thought she was alone, she used to sing a silly little song, with the refrain: *'Je suis malade d'être trop pure,'* so am I, but not in the crude physical sense. How can I make you understand? Everything is like English cooking, neutralized, asepticized, castrated. All the good natural juices have been squeezed out. Though they have the richest vocabulary in the world (I have begun to read Shakespeare with relative ease) they only use about five hundred words: in every sentence the word 'nice' occurs at least once. Otherwise, it isn't nice. Then, there is their understatement as opposed to our overstatement: 'Poor old So and So, he wasn't feeling quite the thing, then all of a sudden, he snuffed out.' Their vocabulary is not only restricted, it is cowardly. They refer to diseases by their initials, as though they were old schoolmates, T.B., V.D., etc. They cannot bring themselves to say someone is dead, they say he has 'passed away' or 'gone over,' or 'passed on,' or something equally silly. Infantilism is carried to incredible lengths. Popularity or *odium* both have the same result; a nickname. Hence 'Dizzy,' hence 'Boney,' etc.

In spite of all these idiosyncrasies, they have beautiful manners, and are naturally tolerant, they long to be kind. It is very difficult for them really to dislike anyone. They are too lazy to hate, it is too much of an effort. The climate is one of affectionate indifference, they are not particularly interested in you, but neither are they particularly interested in themselves.

On the other hand, they are passionately interested in dogs, birds, flowers. Never go for a walk with an Englishman and a dog. You will not be able to get a word in edgeways. As for birds, they are equally sacred; the smaller, the more sacred. The other day at luncheon, we were eating partridge, Lord Canterdown asked me: 'If I was enjoying my "bird".' I replied yes, but that I preferred larks. There was a shocked silence; I realized I must have said an enormity. Lord Canterdown snorted: 'Ho! And what about a nice roast fox?'

Mercifully, I unconsciously rehabilitated myself the same day, on arranging a vase to Lady Canterdown's liking. *Poveretta*, she said pathetically: 'So I see you are not cruel to flowers *as well*.'

Ugo, by the way, had a *succés fou* with her. He made wreaths for all the male statues, and necklaces for the female ones which she thought were quite charming. Lord Canterdown was less appreciative. 'Umph!' he grunted. 'They'll think they're all in Honolulu!'

I know you are longing to hear about Charles. He is charming to me, no, do not frown, *tesoro*, we are no more intimate morally than before we married. He is quite content with what I give him, he does not attempt to penetrate any deeper, perhaps he is scared of what he might find there? I am not unhappy, I am too inquisitive to be unhappy. Each day I make a fresh discovery; besides, it amuses me to tame, no, that is a lie, they are tame already, rather, to disturb this too acquiescent family. I shall shake them to their foundations before I have done with them. The only person you might be slightly jealous of is Peter, he is more intelligent than I thought, and not in the least bit taken in by me, very different from the others. Perhaps

the Englishman is like this before he is pruned and 'licked
into shape,' as they say. Peter has not been 'licked,' or, if
he has, it is the wrong shape. He is neither polite, lazy, nor
indifferent, he dislikes me, but I amuse him. We sharpen
our claws on each other. . . .

Elizabeth and he are very happy together, but some day
he will have a desperate affair with some plain irresistible
elderly Frenchwoman, who will resemble the photograph
of Réjane on Mamma's writing table, and who will nightly
dress the wounds she has inflicted during the day.
Can't you see I am trying to cheer you up, *amor mio*,
soon, very soon now, I will ask if I may have you to stay.
Sii tranquillo, they will not refuse. *Ti abbraccio.*

Vica

*Your little San Cristoforo never leaves my neck. Is it not
queer, I am glad now I did not marry Gian Galeazzo.*

Lord and Lady Canterdown decided to give a party for the
young couple, to which all the county would be invited.

In England, it is possible to be as social in the country as in
town, marvelled Vica. Neighbours sprang up like mushrooms,
the country houses are so vast, and contain so many guests
(not just the family, like in Italy) that the inmates of three
country houses equal one fairly large party. People even go
to the length of *preferring* to live in the country, she discovered, not because they were trying to escape from the glare
of some social scandal, but because they were insensible to
the appeal of urban life. The country was not looked upon as
the site of an ephemeral picnic, or an occasionally becoming
décor for lovers who would be private, one liked the country
per se, one knew the names of flowers, even trees and birds;
one knew the name of everybody who lived in the village,
also the names of their parents, *and* their grandparents. . . .

Then there was the Compulsory Laugh that formed part of
good manners. When you could not think of anything to say
you laughed: it was exhausting.

There were, of course, different categories of neighbours, Vica was quick to note. The neighbours of the same class as her in-laws, for instance, who were more or less acquainted with Italy, and who plied Vica with inquiries about people she had never heard of: Was 'Cora' as beautiful as ever? Did 'Dora' still wear an arum lily over her left shoulder? Did she think 'Vittoria' would be coming over soon? Who was 'Mario's' latest? They seemed very surprised when Vica confessed her complete ignorance about these people and their mode of life. It didn't occur to them that she belonged to the Italian 'bourgeoisie,' that she was middle-class, in fact. Maybe she was Sicilian? Sicilians are very parochial, it appears. . . .

To quite a different category belonged the honest-to-God huntin', shootin', fishin' type, who lived in less grand houses, and who boasted more dogs than guests. These, beyond a fleeting and rather shamefaced allusion to the 'lakes' or Venice (as quickly dismissed as condolence or congratulation) did not wish to converse on the subject of Italy. They talked mostly about the 'run' of the previous day, their children and their servants. Vica found them, on the whole, a rest. The men simply sat and gaped at her, blushed when she addressed them, then guffawed guiltily, to cover up the blushes.

The party was made to coincide with the visit of a relation, whose name was continually on their lips. Vica had heard much about Aunt Sybil from Charles, who assured her that the reason they were all so stupid was that Aunt Sybil had monopolized the brains of the family, there hadn't been enough to go round, so to speak.

Aunt Sybil turned out to be Vica's first contact with British tolerance of unconventionality.

'What is her husband like?' she inquired, on the lookout for data.

Charles giggled: 'She hasn't got one.'

'I see. One of those pedantic, though sentimental old maids, who derive a vicarious pleasure from other people's love affairs.'

'She doesn't need to do that. She's had plenty of her own.'

'I thought you said she was unmarried?'

Don't people have love affairs in Italy even though they are unmarried?'

'Of course, but not the female equivalent of your aunt, I imagine.'

'Well, she's had as many lovers as anyone in Italy, I should think, though she *did* wait until she was thirty, before she started; she said she was willing to give respectability a chance, but none of the chaps she fancied proposed, so, on her thirtieth birthday, she gave a party, in the course of which she announced that she was about to take a lover, so that the members of her family who proposed to cut her should know exactly where they stood. Since then, she has never looked back. Apparently the chaps who did not fancy her as a wife, were mad keen to have her as a mistress. The family was shocked at first, then, they shut their eyes, Aunt Syb gave such amusing dinners, to which people literally fought to be invited. Besides, her lovers were always jolly distinguished – one was a Prime Minister – in the end the family decided it was an honour to be related to Aunt Sybil. Her, what do you call it, celibacy, has become a legend, something rather rare and beautiful, in fact, I think we should all disown her if she got married now!'

Vica gasped, 'But she must be quite old!'

'Quite, round about sixty, I should say. But there's life in the old girl yet, she doesn't half wake us up, when she comes to stay.'

'Is she bringing – her lover?' Vica faltered.

'No.' Charles grinned. 'He's lecturing in America for the moment.'

'Was she – very beautiful – ?'

Charles laughed outright, 'As plain as a pikestaff, but she has the best legs in England.'

'Will she like me?' Vica sensed an enemy.

'My darling, who doesn't like you? She'll draw you out,

you'll find yourself telling her the story of your young life before she's been here twenty-four hours.'

'*Forse che si, forse che no.*' No one could look more secretive, more cloistered than Vica. With his hand, Charles made the gesture of brushing away an invisible cobweb.

'Please, darling, I'm scared of sphinxes.'

As usual, Vica mapped out a plan of campaign: the unsophisticated grateful girl, half peasant, dazzled by all she saw, thrilled at meeting a celebrity. . . .

Aunt Sybil arrived the next day, in time for the party. Contrary to Vica's expectations and the traditional family dimensions, she was shortish, inclined to be stout, with remarkable hands and legs for a woman of her age. A shock of short, coarse, white hair, like winter grass, enclosed a face smooth and brown as a pheasant's egg. Eyes that were a frosty blue glittered in the matt surface, like small pieces of ice in a rut.

There was something curiously earthy, about Aunt Sybil, something animal and robust.

'So here is the siren from Italy! Come and be introduced to your old aunt, siren. I shall call you Calypso, for if ever anyone had their vocation written all over their face, it is you.' Vica realized that the unsophisticated grateful girl must be scrapped, and that, immediately.

'I have heard so much about you, Aunt Sybil,' she temporized, 'I have been longing to make your acquaintance.'

'No wonder! I am the only member of this family whose acquaintance is worth making. Come and sit by me, child. I want to have a good look at you. H'm. This family will never be the same again. Have you ever read "La figlia di Jorio"? No? Well, you should. It describes the havoc wrought on a whole community by a young woman not unlike you. What are you going to do with Charles? If anyone could galvanize him, you could. You could become Charles' Pygmalion. Does the part appeal to you?'

Vica had the uncomfortable feeling that she was being

X-rayed. Shift as she might, the indomitable blue gaze pinned her down.

'Suppose I find him satisfactory as he is?' she hazarded, aware of her temerity.

Sybil chuckled, 'Touchée, I was told you were no fool. You interest me, I have never encountered an Italian like you. Not a drop of foreign blood?'

'My grandmother was Irish.'

'Ah! That accounts for much. A formidable combination. I could be useful to you if I choose, you must need an interpreter. O, I don't mean literally, but someone who could give you a clue as to the nature of the unfamiliar fauna that abounds in these parts. . . . But I mustn't monopolize the guest of honour. I see people beginning to arrive. Go and make yourself pleasant, my dear.'

A posse of guests, shepherded by Lady Canterdown, was bearing down on them; Vica braced herself for a fresh effort, she tried to size them up. To which category did they belong? Local or cosmopolitan, subjective or objective, horticultural or ornithological?

She was not left long in doubt.

A tall ascetic-looking man came up to her with out-stretched hand: 'Didn't we meet at Princess Arrivamale's ball in Florence? We came in after dinner.'

'What fun it was.'

A tiny chic woman, presumably his wife, chimed in: 'I couldn't have enjoyed it more. Besides, I adore the Princess, don't you? She's like a small black ant, and every bit as purposeful. Camilla, come and be introduced to Lady Risingdale. Camilla simply *lives* for the day she can return to Italy. Don't you, Camilla?'

The young woman so designated gave Vica a handshake that was unexpectedly downright, and a look that evidently prided itself on its steadfastness. She was very pretty, but Vica felt that she was trying to live up to some preconceived ideal, or picture, someone had once told her she resembled. It is time I clipped my antennæ, thought Vica, let's hope I'm wrong for once. . . . She was introduced to yet another couple, tall, blond, and slightly 'chapped'-looking.

They all flopped into chairs, round Vica, gazing expectantly at Camilla, as dogs who expect to be thrown a bone. She took her cue, with practised aplomb: '*How* I envy you your Italy: Cimabue, Giotto, Donatello, Fra Angelico, Simone Martini, Piero della Francesca, Bennozzo Gozzoli, Dosso Dossi – '

'Ah,' inserted Vica profoundly, as soon as she paused for breath, 'and what about those early Isotto Fraschini?' Camilla put on a look of slightly controversial academic concentration.

'*Which*? The ones in Siena?'

'No, the ones in garages, those *very, very noisy ones*, that used to go whizzing round the Futa, with the cutter out?'

There was a dreadful silence. Camilla at a loss, desperately wondered what new kind of Art jargon was this, then the silence was broken by a hoot of laughter, in which the others immediately joined. 'Darling, she's getting at you, can't you see? Isotta Fraschini is a make of car, like Rolls Royce.'

The earnest man-to-man look fell from the wretched Camilla's face, was replaced by the tremulous Greuze *frimousse* it had originally ousted.

'I don't think it's in the least funny,' she stammered, on the verge of tears, 'I call it a joke in very bad taste!'

'So it is,' appeased the wicked Vica, 'I couldn't help it, please forgive me, it was a joke in execrable taste, please do not be angry with me.'

'Don't be such an old goose, Camilla,' chided her friend, 'she meant no harm, did you, Lady Risingdale? Camilla was asking for trouble.' ('She never lets one down,' murmured the tall husband gratefully.) 'O yes, you were darling, you were trying to dazzle us with your knowledge of Italian painters. Take her away, darling, and give her a drink.' Vica genuinely conscience-stricken, leant apologetically forward.

'It was unpardonable of me, but the temptation was too great.'

'It will do her all the good in the world,' her victim's friend hastened to assure her, 'she was asking for it. When I first knew Camilla,' she resumed cheerfully, lighting a cigarette, 'she had a beautifully organized appearance, and a small plot of mind, full of smaller plots, and counter-plots. It had been originally designed to contain nothing but vegetables. . . . All would have gone well, had not some mischievous passer-by cast a handful of Sutton's Best (large flowering annuals) on the neat row of salads. . . . O woe! They all came up in Glorious Technicolor, in a perfect riot of roguish irrelevance, smothering the smug rows of vegetables with their pretensions, wantoning up the broad beans, sprawling across the marrows. . . . Now it's too late to do anything about it. The *potager*, forgetting its lowly useful past, is convinced it was never anything but a pleasure garden!'

Though one or two allusions escaped her, what, for instance was 'Sutton's Best,' the wisp, Vica realized, had wit.

She mentally made room for a new category of English women, the cultured, the cynical, the tolerant and genial . . . The Wisp reminded Vica of someone? . . .

The Princess, of course . . .

And Aunt Sybil? She, too, belonged to the same category, with a subtle difference. Vica's mind hovered, swooped, closed; the Princess, all things taken into consideration, had never openly flouted Convention. These ladies, she divined, had made Convention their handmaiden. She gazed at her companion with a new respect.

'God!' exclaimed the latter, 'you must be bored here! I once had an Italian lover, I have never ceased regretting him. . . . ' Vica, forewarned, not in the least surprised, experienced a sudden violent fit of homesickness. . . .

It got worse, of course, as the novelty wore off, and she was confronted with an endless perspective of unanimous days, each differing from its fellow, only in the length of the walk, the length of the game, the length of the anecdote.

The Canterdowns said to each other: 'It's really wonderful how Vica has adapted herself, who ever would guess she was a dentist's daughter?'

Who, indeed! Who would guess that Vica pined for *burischio* and *trippa alla parmigiana* instead of sole and roast chicken, that the decorous silence of Canterdown made her want to scream, that she surreptitiously gave the dogs a kick, that she would have liked to live with drawn curtains, in order not to see the punctual downpour which seemed to be part of the daily programme, who indeed?

O for the clamorous family circle, the admiring, exclamatory brothers, Mamma's facile tears, Gina's *pasta*, the train of compliments that sprang up so spontaneously in one's wake!

Then came the day, when she could bear it no longer, and when she asked her mother-in-law, if she might have Guido to stay. . . .

CHAPTER NINE
Three Bedrooms

LADY CANTERDOWN is reading, in a wide, shabby, chintz-covered bed, the latest Michael Arlen, which she makes it her duty to read, for she prides herself on being 'no prude' and 'keeping in touch' with the younger generation.

She cannot help wondering if people really behave like this, though, of course, she's quite willing to take Mr. Arlen's word for it. They say no woman can resist Mr. Arlen. . . . He must resemble one of those frightfully handsome, rather nordic-looking men, you see in advertisements, lighting their pipe in a hurricane.

Arlen, Arlen, the name rings a bell, I once knew an Arlen. Polly Arlen, no, that was the name of the children's nursery maid. Now, let me see: there was Nasturtium (Nasty as we used to call her) Arlen, that spotty girl we were told to be nice to at Christmas parties. No, that was Arden, not Arlen, I'm getting so bad at names. . . . Surely, I once knew a Sir Lionel Arlen? Of course, how stupid; he used to hunt with the Old Berkeley, we thought he might do for Syb. . . . I wonder if this Michael Arlen is any relation. I must remember to look up the name to-morrow. Now, supposing . . . There came a 'code knock' at the door, a kind of syncopated tattoo, which Christopher had used ever since they were married. Almost simultaneously, his fine magenta nose peered round the door. 'May I come in?'

'Of course, darling, sit yourself down,' Lady Canterdown moved her legs from one side of the bed to the other.

Lord Canterdown sank heavily on to the sagging mattress, 'I must say, that girl's got cheek,' he burst out with his customary petulance.

'Which?' queried Lady Canterdown brightly. 'We have two cheeky girls in this house!'

'That's only too true, Sylvia. This time I am referring to Vica. Vica's request that she might have her brother to stay. Damn it all, the whole family may settle on us sooner or later!'

'*Sooner*,' came the sprightly retort. (I feel in very good form, Sylvia was thinking, it must be that Mr. Arlen.) 'After all,' she amplified, 'it's only natural that the poor girl should be feeling homesick, none of us can speak a word of Italian but Liz, who can, but won't. I see no harm in having an occasional brother to stay.'

'Yes, but you yourself say that it's only the thin edge of the wedge.'

'I'd rather it were the thin, than the fat,' chuckled Lady Canterdown, drunk with her own wit, 'you should see the mother's photograph, she's exactly like Tetrazzini!'

'Charles says the brothers are not too bad,' pursued Lord Canterdown moodily, 'but on the soft side, that's to be expected. . . . I like the girl well enough, she's damn pretty, but I don't want the house to resemble a back street in Naples.'

'O, Christopher, you are funny – ' Lady Canterdown was feeling incurably frivolous, 'do you think that Nana will take to telling fortunes?'

'And Crawle to selling "feelthy postcards" under the lapel of his coat?' roared her husband, slapping his thigh, and suddenly falling in with her mood.

'We might introduce the *tarantella* at the Hunt Ball,' suggested Lady Canterdown weakly, wiping her eyes.

'Liz says they sing Caracoli, Caracola to the tune of Funicoli,

Funicola,' proffered Lord Canterdown, swaying backwards and forwards with mirth.

'Christopher, darling, you're ruining the springs of my bed. I wonder if the Count and Countess are as silly as we are!'

Elizabeth sat rather sulkily in front of her looking-glass, removing the make-up from her beautiful, humourless face. Its humourlessness struck her, not for the first time. What a mercy I have one all the same, though I suppose it *is* difficult for beauty to look amusing, *or* amused, for that matter! Well, East, West, Beauty's best, it saves a lot of trouble. She gave a vicious dab at her solemn incomparable nose. . . . If only Englishmen weren't so fond of one another's company! What on earth can Peter have to say to Charles at this hour? They've been shooting all the afternoon, one would have thought that would have sufficed. But no. All Englishmen, that is to say all *nice* Englishmen, are like that, they'd chuck Venus in order to play golf with a pal. I wonder if Vica minds? But she doesn't seem to mind the things one thought she would, such as men remaining in the dining-room after dinner and never noticing one's clothes. . . . She spends a lot of time in her room writing letters, to whom? All those precious brothers of hers, no doubt. Poor Vica, she was transfigured when Father said she might have Guido to stay. I know enough about Italians to realize that things must grate on her nerves. . . . One must admit that she's extraordinarily good-tempered, she talks to Charles as if he were a child, which, indeed, he is. . . . I don't feel that I shall ever get to know Vica any better, I like her more in England than I did in Italy, she's so adaptable, she was even able to handle the Parson, all things to all men, should be her motto. . . . 'Ah, there you are at last!' she exclaimed, as Peter entered, rather flushed, smoking the fag-end of a cigar. 'Put that out, will you, darling, it's most unbecoming, you haven't the right face for a cigar, you look as though you had picked it up off the pavement.'

'Do I?' he squashed it out obediently in the ashtray on her dressing-table. 'You bloated little plutocrat! You wait!' he hugged her, thereby covering his face with cleansing cream. 'You wait,' he repeated, wiping it off with his handkerchief, 'until I have made my pile, I'm convinced I shall end by keeping your entire family!'

'I shouldn't be surprised, they're an extravagant lot, although it doesn't show on the surface. Mummy spends hundreds on her bulbs, and Father, far more than he can afford, on his hunters, but that is beside the point; what I really want to know is what you can have to say to Charles after having been out shooting with him all day? How dare you keep me mopping away at my face, while you two zanys evoke your schooldays in the billiard-room?'

Peter thrust his fingers through his chunky hair: 'As a matter of fact, it was Charles who wanted to go to bed, and *I* who kept on talking. I told him to "stand" when he is a bit older. It's awfully difficult to get him started; he's so damn frivolous he might be Italian!'

Elizabeth laughed. 'And Vica is so damn serious – '

'Not serious, my sweet, concentrated, concentrated on being a success, on her brothers being a success, on her mission, in short. What a pity dear Charles isn't in the Diplomatic Service, he would become our youngest Ambassador!'

'Come here, you old silly! No. Nearer. You don't deserve a kiss, but you're going to get one, for I love you very, very much. . . . There! . . . Now you may smoke a cigarette while I finish undressing in the bathroom.'

'Liza darling, don't be long! I'm really furious with myself for having wasted an hour with Charles, when I might have been making love to you. . . .'

Vica was writing against time. She wanted to get her letters finished, before Charles came upstairs. *Sia lodato il cielo*, the one to Guido is already in its envelope, then there was a collective one to the family, and another on Anglo-Saxon *mœurs* to Crispa, this was the one she was trying to finish now.

I think you would be pleased with me, Crispina *cara. Je crois que je vous fais honneur.* They have swallowed me whole! hook and all! I don't think they even realize there is a hook, and a pretty big one at that! They are, thank God, neither critical, not analytical. If they like one, unlike *you, ils ne cherchent pas la petite bête.* It is a mercy I didn't marry into a French family. Such good looks as I possess would have been of little avail with my in-laws, unless, perchance, there was a *collégien* among them.

I clearly see why there has never been much love between the French and the Italians: When Latin meets Latin! *Mais quoique vous en disiez*, we are much nicer that you are, we have more charm, more beauty, as far as I can judge, on the strength of my forty-eight hours in Paris.

The English are not without a shy, violet-like charm, especially the men. The men are nearly all violets, so modest, so unassuming, it is not to be believed! When I think how we brag about everything! Why, they do not even seem to be aware that they have beautiful fingers, and the most *signorile* homes in Europe. I like the men much better than the women. The women are either completely unfeminine (like hospital nurses) or so oversexed that they give you the impression that it is not safe for a man to be alone with them. There seems to be no *juste milieu*.

They are much nicer to one another than we are, and really appear to practise the art of friendship, which we Latins are apt to look upon as a purely masculine monopoly.

It is very sweet of my father-in-law to allow me to invite Guido; I have had an awful fit of nostalgia ever since the party, the climate perhaps, has also something to do with it; it rains so little and so often, not a cloud-burst, as with us, but a busy little drizzle, just enough to make your clothes damp, but never enough to keep you indoors.

Please, Crispa, make a point of going through Guido's clothes before he leaves, suppress the so-called 'British' numbers, especially the overcoat with all those buckles. . . . Do not let the others feel out of it, tell them they will each have their turn, especially Leone, there should be a fine sporting future for him in this country. I would naturally like Mamma to visit us, but, *entre nous*, they are not ripe for Mamma yet. I do not despair of finding jobs on the estate for all my brothers, excepting, perhaps, Rigo. Ma zitto! I hear footsteps, no more for the present –

She had started to write the address when Charles entered, as he hoped, noiselessly; he planned to creep up behind her and steal his arms round her neck. Without looking round, she said, inconsiderately: 'What, up already, *tesoro*? I thought you were going to have a nice talk with Peter in the billiard-room.'

'But we *did* have a nice talk,' he sounded crestfallen, 'I thought you might be getting impatient.' This would never do, she pulled herself together.

'But I was, *tesoro*, I was, I was just writing the good news to Guido, to pass the time away.' Charles sank into a chair by the writing-table. 'You're always writing to Guido,' he pouted, 'I should think you wrote every other day.'

'Didn't you write to Elizabeth when she was in Italy?'

'Yes, from time to time, but not every other day, and not *screeds*.' Vica stretched out her arm, caught him to her, peered into his eyes. 'Jealous?'

'A little,' he confessed.

'How can you be jealous of my brothers? It is absurd.'

'Let me go, darling, I don't want to be mesmerized. It is hitting below the belt.'

She let him go, lit a cigarette, offered him one. 'That is a very popular axiom, *è vero*? Hitting below the belt . . .' Characteristically she threw back her head, blew a cloud of smoke to conceal her thoughts.

'It means,' he explained, 'to take a mean advantage.'

'I know it does, I'm getting very good at English.'

'You're getting very good at most things,' he rose abruptly, stood over her, pressing her head to his side. 'Supposing we went to bed? It is getting past our bedtime.'

'Darling Charles, just let me finish this cigarette, you are always in such a hurry.'

'Can you be surprised?'

'Charles, do sit down for a minute, you are so restless. Tell me, does your aunt like me?'

Charles was an essentially truthful person; what Aunt Sybil had actually said was: 'Vica is a queer and beautiful fish that needs watching.' 'She admires you very much,' he compromised.

'I did not say "admire," I said "like"?'

The truthful Charles fidgeted. 'She takes a long time to get to like people.'

'I see. She doesn't, yet. But she will, before she leaves here!'

'That goes without saying.' Charles' relief was manifest. He hated to be pinned down. She suddenly felt mean, like a smuggler masquerading as a Customs House official. Poor Charles, his defencelessness deserved a gesture. She stubbed out her cigarette. . . .

Guido's visit did not work out according to plan.

He hated Canterdown from the word go, hated the park, with its insistence on cows and privacy; hated the house, vast as the Palazzo Pitti, but less straightforward, full of misleading staircases and intimidating neo-gothic lavatories; he hated his chilly virginal bedroom, with its spiteful little coal fire, the drawing-rooms, full of draughts and mute reproaches, the billiard-room's silent smoking masculinity; he hated the rattling windows, the perpetual reminder to wash your hands in the shape of a can of hot water, he hated the servants, the food, the dogs, he even hated his host's and hostess' patient civility.

He was miserably aware that everything about him was wrong; his hair, his clothes, the way he ate. Even his good looks; fruity, exotic, they were as unseemly as a vine rioting round an oak tree. A man, in order to be considered good looking in this country, must be thin to the point of desiccation, shaved until he bled, shorn until his scalp smarted.

Three days after his arrival, Vica was stricken down with pneumonia, caught, she wheezed, from taking the dogs for a run in the rain. Guido was demented, convinced that she was going to die; he spent half his time in prayer, and the rest getting in everyone's way. The staff never referred to him as anything but 'that dratted dago,' the men-servants snubbed him, the housemaids made fun of him, the trained nurse simply ignored him. The only person who was in the least kind to him was Aunt Sybil, who was disarmed by his beauty and helplessness. (Many were the unofficial honeymoons she had spent in Italy.) She did her best to pacify the wretched boy. 'Do sit down, smoke, drink, do anything, but stop pacing up and down, like a caged panther!'

'I cannot smoke-a, I cannot drink-a, my sister, she may be *in extremis* at this moment. If she die, I die also.'

'Now listen to me, young man: hundreds of people have pneumonia, hundreds of people recover from pneumonia, why should your sister be the one exception? Look at Charles, he adores his wife, yet he doesn't carry on like you!'

'I know. I could-a kill eem. He will not let me go near Vica. As for that *infermiera*, why wear spectacles if not to see? I am no *spirito*, yet she look-a straight-a through me. I shall go mad!' he moaned, flinging himself on the sofa beside Aunt Sybil, burying his curly head in his hands.

At that moment, Charles, looking more unfocussed than ever, entered the library in search of company, other than his parents. 'Come and cheer up Guido, for goodness sake! I can do nothing with the boy,' his aunt entreated. The 'boy's' response was immediate, he sat up, flattened his hair, contrived a wan smile. It was important to give Vica's husband an impression of virility. Charles perched himself affectionately on the arm of the sofa. 'I say, old thing, you mustn't give way like this. Vica's no worse, Sister is quite satisfied. It has to run its course. It's bad for you, moping indoors like this. Why not come for a stroll with me?'

Guido glanced at the bedewed window-pane, repressed a shudder and said he would be pleased to go for a stroll. He suddenly recalled a frightening adage of his father: 'The English only admit to one illness, the one that kills them.'

Vica was in the most unpleasant state of being neither quite conscious, nor entirely insensible. She allowed her mind to drift fatuously along in a flooded landscape, as acquiescent as it was impotent. If there had been any resistance, it was over now: half-drowned objects, she did not attempt to grasp or identify, floated past her, the embodiment of *laisser faire, laisser mourir*. . . .

Abdication was sweet: where there had been mountains, jagged as a temperature chart, there was now nothing. The mountains had vanished, leaving a blameless vacancy, a Cuyp-like blandness. There was no boundary, no limit, she might go drifting on for ever; no hand was raised to detain her. She travelled without jolt or impediment, gently rocked, as by an outgoing tide. . . .

In her wicker chair, watertight, immune, Sister Margaret knitted placidly, her thoughts keeping pace with her needles, the unspoken commentary of the sick bed: purl, plain, purl, plain, wax, wane, wax, wane. . . . From time to time she would glance at the face on the pillow. Looks a bit better to me; less flushed, breathing easier. But it's difficult to tell with these foreigners, they don't seem to react the same way as we do. Sweetly pretty, though, I must say, it's touching to see him with her, just a smile and a pat, ever so quiet and considerate, very different from that crazy brother of hers, I soon sent him about his business, he won't come bothering me again in a hurry. . . . Wonder if it would be safe to leave her for a minute,

I want my cupper tea, it's now or never. Let's have another
look. The wicker chair creaked loudly as she rose, bent
over Vica, took her pulse. I was right, it's going down. She's
actually dropped off. Me for tea. I'll be back in a minute. . . .

. . . Now the lovely abstraction of which she was the
centre, showed signs of losing its fluidity. Were the floods
receding? Here and there, a patch of brown earth emerged,
a drowned tree reared its haggard head, recognizable sounds
pierced her semi-consciousness, where it had worn a trifle
thin; the creak of Sister's chair, for instance. . . . Resentful, she
tried to slip her moorings again, it was less easy this time,
things snatched at her consciousness, threatened to become
concrete. Down, Reality, down! I do not like being pawed.
. . . O my bubble world, my rainbow-coloured world, all
iridescence and fluency, forsake me not. But no! However
much we object, *things* will be *things*. The mahogany
cupboard opposite her bed, insisted on being a mahogany
cupboard, the picture of Charles' grandfather was again,
incorruptibly, triumphantly, Charles' grandfather. Instinctively
she looked for the stiff bent figure in the wicker chair. It was
empty, she sighed with ease, closed her eyes, really dozed
this time. . . . Then, another sound was born, stealthy yet
urgent. The door opened, an inch at a time, finally admitting,
not Sister Margaret, but Guido. Guido on tiptoe, deafened by
his own heart beats, terrified of being surprised by Sister, of
disturbing Vica. He had seen the nurse go along the passage
to her tea. This was his opportunity.

On tiptoe he approached her bed, greatly daring, he knelt,
brushing the cool sheets with his lips. A tremor shook her
narrow frame, all that was submerged, derelict, all that was
vanquished, dispossessed, threw off the last lingering mists,
she was rescued, safe. 'Guido,' she whispered, just able to
touch his hair, '*sei tu, Guido? Ti voglio bene, sai . . .*'

On the day Vica was pronounced convalescent, Aunt Sybil,
her arms laden with hot-house flowers she had wrested from

the recalcitrant head gardener, was on her way to Vica's room.

Illness had accomplished what, perhaps, months of health would not have succeeded in achieving, i.e. the subjugation of Aunt Sybil. Vica's white shadowy face, her narrow gothic hands plucking at the sheets, the crucifix over her bed, the photograph of the ballet-like group of her brilliantined brothers by the bedside, all combined to produce an atmosphere subtly exotic, unsettling in more ways than one. How was Canterdown to assimilate Vica, how could Vica ever really assimilate Canterdown, was one of the questions Aunt Sybil was continually asking herself. . . .

When she opened the door, brother and sister were engaged in such animated conversation that they did not immediately notice her entrance. The rapid southern voices, articulated, sonorous, seemed to generate heat. The room was heated by their voices.

Guido was, as usual, kneeling on the floor, by the bed. Vica, propped up on many pillows, was gazing into his upturned face. Sybil scarcely liked to intrude on their massive intimacy. . . . Vica saw her first: '*Cara*,' she exclaimed, with genuine pleasure, 'I was hoping you would come. Guido, *porti una sedia per la Zia*. We were discussing Guido's future. I was urging him to find a job in England, but I would not care to tell you his reaction.'

Aunt Sybil settled herself on the proffered chair, threw Guido one of her shrewdest glances: 'I think I can guess; Guido is not exactly in his element in England. He will never settle down here.' The boy impulsively took her hand, 'You are all so kind-a, yet I feel outsid-a, never insid-a, yet I cannot leave Vica,' he raised his great tragic eyes to hers.

Sybil, vulnerable to beauty, suddenly thanked her stars she was not twenty years younger. 'Well, well,' her voice was gruff, 'and so what is to be done? We must find a solution, but there doesn't seem to be any.'

'There might be, Aunt Sybil,' said Vica softly, trying on a

voice as one tries on a jewel, 'but it would only be a temporary one, and you would have to help us.'

'Italia,' cried Guido, in a voice that lit, as it were, all the chandeliers in Canterdown. 'Italy! Vica has been so ill-a, would she not-a be allowed to return with me, to eskepp this socold-a winter, she might have drop-back –'

'Might have *what*?'

'He means a setback, a relapse.'

'Oh, I see, yes, I suppose she might. Well, Charles is the person you will have to persuade, not me,' said Sybil soberly, though she was secretly touched that they should have appealed to her. Unlike Guido, Vica hastened to atone.

'I love England, I have been very happy all these months. Poor Guido is different – *per forza*! Unlike most people who say they cannot speak a foreign language, but that they *understand* every word, Guido can speak English, after a fashion, but he seldom if ever understands the answer. Besides – *look at him*!' She made a gesture of comic despair – 'Some Italians would look all right, but not my Guido, he has too much of what the English have too little of, and vice versa. Too much hair; too large eyes; too long eyelashes; too small teeth; too small feet. . . . '

'I get your meaning,' Sybil twinkled, 'whereas, *we* have too large teeth, too large feet –'

'No, no, I do not mean that, I just mean that the formula is different; he will never look right, nor feel right.'

Sybil thought that this was more likely, though she did not say so.

'Yet,' sighed Guido, 'I look so British in Florence. Pipple were always asking me the way in English.'

Vica bestowed on him the smile of a fond parent. '*Poveretto*! Leave him his illusions! But you *will* help us, won't you, Aunt Sybil?'

Simultaneously the two exiled, homesick faces turned towards her. She realized she was done for: they had made her their accomplice.

*

'I don't see why not,' said Lady Canterdown, with her usual mildness, 'after all, she has been very ill. I find the climate pretty trying myself at times.'

'Nonsense, Sylvia. It's no use trying to pass for a little hot-house flower at your time of life! It won't wash!' Lord Canterdown turned to his son: 'When I think that your mother spends most of the year kneeling on damp clay, I wonder she is still alive. But it's for you, my boy, to decide whether Vica is to return to Italy, with her brother, or not.'

Charles flushed. The idea was distasteful. During Vica's illness, Guido had not endeared himself to Charles, by continually hinting that there was much in Vica's life, that Charles would not, could not, understand. A whole aspect of her life which escaped him.

'I, I have no objection to Vica's returning to Italy for the colder months, but I don't see why I shouldn't go too,' he stammered, turning instinctively to his father. Mummy could be such a broken reed.

Aunt Sybil, feeling a traitor to her family, knew that it was now or never, 'I think Charles dear, that what Vica needs is a rest in her own home, surrounded by her own family. She is very homesick, and no wonder. After all, the poor girl has never been away from her country, let alone her family, since she was born. For the last five months, she has done everything she could to humour us, to fall in with our ways. Although it has been an unqualified success, it must have been a great strain. On the top of all this, she falls seriously ill. She returns to life and winter, with the nostalgia she already experienced before her illness, sharpened, intensified. Can you be surprised?'

The weather, which was also, apparently, on Vica's side, took its cue. Sybil pointed to the streaming pane: 'Of course, she must return to Italy for the next few months. . . . Personally, I think she ought to have a month or so in her family, *with* her family, wallowing in spaghetti, at the end of which time Charles could join her. Otherwise she will have to spend her time playing the part of interpreter. . . . After all, Charles darling, you must be rather a liability in Italy, aren't you?'

'Not more than most Englishmen,' said Charles ruefully, kicking the fender. Of course, Aunt Syb was getting away with it. Of course, Aunt Syb was creating a diversion. Of course, Aunt Syb had been vamped by the wretched Guido. It stuck out a mile. 'Well, in another six weeks, you can become as much of a liability as you like, but for the present, I think we should leave Vica to her family.

Lord Canterdown had been listening to this demonstration on the art of getting one's own way, a sardonic smile playing about his lips. The smile was not untinged with exasperation. Poor Charles, he was doomed to be ruled by women, as a baby by Nana, as a boy by Liz, as an adult by Vica. Not that he was over vulnerable to their charm, in his case, it was just laziness. He could not be bothered. If ever he was going to stand up for his prerogatives it would be now. Look at him. Reduced to silence by a persuasive old woman. Meanwhile, all waited, Lady Canterdown with a small measure of anxiety, she hated unpleasantness, hoped it was all going to turn out for the best, her son took after her; Sybil with embarrassed impatience. Embarrassed for herself, embarrassed for Charles, surely he ought to have more guts? She wanted to lose her case, but no. Under the collective scrutiny, Charles gave the fender a final kick: 'O well, have it your own way. I suppose you all know best. I'll join Vica in a month.'

Chapter Ten
Prodigal Daughter

THE table was laid for seven. Beppino of the Buca placed two two-litre bottles of Chianti, one white, one red, at either extremity. Under his arm he carried a basket of curiously phallic-looking rolls, specially imported from Bologna; they were very popular with his clientèle, and led to many a pleasantry. A small respectful satellite, not yet promoted to the status of waiter, accompanied him; he never took his eyes off Beppino's face, so anxious was he to anticipate any jerk of the head, which might signify more knives, more forks, for Beppino excelled in conveying what he meant by gesture, not that he was, by any means, a silent man, but he liked to economize his strength for the dinner hour; besides, the baby novice must learn to interpret the shrug of an eyebrow if he is to be any good. . . .

Moreover, a waiter should be neither seen nor heard. He owed part of the success of his establishment to the fact that il padrone was reputed to do most of the waiting himself, a feature which greatly appealed to the thrifty Florentines.

From time to time, he consulted the menu in his left hand, the Contessa had said she would leave it to him. How wise. How satisfactory. And what a dinner they were going to have! *Minestrone, fondu' con tartufi, osso bucco, pasticceria, caccia cavallo*. A dinner fit for a diva, but hadn't the Contessa been one in her youth? Perhaps, who knows, she would oblige with an aria at the end of the dinner, especially as Rigo was bringing his guitar? (We must remember not to call Rigo, Rigo, as he will be with his family, Beppino made a mental note.) Then there will be the lovely young Contessa, married to an English 'milor,' just returned from England, after what, the Contessa had informed him, on the telephone (*con tremolo*), had been *una pleurite molto grave*. The dinner was precisely to celebrate her return. Of all the restaurants in Florence, Beppino had been given preference; of course, Rigo was responsible for this; on one memorable occasion, he had even brought his sister to dine there. The place had evolved since last we mentioned it. It had become fashionable: Beppino could have had six waiters, had he so chosen, but the wise old fox knew better. Bohemian it was, Bohemian it must remain. The waiters, if any, must be invisible, or else passed off as relations (such a hardworking family, it is wonderful how every member pulls his weight!) It would be a mistake to keep the place too clean. . . . He hoped that a few writers of renown, Norman Douglas, or Osbert Sitwell, would put in an appearance so that he could point them out to the Papagallis; one never knew, especially at this time of the year, not many *forestieri* came to Florence in January, but il Douglas and il Sitwell, scarcely came under that heading, as for il Signor Asche, he was more local colour than anyone; he would sometimes bring a ravishing young lady of the aristocracy to show her the low life of the town. . . .

Well, well . . . Beppino wondered if he might indulge in a shave? Better not. Never shave on a gala night, was one of his axioms. Never shave on Papagallo nights, either, if it comes to that. He gave a sudden chuckle, which so frightened the novice that he came running to his side: 'Va be, va be,' he shooed the boy away. Time he went to the kitchen.

What a dinner they had!

Never had the *fondu* been so succulent, never the Chianti so heady. Vica looked proudly round the table. If anything,

they were better-looking than ever, her brothers; plagiarists
no longer, for they had no one to copy, they dared be themselves: Rigo did conjuring tricks with three glasses and a
toothpick; Leone shot his linen and insisted on your feeling
his biceps; Mario did an irresistible imitation of Charlie
Chaplin's *danse des petits pains*, with the phallic rolls;
Ugoccione, of course, told side-splitting stories to Mamma,
which made her laugh till the top button of her bodice burst
– as for Guido, he was just Guido. . . .

Pappà would have been *de la partie*, had not the stopping
elected to come out of one of the Pope's molars just the day
before. In a way, they were rather relieved, as his presence
was apt to cast a chill over parties. . . .

Vica could be very funny. She was now. She did a mute
imitation of breakfast at Canterdown. For quite a minute, only
her maxillaries moved. '*Ma non parlano?*' enquired the family
with interest. '*Mai. Non si deve parlare. Si ascolta la pioggia*,
one listens to the rain; in desperation, I sometimes knock
over a cup, in order to oblige them to say something.'

Then she did Lord Canterdown, protected from his family
by *The Times*, with Mamma's borrowed pince-nez, precariously
poised on the tip of her nose; then she did herself, lifting the
cover of empty dish after empty dish, as she was always late.
The family went into paroxysms of laughter: all except Guido,
to whom the ritual was too familiar to be funny.

'And you want to lure us to this country, where nobody
speaks?' demanded Leone, dexterously popping a lump of
Gorgonzola into his mouth with his knife.

'*Bambini*,' Vica was serious again, 'you have *got* to go
through it: it's like having measles, you won't be grown up
until you have, when I say grown up, I mean you won't be
men of the world. . . .'

'*Diamine!*' broke from Leone, 'I think I would rather stay
as I am.'

Vica put her hand on his muscular forearm, 'But you cannot, *tesoro*, I have already made enquiries, I may have some

good news for you in a few days.' An awed silence spread
round the table which Mamma was the first to break: 'Vica!
I must say you are the most exceptional sister. The boys should
be at your feet.' The ready tears welled to her eyes, 'But that
is not all!' Vica sparkled like a Christmas tree. 'I have something in view for each of you – I do not despair of getting you
all to England within the year, of course, darling Mamma
would come to stay with us. In two years, my children, you
will be rich and fashionable!'

'What may I ask, do you envisage for me, *cara*?' questioned
Ugo's caressing tenor.

'A rich wife.'

'If she is plain, I will have none of her.'

'*Non è una bellezza*, but she is so rich, it does not matter.
Rich and well born.'

'Then she will not look at me,' he said, already slightly
dashed.

'O yes she will, you have only to look at her as you used
to look at Elizabeth, and the trick is done.' Guido was the
only member of the family who showed no interest.

'*Non ti piace l'Inghilterra?*' Rigo threw at him. Guido
shook his head mournfully.

'*Affatto.*'

'*Tesoro*,' Vica rebuked him, 'nobody asked you to look
upon England as *pleasure*, it is work, hard work all the time,
but there are compensations.'

'Which?' he pouted.

She pinched his sleeve. 'Your new suit, for instance. Ugo's
overcoat. Pappà's wrist-watch. Mamma's furs. Leone's plus-
fours. Do you want me to go on, if so –'

'I think,' interrupted Leone weightily, with a look of inner
exultation, nodding in the direction of Mario, 'that it is time
to tell our secrets. We have not been idle in your absence,
cara. For my part, I am engaged to be married.'

'What!' This was nothing short of treachery. Were all these
months of patient probing for jobs to prove in vain? With

quivering nostrils (her 'runaway horse' look) Vica waited, containing herself with difficulty. 'You are bound to approve, *cara*,' the imprudent young man continued, 'she's an American, a widow, rich, a little older than I am.'

'How much older?' Vica pounced.

'A few years.'

'How many?'

'Eight or nine, but she looks much younger.'

'Just as I thought,' she snorted, 'old enough to be your mother!'

'Scarcely. But Vica, you have just been urging Ugo to marry a plain rich lady; mine, at least, is pretty. After all, one can be pretty at thirty-three.'

'And when am I to see this paragon?'

'She has gone to America to make arrangements and is returning in the spring.'

'I see. No doubt you will send us an invitation to the wedding, but now I come to think of it, you said "our" secrets. Does "our" mean that Mario is also keeping something from me?'

'O, that's quite different.'

Was it her imagination, or did Leone sound a trifle contemptuous? 'Well, out with it then,' she rapped. (That is the voice she will have as an old woman, Guido thought with a shudder.) Mario quickly moved round to her side. All listened, their hearts in their mouths. They knew what this meant to Vica.

'I have found a job as a secretary to an English writer of great distinction. The salary is large, and the work – negligible.' His voice was not as firm as he could have wished.

'How can you be a secretary, you have none of the qualifications.' (Vica's tone was measured, measured but glacial, it struck terror into the heart of her listeners.) 'You cannot type, neither do you know shorthand. Spelling was never your strong point. What, then, do your duties consist of?'

Mario paled. He had been dreading this moment all day, putting it off until now, when he knew he could relay on his family's tacit backing. 'I . . . I . . . order the meals, and arrange the flowers, I also take him sightseeing.'

'And that, in your opinion, constitutes the duties of a secretary. How charmingly naïve! And the name of your patron?'

'Wetherby Solent.'

'I have read some of his books. It is, at any rate, true that he is a writer of distinction. I will make enquiries about his private life.'

'Is that necessary, Vica? He's wealthy and honest. Ask the *antiquari* of Florence.'

'The *antiquari* of Florence will tell me nothing. I will wait until I return to England.'

He looked round imploringly: the public part of his avowal was at an end, he must be allowed to use what private arguments he could find, to convince Vica it was all for the best. The family understood, and immediately engaged one another in feverish conversation. Guido moved down the table, Mario attempted to take one of her frozen hands, which she withdrew. 'Vica, you *must* listen to me.'

'I *am* listening.' She felt numbed, betrayed, first Leone, now Mario! This was her reward for having sacrificed her life to these boys. One by one, they were forsaking her, mapping out careers for themselves, eliminating her from their lives. Mario grasped the necessity of saying something drastic, something that would act as a brake on that runaway face.

'Vica, I can never love any woman but you.' It had the advantage of being true. She was stayed in her course. The 'runaway face' came, as it were, to a standstill.

'Mario, that is a childish statement. Of course, you will love other women, but why have you hidden this from me all these months?'

If only they could have envisaged it together, it would have lost its sting.

'You were not here, it was difficult to explain by letter. *Carissima*, if only you knew him, I honestly think you would like him. He has taught me so much, he is so understanding, so human, so infinitely cultured. He has revealed the meaning of so many beautiful things in Florence which I took for granted –' Mario paused, vainly trying to decipher Vica's face. She was, in point of fact, trying to weigh the pros and cons of this new outlook; it was hard to be entirely objective, what would it lead to, that was the question? Were elderly English writers a sinecure? Such was her possessive and protective instinct with regard to her brothers, that she could not succeed in stifling a sense of outraged decorum, surely, the elderly English writer should have asked Vica for Mario's hand, so to speak? Well, it is about time I thought for myself, of my own pleasure. Why should I go on sacrificing myself for my ungrateful family? Henceforth they can fend for themselves. . . .

As though in answer to her unspoken thoughts, a shadowy, unnoticed figure, sitting at the back of the room, rose, crossed over to their table, bowed over Mamma's hand, kissed Vica's. A glad cry broke from her: 'Gian Galeazzo!'

He said courteously, ceremoniously, '*Ben tornata, Contessa!*'

He left her two days without news. On the third day, came an invitation from the Princess, to dine *dans l'intimité*, just ourselves?

The implication of this was not lost on the recipient of the letter, the gracious sanction, the permission to love Gian Galeazzo at long last. . . .

Her mind was made up.

Her brothers no longer needed her. No matter. They would again. Why give to the gorged, was it not kinder to give to the famished? Gian Galeazzo was surely entitled to a reward for his perseverance, besides, she loved him, had always loved him; only her family, especially Guido, had come first. Now they would see what it was like to be without her. Serve them right! Meanwhile, the brothers had no illusions about the significance of the dinner: a *lettre de faire-part* could not have made things clearer. Leone and Ugo could not find it in their hearts to condemn Vica for her surmised surrender to a sentiment which had only owed its repression to a superior sense of duty. After duty, pleasure? It was only fair she should have compensations.

As to Mario, dual, dubious, he was so disagreeable to his employer, that the latter wondered, not for the first time, if it was worth while continuing his education?

Guido, for his part, appeared to take no interest in the proceedings. Bland, impervious, he affected to look upon the fateful dinner as a mere social engagement. He was well aware that it was the attitude best calculated to unnerve Vica; it needed not her intuition to guess that he was jealous; normally, they would have discussed the evening down to its smallest detail. . . .

Charles, she knew, he had accepted. Charles was a necessary evil, whereas he undoubtedly saw in Gian Galeazzo, a deliberate act of lèse-Guido, gratuitous, insulting. She was troubled when she heard him whistling himself defiantly out of the house. It was the first time he had not been in to sit with her while she dressed for dinner. . . .

The ancient family car wheezed round to fetch her; her dress, she knew, was a masterpiece of line, of simplicity. She wore no jewels except the famous Canterdown black pearls.

She arrived five minutes late, not more, because the Princess was too old to be kept waiting. Gian Galeazzo met her in the hall. She thought he looked older, more ascetic. 'I have no words to express my happiness,' he murmured over her hand. Side by side, they went upstairs, he threw open the door of the *salottino*: the tiny familiar figure, in the latest Chanel creation, rushed to greet her, as though she were a long lost daughter: 'Vica! *Ben tornata*! How I have missed you all these months! Let's have a look at you, my child.

More seductive than ever! One should always live six months in England for one's complexion, and six months in Italy for one's eyes. . . . This is really a family party, as you see. . . . ' She pointed to a little round table laid for three. A magnum of champagne stood in an ice-bucket.

At dinner, the Princess surpassed herself, plying her with questions, about her mother-in-law, Canterdown, Charles, every question accompanied by a 'mot,' in the best Zia manner. 'Canterdown. I can see it from here. A cosy Escurial. Sylvia, of course, a sexagenarian Ophelia, as for Charles, he sounds like a guilty *putto*, who has been told not to play with the matches.'

Gian Galeazzo took no part in the fireworks, he was busy observing Vica: Vica the outwardly self-possessed; Vica, the poised; Vica, the chatelaine; Vica who was charming to him, as one is charming to an old friend, but who appeared to have really more to say to his aunt.

The latter, it was easy to see, was delighted with her one-time protégée; few girls could have played the game, *her* game, with such success, such *savoir-faire*. . . . In fact, a medium had taken possession of Vica, prompting each remark, each gesture. She had always known it would end like this, it was a foregone conclusion, this play of three wills, by the Princess, who was also responsible for the *mis en scène*. Everything conspired to make it a success, the suggestive Venetian furniture, the pampered fire, resinous and rich, the mirrors charged with reminiscences. . . .

She was but playing her predestined part, the conspiritorial palace was the silent auditor, the scene was so familiar that had she been at a loss for a word, the word would surely have been whispered. . . .

'We should have invited Rigo,' observed the zealous Producer, 'he would have sounded charming. . . . ' Vica smiled ruefully.

'Do you think, Princess, that poor Rigo has forgotten how he behaved on the night of the ball?'

'How he behaved? But he was the soul of discretion! he drank himself quietly into a stupor, instead of setting fire to the curtains, which is what I would have done in his place. I consider Rigo behaved in the most gentlemanly manner, worthy of an English lord.'

'O, Zia, you are perverse,' teased Gian Galeazzo. 'If only Valka could hear you!'

'How can you expect Valka to appreciate Rigo? She's far too middle-class.'

'And Elizabeth, is she happy with her yokel?' asked Gian Galeazzo, with sudden rancour. He had not forgotten the slight to his honour, though her happiness was a matter of complete indifference to him.

'Very. I think she is going to have a baby.'

His face darkened, 'No doubt it will be a son.'

'And supposing it is, what of it?' The Princess cracked her whip, she would be hanged if Gian Galeazzo was going to be allowed to upset her design for loving. 'My dear Gigi, as we both know you never looked on Elizabeth as anything but an obligation, why try to dramatize her? We are not taken in.'

He tossed his gloom away, as though it were a cigarette stub. He was for ever trying on moods, to see if they became him; his mind was always full of pins, his eyes danced, he inwardly bubbled. Was not everything going according to plan? The lovely Vica, something told him, would be his before the evening was out. Her English anecdotes were, in spite of herself, revelatory. The boredom showed through the persiflage. All these months she had been at the back of his thoughts. Time worked in his favour, he knew she would return. Who could better supply the element she lacked but himself? England was his ally, he relied on England to dispel, once and for all, the sense of inferiority which had, so far, wrecked their relationship. They met now as equals, there was no longer any obstacle, though he had not said as much to la Zia, he knew that she divined and approved of

his intentions. They deserved some recompense for their
forbearance: they deserved each other. After work, pleasure.
Yet, another facet of the Princess' curious character came
into play. She was a born *entr'-metteuse*, once the family
exigencies were satisfied, the tribute to decorum paid, why
stint yourself? Why deprive yourself of the one thing that
makes life worthy living? Once the Prince had safely married
the Princess, the fairy godmother was perfectly prepared
to further less orthodox projects. . . . The main thing was
that they should live happily ever afterwards, she did not
specify with whom. Hence this deep-laid plot, this well-laid
dinner table. . . . It was up to them to make the most of their
opportunity!

'*Ci vuol esser lieto, sia.*' A realist, she had no patience
with people who did not know their own mind. Meanwhile,
the smoke from their cigarettes mounted. What djinn, what
subservient spirit would presently emerge?

'Do you know, children,' the Princess began to weave her
spell, the 'children' swept them under her protection, 'I have
a name for you both. My name for you, Gian Galeazzo, is
Thlaspi, and for you, Vica, Egusa. I will tell you why: "V'è
un herba rossa che si chiama Thlaspi, ed'un altra brancia che
si chiama Egusa. E crescono lontano l'una dell'altra. Ma le
loro radiche si trovano, sotto la terra cieca. E lì s'annodano.
. . . Diverse hanno le foglie, ma fanno l'istesso fiore ogni
sett'anni. . . . *

'But where did you find this exquisite legend, Zia?'
questioned Gian Galeazzo, deeply moved.

'It is in "La Figlia di Jorio." I know my d'Annunzio by heart,
or ought to!'

'E crescono lontano l'una dell'altra,' murmured Vica, 'it is
true we grow far apart. . . .'

---

* There is a red flower called Thlaspi and another white one called
Egusa. The two grow far apart, but their roots find each other and
intertwine deep in the blind earth. Their leaves are different, but
every seven years the same flower grows in both.

'Only *you* could have found such suitable names for us, Zia,' he kissed the tips of her fingers. 'Henceforth,' (he used the lovely adverb, *Ormai*), 'Ormai, I shall call you Egusa, Vica.'

'There is, however, no occasion for you to wait seven years,' said the witch briskly, in her hurry to turn the page – these two had dallied quite long enough in her opinion. She had no wish to prolong this atmosphere of inoperative regret. As though in reply to a given signal, the youngest browbeaten footman appeared:

'The Countess' car has arrived.'

He would never know why he got a dazzling smile from his employer.

'Tell it to go away again,' ordered Gian Galeazzo, at his most peremptory. 'I will drive you home' – la Zia frowned – 'that is, if you are willing,' he amended.

'*Volentieri*: both car and chauffeur are so old, it is a wonder they hold together,' said Vica easily, having anticipated this.

'It is getting late,' Gian Galeazzo glanced at his wrist-watch. The Princess put on what she hoped was her most innocent expression, 'So soon must you go? I had hoped –'

'*Cara Zia*, we will return.'

'Please, please, I cannot see enough of dear Vica.' She embraced them both, '*Vaya usted con Dios*,' she said with some emotion, aware that she was sending the girl to her lover.

Gian Galeazzo's sports car, designed for noise and speed, slid up the Lung'arno, past the Palazzo Pitti, past the Porta Romana. It was only when they began the ascension to Bellosguardo that he slid his disengaged arm about her shoulders, without attempting to kiss her. Why mar a perfect kiss by changing speed in the middle?

When they reached the villa, he let himself in by the side-door. They found themselves in Gian Galeazzo's study, where a great fire caracoled; the monastic, scholastic furniture looked as though it were expecting the visit of Savonarola.

... The family *stemma*, a leopard rampant, in the sinuous
Italian escutcheon, pranced over the fireplace. How often had
the austere room been violated, she could not help wondering, in spite of the fact that Gian Galeazzo had her in his arms,
was kissing her ravenously. '*Ti amo, ti amo*,' he murmured
over and over again. It was no use holding out any longer.
She gave in, '*Anch'io*,' she whispered. . . .

Night clung to the steep, virginal room. Presently the sun,
ostentatious as a giant chrysanthemum, would splash the
shrinking walls with colour. The room might have been
designed for Santa Fina, so narrow was it, so bleak. *Levitate*,
it would appear to insinuate, who knows but what stigmata
will visit these pale predestined hands?

Vica stirred uneasily. The enormity of her presence in such
a room seemed to weigh on her subconsciousness. A lover,
newly born, tossed on the grudging pillows. At three o'clock
in the morning, Gian Galeazzo's tactlessly snorting car had
drawn up at number 42. Unobserved, a vigilant head had
hastily withdrawn from an uncurtained window of the *piano
nobile*. Guido, after a night's vigil, returned to his room
where, smoking cigarette upon cigarette, he would pace until
dawn. . . .

The never completely stilled city started to whimper;
somewhere on the horizon a dog barked; a cock crowed.

At six o'clock the first campanile began to stutter. One
after the other it was joined by the flagging, sleep-bemused
bells. On the banks of the Arno, a punctual donkey tore the
night to shreds.

The hour of waking, veiled in mists, but unmistakable, had
struck. It was as though an orchestra, obeying the arbitrary
baton, attacked an *aubade*. Immediately bells, klaxons,
sirens, raucous voices, joined in the morning cacophony.

Deafeningly, Gina's alarm clock rang. She opened an eye
brown as a bee. Outside, a false darkness attempted to lure
her back to sleep. She turned over. Her harsh mattress

creaked admonishment. With a tremendous effort, she disengaged one plump leg from the bedclothes. She had to get up in order to light the cruel bald bulb in the middle of the room. In sudden panic, she splashed icy water from the jug on her furry cheeks, struggled into the discarded clothes lying at the foot of the bed.

There was la Crispa's coffee, la Contessa's tea and rusks (she was doing her annual slimming cure) to be got ready, the boys' coffee and rolls, the young Contessa's China tea (an innovation) . . . *Spicciati, spicciati*, she staggered to the sticky pitchpine door. . . .

Crispa, always an early waker, lay motionless on her bed, staring up at the officious, scroll-carrying eagles. She was vainly trying to recapture a fugitive dream, but dreams, she reflected, are like wild flowers, they fade as soon as grasped.

The dream had centred, as did nearly all her dreams, round Vica, Vica receiving at the head of the stair of some grand house. As the guests were ushered up, she bent solicitously over each in turn: 'Are you wearing the badge, my badge? Otherwise, you know, you cannot be admitted.' . . . Here, it broke off, but there had been much more to it than that. What *could* be the meaning of dreams such as these? A little book by Crispa's bed, *la Clef des Songes*, was hardly up to their standard. It only envisaged dreams of a cruder symbolism: bells, a ship, a wreath of white flowers. Freud, of course, had scarcely penetrated to Italy.

. . . O dear! What a worry Vica was! She had never ceased to be a worry. The significance of her two hours' toilette had not been wasted on Crispa; the whole household, of course, knew where she was dining. God knows at what unseemly hour she had returned! Crispa's room, did not, unfortunately, overlook the Lung'arno, it 'gave' on a clamorous garage which obliterated all lesser noises.

Why couldn't Vica be content with what she'd got? She had

made an undreamt-of marriage. *Charles est un charmant garçon qui n'a pas inventé la poudre, c'est une affaire entendue, mais on ne saurait tout avoir. . . . Il l'adore, la preuve, c'est qu'il l'a laissée partir sans lui, il lui a fait confiance. . . . Il faut être fou pour avoir confiance en Vica!*

She smashed a small fist into her unoffending pillow, and sat up. Whether Vica liked it or not, she was going to get a talking to from Crispa that very morning!

Gina had called Crispa, called the Countess, roused the brothers, she was now coming to the last on the list, her treat, her recompense: her adulation for Vica was such that she really *did* try to tiptoe noiselessly from the door to the window without turning on the light. It was only five minutes later, when she laid the tray on the bed, that Vica awoke.

A tremor, like some delicious form of seismic shock coursed through her body, conveying the delectable message from limb to limb. I'm in love at last! He is mine, I am his! How could I have waited so long! What a fool I've been! Strange that something that could be so monotonous with one person could be so entrancing with another. 'Gina, come and embrace me this minute!' The startled girl couldn't believe her ears. Trembling, she approached the bed. Vica threw her arms round her neck, gave her a resounding kiss on both cheeks. 'I could hug the universe! O Gina, isn't it wonderful to be alive? Come and sit here, Gina, on the edge of the bed. Have you a lover, Gina? If not, why not?'

'*Ma*. Signorina – '

'What! Can that mean you haven't one already? You must see to it at once, this very day! What are you dreaming of, girl? A fine healthy young woman like you! *Vergogna!*'

Gina stared at the signorina in open-mouthed astonishment. What had happened to her during the last twenty-four hours? Not only her manner, but her face had changed. It was as though a curtain had lifted, unimpeded, unashamed, happiness shone forth as the rising sun, Gina recoiled in sudden shyness. Was this apotheosis meant for her? 'Signorina,' she stammered, 'I have work to do – '

Vica gave her a push which seemed part of her new personality. . . . 'Be off with you then, and don't dare show your face again until you have secured a lover!'

The girl went out backwards, still agape. It was impossible to lie in bed doing nothing. Gian Galeazzo was coming to take her out to lunch, there were still three hours to go. What to do, in the meanwhile? On a sudden inspiration, she leapt from her bed, rushed to the looking-glass, in need of immediate reassurance. So this was the face that had inspired such passionate, such tender lovemaking, this and no other! . . . As she admired herself in her hand-glass, turning her head this way and that, there came a crisp tap at the door. Guido, his hour. '*Avanti, tesoro*,' she cried superfluously, as he was already in the room.

He gave a glance of almost quakerish condemnation at the diaphanously-clad figure in front of the looking-glass. 'Don't you think,' he suggested primly, 'that you would be better in bed? One can do this sort of thing in June, not in February.'

'But it is a lovely day, *tesoro*, February or no February. However, to please you, I will do as you suggest.'

Guido averted his eyes as his sister bounced into bed. Really, she had no shame. What were women coming to? With pursed lips, he sat down on the rickety chair by the bed.

'What is the matter with you, *tesoro*? You look as though you needed a purge,' remarked Vica, with unnecessary coarseness.

'I have been thinking,' he announced ominously, deliberately adopting the pose of Rodin's *penseur*.

'It happens to all of us at times,' came the flippant retort.

'I have been thinking,' he pursued in an even loftier tone, 'that there is a lot to be said for the Protestant Church!'

Her sudden laughter was surely not in the best of taste?

'And what,' she enquired with mock seriousness, 'strikes you as particularly commendable in the Protestant Church?'

'*Convenient*, rather than commendable,' he said meaningly. 'There is no confession, for instance you can commit any atrocity and you don't have to go and blurt it out to the parish priest,' he completed with more heat and less eloquence.

'Aha! I think I see what you are driving at, my little Guido, this is a covert hit at me.'

'Can you pretend you have nothing on your conscience? Can you pretend you have not done something so abominable that you should be, even now, on your way to the confessional?' He was flushed and furious.

'But I still do not see why *you* should wish to become a Protestant, Guido mio, unless, perhaps, you too have something on your conscience you would rather not confess?'

In argument Guido was no match for his sister, and he knew it. Very well. He would take another line.

'When I think that your husband, *un uomo per bene*, a man of the highest integrity, allows you to travel about Europe, unchaperoned, because he trusts you!' Guido raised his hands to the Heavens.

'I was under the impression that *you* were my chaperone, and that he had entrusted me to *you*,' observed Vica sweetly.

'Ah! he little knew! He little knew what pitfalls awaited you in Florence. He little knew that a professional seducer, a man who causes mothers to affix bars to their innocent daughters' bedroom windows, waited round the corner.'

'I don't like "round the corner" much,' drawled Vica, starting to polish her nails, 'it is not worthy of the first part of your sentence.'

'Vica, you will drive me mad. Your attitude is a studied insult. It is with the greatest difficulty that I keep my hands off you!'

For a split second, Vica lifted her eyes from her polishing. They were deadly. 'You try. You'll get as good as you give.'

The scene of denunciation was not going according to

plan. Vica was so slippery, it was impossible to pin her down.

'I am in no mood for a rough-and-tumble,' he said, with a return to Fig. I. Hauteur appeared to be his best suit. 'The situation is too serious to admit of such crude solutions.'

'*Tesoro*,' she said, holding her hand at arm's length, admiring her exquisite nails, 'do you know that you are becoming a bore, and that that is a thing you must never, *never* permit yourself to be? Now bustle off. I shall be seeing you to-morrow.'

'But, Vica,' he pleaded, all hauteur discarded, 'not until to-morrow?'

For the first time she was serious: 'It is better so.'

'O Vica,' there were now tears in his eyes, 'don't you love me any more, what *have* I done?'

He laid his curly head on her knees. This was the Guido she feared, the doting child, the defenceless twin. Placing her hand on his bent head, she said in a voice hoarse with tenderness: 'Listen, *amore*: I love you, I shall always love you, in a way, better than anyone else, but you must not attempt to interfere in this. It has nothing to do with you. I must fulfil myself in the way I have chosen. Until yesterday I was only half a woman. No. Do not wince. You should rejoice with me. You will see, I will become much nicer, you do not want me to be unhappy, do you?' Though his shoulders heaved, the curls shook their dissent. 'Of course, my darling,' she soothed, 'I know you want me to be happy. One day the same thing will happen to you. No, no, don't shake your head. I *know* it will. *Pazienza*. . . . Now go.'

Vica's next visitor was Mademoiselle Crispin.

Vica saw at once that it was not of the slightest use attempting to bluff Crispa. With a sigh, she settled down to what was bound to be a very unpleasant quarter of an hour indeed.

'What a pity,' remarked Crispa conversationally, seating herself on Vica's bed, 'that you are such an old muddler.'

This was the last accusation Vica had expected. 'Muddler!' she gasped, thrusting her hair back from her forehead, as though in order to see better. '*Muddler*, what have I muddled?'

'*Everything*. Your life, your brothers' lives, and now, your married life. Such a pity. First let us take your brothers. You deliberately made them completely dependent on you. It is difficult enough to run one's own life, let alone four others. So fatiguing. You remind me of one of those unpleasant little chess prodigies, rushing from table to table, displacing a pawn here, a pawn there. When do they have time to play their own game, or rather, games? Why couldn't you leave them alone? Do you suppose it has made them happy to have ideas above their station? Leone is marrying a rich American. Why? In order to *épater* you, though he doesn't realize it. Mario is educating himself under the auspices of a suspect old sybarite. Why? Again, in order to *épater* you. As for Guido, he is making himself both ridiculous and conspicuous.'

'I have just told him so,' murmured the abashed Vica.

'Even if you have, it is too late to do anything about it,' Crispa swept on. 'Do you suppose that, in later life, these men won't turn on you and rend you? Of course they will! The only one you respect is poor little Rigo, because he refused to play the game, *your* game! Your thirst for power will be your undoing –'

'That is why,' intercepted Vica, with considerable pluck, 'it is good for me to have Gian Galeazzo for my lover. It is *he* who will have the upper hand, not I.'

Crispa cast a speculative Gallic eye, half appreciative, half cynical, over Vica's displayed and dedicated beauty, assessing each item, as it were, at its true value. She shrugged. 'Unfortunately, it won't last long, his ascendency, I mean. You will not let him rest until he has given in.'

'But he *has* given in, I tell you, we love each other,' cried Vica, at bay.

'I am sure you do,' acknowledged the unrelenting Crispa, 'but that won't be enough, not for the little Pygmalion that you are. You will want to change him, to modify this, retouch that. If he is a sporting type, you will want to make him into an intellectual, or vice versa. You cannot leave people alone. You are not only a muddler, but also a meddler. Why can't you be content with what you've got? I should have thought it would have been sufficient for most women.'

Vica caught Crispa's hand, briefly pressed it to her breast. She was really fond of the indomitable Frenchwoman, anxious to soothe and placate her. (But it is her eyes, not her hands, that have fingers to lull, disarm, efface, the cautious Crispa warned herself.)

'Listen, Crispa, you know, I struggle a little, but I always tell you the truth – in the end. I have never been in love before. If you *must* know, I was beginning to think I was quite sexless. I have fought against Gian Galeazzo's attraction for months. If I married Charles, it was partly to get away from Gian Galeazzo. Had I married him in the first place, it is quite on the cards I would have made him an impeccable wife. . . . But this is where it went wrong. He wounded my pride, he humiliated me and my brothers. I could not forgive that. I married Charles in order to avenge myself on Gian Galeazzo.'

'What an extraordinary creature you are, Vica!' exclaimed the governess, awed, in spite of herself, by so much pride, so few scruples. 'You are like something out of another epoch.' (It always pays to tell the truth to people of character, Vica noted, not for the first time.) what are you going to do now?' Crispa enquired in a tone that had lost its stringency.

'*That* will depend on Gian Galeazzo. Supposing, when you first became Angiolino's mistress, someone had asked you what your plans were, what would have been your answer?'

'*Touchée*, Vica.' She could not help smiling, the girl was

astute. '*Tu me fais peur*. I see that I am wasting my breath.
Promise me one thing?'

'Yes?' encouraged Vica, quietly victorious. . . .

'That you will keep me *au courant*, that you will not do
anything reckless without telling me?'

She was rewarded by Vica's most significant look. 'Crispa,
I promise.'

Though the month was only February, up at Bellosguardo,
it was possible to believe in a kind of precocious Spring.
The motionless invariable ilexes glittered impartially through
Winter and Summer; the cypresses, too, knew nothing of
transition, only the absence of flowers, the gentleness of the
shadows, gave the show away. Spring is less kind, less
temperate.

Gian Galeazzo, humming in his pleasant tenor, was piling
logs on a fire he was already beginning to consider superfluous. For an Italian he was singularly impervious to cold.
The fire was in honour of Vica, who should be here at any
minute now. The Alfa Romeo, driven by his chauffeur-valet,
had gone to fetch her. Beloved, beautiful Vica! He profoundly
believed he had never known real happiness until now. He
could not recall a single mistress who had given him the
same serene satisfaction, as of owning a perfect work of art,
unique, without precedent. He was unaware how much he
had improved under Vica's auspices. No longer on his mettle,
the wish to show off had subsided, his protracted conquest
of Vica had assuaged his vanity, once and for all. A very
different side of his character, long neglected, had reasserted
itself; fostered by Vica, his latent love of music, of poetry,
blossomed anew. While she drew, he read to her; while she
wrote, he sang. La Zia, to whom illicit love spelt Romance,
watched over them with the fervour of Juliet's nurse. There
was only one cloud on the horizon: the arrival of Vica's
husband which could not now be long delayed. Whenever he

was reminded of this, something in Gian Galeazzo's stomach would uncoil like a snake about to strike. . . .

It was unthinkable that he should ever allow Vica to sleep with this man again.

With a flourish like a signature in the gravel, Cesare drew up at the villa door. He was inordinately proud of his car, his master, his master's mistress. It was a privilege to be seen driving her up to the Villa.

Vica sprang out with her usual impetuosity. Gian Galeazzo was already at the door. They had hardly got inside before he crushed her to him, kissing her as though he hadn't kissed her for months. In the middle, however, she pushed him away distressfully. '*Amore*, not now. I must talk to you. Something has happened.'

Unconsciously his hand flew to his heart. 'He is not arriving?'

'He is. I must sit down, I feel quite faint.' He led her to the study, to the divan. There was a bitter taste in his mouth, it was difficult to swallow.

'He – he is on his way?'

'Not yet. He is leaving England on Saturday.'

'You cannot return to him.' This was so self-evident that neither attempted to speak for nearly a minute. Then Gian Galeazzo's voice fell, final as the guillotine: 'You must write at once. This is only Monday, he should get it in time.'

'But what can I say?' Her tone was perhaps more specula-tive than despairing.

'The truth,' he rapped. 'Tell him the truth, that I am your lover, that you cannot possibly return to him.'

'Poor Charles,' sighed Vica, already resigned to his fate. 'he will be very sad.'

'It won't last, he is not one of those who pine. There is not a minute to waste. Sit there, at my desk. You will find all you want.' Obediently Vica seated herself at the high, scholarly writing-table. She selected a large sheet of vellum with a tiny coronet on the top left-hand corner. She sat there, sucking her pen at a loss.

But not for long.

This is what she wrote:

Darling Charles,

This is going to be a very painful letter, painful for you, painful for me. Try to be brave. You were very brave when you asked me to marry you, but believe me, you would have to be braver still to go on being married to me. I am not a nice person, in any sense of the word. With one quick wrench you can get rid of me. A year hence you will congratulate yourself on having taken this step. Your father will be furious, your mother disappointed, Elizabeth will not be in the least surprised, neither will Aunt Sybil. Nana and Mademoiselle Cujac will probably dance the can-can together, but that is beside the point. Gian Galeazzo, who is reading over my shoulder says that I am beating about the bush, which brings me to him, the bush. I am sorry to say we have become lovers, but we were already lovers before we became lovers, if you know what I mean? In fact, we fell in love the first day we met, at his aunt's party. We should have married straight away, is it not cruel that I could not marry him, at least not until I had married you?

'Vica, you cannot possibly put that!'

'But it's true!'

'*Toute vérité n'est pas bonne à dire!*'

'Very well, I'll cross it out then. She substituted.

. . . but his aunt had made other plans.

I think, Charles, it would be best for you to divorce me, or for me to divorce you. I think it is unlikely we should have children; you had much better marry some nice young neighbour with feathery yellow hair like yourself, and no brothers.

As I am a Catholic and you a Protestant, it makes things much easier, as we do not then have to obtain an *annulamento*. I am truly sorry this has happened. I shall always be very fond of you, and your mother, and Liz –

she paused, pen suspended – È vero, sai – I really love Lady Canterdown, I think I shall write her another letter, explaining. . . . She is so sweet and gentle, not in the least like a mother-in-law –

'Every woman contains a mother-in-law, however sweet and gentle,' remarked her lover grimly, 'you wait – '

I shall always keep the sketch your mother made of me (*the writer resumed*), which makes me look like a Luini Madonna. Please tell me, dear Charles, what steps I should take legally, I mean, as I have no experience in these matters. (*'I should think not indeed!' growled Gian Galeazzo*.) I cannot thank you enough for all your patience with me, try not to be too unhappy. I will always be your friend.

Vica

She blotted the letter, turned to Gian Galeazzo, raising interrogative eyebrows: 'By the way, I take it for granted you *do* want to marry me?'

It so happened that Aunt Sybil was staying at Canterdown, when Vica's bombshell arrived.

The family were grouped round the breakfast table; each was engaged in characteristic occupation: Lord Canterdown was mentally compiling a reprisal to *The Times* in reply to what he considered an extremely offensive diatribe from a fellow peer; 'Mummy' was fanatically hunting for an unheard-of rock plant in a seed catalogue; Charles had replenished his plate for the third time, as, he reflected, this time to-morrow he would be in the train. . . . It was, consequently, his last

English breakfast for many weeks to come. Sybil, late as usual, had provoked the usual rebuke from Christopher. She had just read, and was inwardly digesting a 'lecture' from her lecturing lover, who complained that he had not heard from her for the last fortnight, when an exclamation broke from her sister-in-law: 'Why, here's a letter from Vica I had completely overlooked! I was so excited over my new catalogue. How odd: it's a letter to me, enclosing one to Charles – here, catch! What can it all be about?' She readjusted her spectacles, began to read. Sybil was watching her covertly: after a few seconds, her still childish chin, over which she was known to have no control, began to quiver, her still childish cheeks became suffused with scarlet. Sybil, in alarm, instinctively put out her hand.

'O-o-h,' came a wail that ended in a sob, 'ooh, it can't be true, Vica is never coming back, she's got a lover!'

'What!' Lord Canterdown sprang to his feet, pushing back his chair which fell with a crash on the floor. He tore the letter from his weeping wife; as he read through his mean steel spectacles, his *samurai* eyebrows rose higher and higher, until they practically vanished in his hair.

'The bitch,' he spluttered, 'the bloody little bitch! If that doesn't beat the band –! Here, read that, Syb,' he thrust the letter at her. Everyone had forgotten Charles, who having read *his* letter, sat staring into space, as though mesmerized. He might have known, he might have guessed, it was too good to last, too good to be true. . . .

'I just want you to listen to this,' roared Lord Canterdown, suddenly snatching back the letter. ' "I wish we could go on being friends, dear Lady Canterdown, I do miss your soft voice, your secateurs and your gardening gloves, you always seemed to me more like a nurse than a gardener, bending solicitously over your patients." ' . . . 'Can you beat that for effrontery?' Almost inarticulate with rage he resumed: ' "Try to forgive my having changed, I haven't changed really, I am like a woman trying to match a pattern, I go from shop to shop, comparing, assessing. And now, I have matched my pattern at last!"'

Lord Canterdown choked, his bubbly eyes protruded; on his forehead, the veins stood out like blue worms. . . . An appalled, an outraged silence descended on the desecrated breakfast table. . . . To her horror, Sybil heard herself humming, quite audibly, 'La donna è mobile,' a tune with which even her brother was familiar. 'If you have any singing to do, Sybil,' he barked at her, 'go and do it outside!'

VIRAGO MODERN CLASSICS
&
CLASSIC NON-FICTION

The first Virago Modern Classic, *Frost in May* by Antonia White, was published in 1978. It launched a list dedicated to the celebration of women writers and to the rediscovery and reprinting of their works. Its aim was, and is, to demonstrate the existence of a female tradition in fiction, and to broaden the sometimes narrow definition of a 'classic' which has often led to the neglect of interesting novels and short stories. Published with new introductions by some of today's best writers, the books are chosen for many reasons: they may be great works of fiction; they may be wonderful period pieces; they may reveal particular aspects of women's lives; they may be classics of comedy or storytelling.

The companion series, Virago Classic Non-Fiction, includes diaries, letters, literary criticism, and biographies – often by and about authors published in the Virago Modern Classics.

'Good news for everyone writing and reading today' – *Hilary Mantel*

'A continuingly magnificent imprint' – *Joanna Trollope*

'The Virago Modern Classics have reshaped literary history and enriched the reading of us all. No library is complete without them' – *Margaret Drabble*